GHOSTS OF IBERIA

JERRY AUTIERI

1

Against the stone of the fortress walls the cold of an indigo night pressed against the few areas of Varro's exposed flesh. He clenched a black wool cloak at his neck, both to keep the heat against his skin and to hide his mail shirt. His other hand rested on the hilt of his pugio. Given the work ahead this night, its shorter blade would serve him better than his gladius. Its comforting weight hung from his right hip.

He tilted his head back and glanced above. The yellow stone walls were streaked black in the thin moonlight. Nothing stirred above, no orange torchlight or the errant glint of metal. No sound of muted conversations between lookouts, or scratch of leather against stone.

Those noises came from the others pressed to the wall with him. He now glared down the line at his raiders and set his finger across his lips. The dark shapes, hardly discernible even to himself, flattened against the wall in response.

Falco nudged Varro with his elbow. His face was lost in the shadow of the black head cover he and everyone else had selected for tonight's operation. But Varro could imagine the impatient expression hidden in the darkness. Curio, who stood on Falco's opposite side, was already portioning out the knotted rope to the iron hook he pressed between his knees. Varro admired his caution to not risk the hook scraping against the rocky ground underfoot. They had taken such pains to reach this Carthaginian fort undetected that it elicited an irrational fear of giving away any sign of their presence. Varro had even held his breath for no reason.

He answered Falco's nudge with a sharp nod of his own. They hadn't come to test if they could touch the walls of a fort said to be unapproachable and impenetrable, like children on some kind of dare.

They had come to prove the belief unfounded and punish the Carthaginians for their crimes.

Before he issued the order to begin the infiltration, Varro glanced out across the barren, rock-studded landscape they had just crossed. The ridges of shallow hills showed a deeper blue against the dark of the night sky. Nothing stirred there either, but that was by plan. Still, his eyes bored into the darkness, searching for reassurance but finding none. He would accept that his primary force was in place. He had no reason to doubt, but he had also done enough operations like these to know nothing ever proceeded as planned.

Varro waved at Curio to begin. He stepped back, twirling the iron hook, then casting it with a stifled grunt.

The rope spooled out of his hands as the hook sailed into the night. For an instant Varro could not see it, and his throat closed. If it missed and rebounded onto the ground, any alert guard would hear it clang and investigate. But Curio had practiced scores of hours on the cliff walls of their Numidian base to prepare for this moment. True to his practice, the hook bit the ledge with the barest chime of iron on stone.

He formed a mouthed cry of success, and even hidden beneath hood and robe his exuberance was contagious. Falco stood by nodding in appreciation and the other raiders followed. As they had learned at Sparta, scaling a wall was a dangerous art and success began with sinking the hook.

Curio tested the rope, yanking it and laying it flat to the ground to ensure both hook and rope endured. A dozen men had to traverse its length, requiring a sturdy lock on the wall. When he was satisfied, he extended the rope in an open palm to Varro. As decided, he would go first, followed by Curio, the rest of the team, then Falco to bring up the rear.

He let his held breath seep from his tight lips, clapped Curio's shoulder, then took up the rope. The wall was rough stone with hardly any gaps. But his soft-sandaled feet could gain enough purchase that he began the climb easily. No one could tarry in this operation. All the men he selected had demonstrated their capacity to scale a cliff wall, and that included himself, Curio, and Falco. None of them could afford to hesitate. They were stealing into a fort that was said to never sleep, that was an unblinking eye ever staring into the glare of the surrounding desert.

But the locals knew it was more legend than truth. Varro imagined a canny fort commander paying merchants to spread the rumors. This was not a trouble-spot where such vigilance was necessary, and Varro smelled the lie in the half-truth. Indeed, a substantial force could not approach this hilltop fortress in the day without detection. But that was true for most of the forts studding the wilderness outposts. The hills of Numidia shaded off into Carthaginian lands to spill into flat grass plains or scrub such as this.

So he raced up the side, aware that guards did watch but less so from this side, where steep hills and rugged terrain would stop attackers better than arrows shot from the walls.

His sandals whispered on the stone. The rope burned in his

calloused hands, but each knot was fat and reassuring. He had the strength in his chest and shoulders to walk sideways up a wall in mail armor. Such was the rigor of his daily training that he possessed strength he would never have imagined possible before he joined the legions.

Without hobnails to aid his grip, he slipped and paused on his ascent. But hobnails would give him away, not to mention he had discovered them rare in Numidia. His old caligae were now down to three hobnails per sole, and a disgrace to legion standards as well as utterly useless for military operations.

Upon reaching the top of the wall, he no longer felt so cold. His arms quivered with the effort of his climb and his shoulders burned. Sweat beaded on his face, both from the exertion and nerves. A wooden walkway was set behind the parapet, leaving enough space for a man to stand and one to slip behind him. Thin wooden rails protected against falling into the yard below, but were flimsy enough to break with a hefty kick.

The rope remained taut as Curio and the others were now behind him in a steady line. Varro searched both left and right, finding no one present on the stretch of walkway.

So much for the never-sleeping fortress, he thought. He would wake them soon enough.

As Curio's hands grabbed the wall edge, Varro shuffled in a crouch toward the nearest ladder. Corner towers were the principal ways patrols reached the walls, but wooden ladders were set at intervals to facilitate rapid response from the defenders. Varro found that trying to move the ladder from this height was impossible, at least from a crouching position. It dragged and made too much noise, and he felt as if it might slip from his hands and crash to the ground below.

So he waved Curio his way, then turned to examine the layout, finding it as expected.

He had done his preparations, paying merchants for intelligence on what they had observed inside the fort. It had been risky to do so, since an unscrupulous merchant could report back to the Carthaginians for a double payout. Most had been willing to just continue on into Numidia, but one merchant had proved loyal to Carthage. To Varro's disgust, he had to resort to violence. He had reconciled killing in warfare, and even in circumstances like tonight. But he could not kill an innocent man, and so had him and his companions bound and sent under guard to Cirta, where they would be too far away to make trouble. It was less expedient than eliminating him and cost him men from his force. But he had to sleep at night.

When Curio joined him, they both started down the ladder into the night-shrouded yard below. The main fortress was better guarded, particularly at the front where four men stood on watch and bathed in the light of several torches. But they were entering a side door for servants and slaves, which might be barred but not guarded.

He stepped off the final rungs onto the hard-packed ground, then sped at a crouch to the broken wagon that one informant said had been left in the corner for months. It made for excellent cover, being shadowed and by the wall.

Still not daring to speak, they both nodded to each other as they waited for the other infiltrators to join. They were hard to see against the parapet and shrouded all in black.

While he waited, he noted the thin dots of orange torchlight connecting along the gatehouse and front wall. If there were a dozen men on watch, he would be surprised. Considering this fort now housed riches stolen from Massylii tribes, he would have counted on a higher alert. The tribes had not been quiet in their outrage, and their holy men had made curses and issued death threats to the fort commander.

But this commander was more greedy than cautious, or so it seemed. It also seemed he believed his own lies about the defenses of his fort.

At last, half the raiders gathered behind the wagon. They were safe from detection in this derelict corner of trash and broken wagon parts. So Varro dared to whisper in his passable Massylii speech.

"Do you have the bar?" he asked Curio, who carried the gear for entrance and escape, but he instead nodded to another man. He opened his robe to display the dark iron pry bar strapped to his side.

"We'll need it for the servant entrance," he said. "It will be barred. After that, I don't know. Keep it ready."

He then assessed the rest of their gear. The brawniest man outside of Falco had a leather sack cinched to his back and would carry their objective out of the fortress. The other had arrows wrapped with pitch-soaked cloth and a short bow which he now strung. It was everything needed to begin.

"Falco has our backs," he whispered. "Let's reclaim what was stolen from us."

The raiders were all Massylii tribesmen, but all part of the standing Numidian army. Even if the stolen treasures were not their own, rage still burned in their hearts. The Carthaginians had made a grievous mistake in stealing a golden statue of their beloved goddess, Tanit. It was a famous treasure, but a series of missteps had placed it in the path of an opportunistic Carthaginian commander. If he had left it alone, he might not be in the danger he faced tonight.

But now every tribesman in the region wanted his blood. King Masinissa, eager to please those who only recently rose in revolt, commanded Varro to deliver that blood and statue to his people.

They sped along under cover of darkness to the servant door.

Varro drew his pugio, and he and Curio flanked the entrance. The man with the pry bar went to work as the others kept careful watch, their long knives drawn and glinting in the moonlight.

The door groaned then planks shattered. To Varro it seemed as loud as thunder, and he feared the front entrance guards might hear. But the tribesman already had his arm through the door and lifted away the bar. It was not a technique for entering a room with armed defenders, but against slaves it was safe enough.

The door opened and Varro was first inside. Even though his eyes were adjusted to the night, this room was black. He stumbled over something soft, and Curio shoved him as he too entered. Wheeling around, he could not keep his balance and fell atop a sleeping body.

A cry of surprise rang in his ear, and a wet breath rolled over his cheek. It was a man's voice, and whoever he landed on screamed.

He clapped his hand over the man's face, searching for his mouth. But as they wrestled, the man shouted in Carthaginian. Varro's palm slipped over the mouth at last, but his little finger pressed into it and the man bit down.

Now he cried out in pain, snapping his hand back.

In the next moment, a heavy thud landed beside his own head, followed by a crack and a hot splash of fluid. The body under him went still.

He could not identify the shape hovering over him other than he was too big to be Curio. He extended a hand to haul Varro to his feet, and he saw the raider held a crowbar that now dripped blood. The moonlight faintly illuminated the room, and he saw the bare legs of slaves kicking back into the corners of the room. One of his men spoke the language of Carthage, and though the words were gibberish to Varro, he knew he commanded the slaves to silence.

"You fell," Curio whispered beside him.

"Yes, thanks for that. Now, we're to go down the corridor, to the right, and down the stairs to the storerooms. There will have to be guards. Let's be quieter."

They slipped into the black corridor, and Varro kept his hand to the west wall as instructed. The merchants he interviewed were instructed to carry their deliveries to the lower supply rooms. The treasures would either be there or in the commander's quarters. In either case, he had to check both.

They traveled in a long line, finding the stairs and seeing the dull flicker of candlelight below. Someone was snoring, and from the top of the stairs Varro could see a shadow and a sandaled foot extended into the archway.

He padded down the stairs, pugio in hand. He stepped out into the small room and stood before a sleeping guard. His head leaned against the wall and his mouth hung open as he snored.

Varro and Curio stared at him. With a shrug, Curio cut his neck. Varro turned aside. Soldiers die, he thought to himself. This one might not have deserved it, but such was his fate and Varro could not risk all his men for one enemy.

With the key retrieved, the door unlocked and swept open. One man raised his candle to show the inside.

The goddess Tanit sat atop a chest that was likely filled with the other riches gained by the Carthaginians. She had the head of a lion and her eyes caught the candlelight. For a moment, Varro shuddered at this foreign and evil visage. But the tribesmen behind him whispered prayers and thanks. Their holy statue would be restored to its temple.

"Load it up," Varro said, and the raiders went to work.

He looked about the room, finding other sacks, crates, and small casks. These were likely the garrison supplies, and Varro thought about destroying them. But it was not his mission.

"This is almost too easy," Curio said. "I mean, other than you falling over someone."

But before Varro could answer, he heard a shout and clash of swords in the corridors above.

"You cursed us," he said instead, then looked to his men. "Secure the statue and get it out no matter what. I'll finish the mission."

In the corridor, the rearguard fought at the top of the stairs. He could not tell who prevailed, or if Falco was among them. Regardless, as the leader he had to push to the front.

The confines of the hall made it impossible for more than one man to fight at once, and Varro emerged onto a scene lit by a wildly swaying lamp. A soldier lay in a dark puddle underfoot, while his black-clad men pressed on another desperate soldier. The swaying light came from the last soldier fleeing back the way he had come.

The one fear Varro had was becoming trapped in the lower fort, as there was only a single escape path he knew of. For the moment, his men prevailed and the struggle ended when the Carthaginian collapsed with a scream.

But before he could even draw a breath of relief, a horn sounded outside, sharp and high pitched like a panicked scream.

"We're caught," Falco said, now speaking plainly out of the darkness. His bulk filled the corridor they had just come down.

"The statue has been recovered," he said. "You've got to get it over the wall. Take the bowman, and stick to our plan."

"What about you? The commander will certainly be guarded now."

"Stick to the plan," Varro snapped. "I'll take Curio and the rest of my team. I'll finish the mission. The commander's head will be on Cirta's walls by tomorrow night. Now get going."

"The plan is madness," Falco said. "But it has to be, since it was yours. Very well, meet you over the wall."

Varro nodded at the shadow of his best friend. The team had already mounted the stairs with the statue of the goddess now secured on the back of his strongest man, whose smile beamed even in the dark.

"Curio and you three, come with me. The rest get over the wall. We're going hunting for a commander's head."

2

The blaring horns echoed down the hallway. Varro only knew the direction that the soldier had fled, but in this near total darkness he could not determine what lay ahead. He could find the side exit by memory, but nothing more. The candlelight below guttered and sparkled on the expanding pool of blood at the bottom of the stairs.

The salty taste of blood tinged his mouth, a splatter left from the servant he had tripped over. Soon it might be his own if he did not act. The entire fortress would converge on them, bringing the commander who was the second half of his mission. But he would never fight through his guards to reach him, and even if he did, he could not escape.

At least not until Falco sent the signal for Baku to begin his feint.

Curio and the three men he selected to remain with him looked expectantly at him. Faint yellow light danced on the stone stairwell behind them, cast by the lone candle by the slain guard at the bottom.

"You have a plan?" Curio asked. "Or you just picked this moment to get us all killed? You could've left me out of that plan."

Varro held up a hand for silence. He could not return to Masinissa with only half the mission completed. A message had to be sent, and punishment dealt, or else the king would appear weak to his enraged subjects. That Varro had spoken so vocally to get this mission meant he had to succeed or risk the king's wrath and embarrass Rome as well.

"I think they're coming," Curio said. "We're out of time."

"Trust the plan," Varro said at last. "Falco and the rest don't have to creep around. They're running, and will send the signal any moment. This may not be where I planned to catch the commander, but it might even be better."

"I don't see how being trapped in the heart of an enemy fort is a better idea," Curio said, peering into the blackness ahead.

In the distance more horns sounded and Varro smiled.

"That's Falco. They've started the fire and Baku will now come."

The archer with the pitch-soaked arrows would send flaming shafts into the stables, which were close to where they had entered. This would panic the animals, possibly start a fire, but most importantly the flaming arrows streaking through the sky would signal Baku, who watched for them.

It would also call attention to the rope and hook used to enter, but Varro had not planned to exit that way.

They heard voices shouting and confusion in the blackness down the hall. Varro had only a moment to decide whether to flee or to trust his hunch that the commander, being greedy and small-minded, would want to see with his own eyes if his treasure had been stolen. It was a small room, with only space for a few men to stand. He would come with few guards, expecting the thieves were already outside his walls and wanting to know if he needed to dispatch riders in pursuit of his stolen wealth.

Voices echoed down the hall, angry and shouting. One was brasher and louder than the others. In another circumstance, Varro might have wondered if he was an officer. But he knew it had to be the commander. His rooms were just a few floors above, making it a quick check to confirm what he had learned from his guard's report.

That thought gave Varro inspiration.

"Get back to the room below," he whispered. "Lie down as if slain. He will expect to find dead bodies and his eyes will seek the statue first. Attack when I do."

They fled down the stairs, where two of his men lay down on them as if killed. Curio dragged the body of the guard he slew over himself and Varro slumped against the wall inside the room and closed his eyes.

He feared his throbbing neck would reveal him. But he heard shouting and cursing drawing closer. Straining his ears, even below ground he could hear the din outside as the alarm intensified. By now they were seeing Baku's line of false soldiers. Certainly there was real cavalry there, but they had constructed two straw dummies in simple robes for every real man, and the murky torchlight that Baku arranged would show them only as shapes that danced and threatened to attack. Each man would hold up a dummy with each of his hands. The ruse would not last long, but would suffice for their purposes.

A shout rang out from atop the stairs, angry and bitter. With his eyes closed, Varro felt even more panic. But his hand tightened on his pugio, hidden under his leg. The voice grumbled and cursed, and he heard quick steps descending closer. He imagined the commander picking through men ready to kill him, never wondering how his few soldiers had killed so many. But the confusion of the moment and the need for haste would cloud his judgement.

He felt the commander's presence outside the opened door. A

sharp intake of breath and a curse burst over his head, letting Varro know his moment.

The commander stepped in and in that instant Varro's arm shot out. He grabbed the commander's ankle and sent him sprawling to the floor.

While the commander screamed and struggled, he staggered upright himself. Being in a heavy mail shirt in a crowded space limited his movements. But while the brawny commander lay flat before the chest where his ill-gotten prize had once rested, Varro now hovered over him. To his rear, Curio and his other men burst into shouting with blades ringing against metal and stone.

The commander flipped onto his back, revealing a bright red face framed in stark black hair. His eyes reminded Varro of a boar's and he seemed to have the same temperament, for he spit curses and reached for his own dagger.

But Varro was faster, the hound at his quarry's throat, and dropped his knee into the commander's gut. The mail shirt crushed against Varro's knee, but the commander's breath rushed out like air forced from a blacksmith's bellows.

The pugio slammed into his neck, plunging down to Varro's hand. Blood erupted onto the floor. The commander grabbed Varro's wrist, but then his eyes unfocused and his body went slack.

"We're clear," Curio said, looking into the room. "He only had two others with him, and not very alert ones."

Varro felt dizzy and out of breath, less from the effort of finishing the commander and more from his nerves. Regaining himself, he brushed away the blood that now puddled in the collar of the commander's mail shirt. His heart raced and he felt faint when his searching found nothing. But then it swept across the gold chain he sought and the silver coin attached.

"Here it is," Varro said, snapping the chain off then dumping it into a pouch. "The commander's so-called lucky coin. Didn't do him much good. He died like a pig."

"So that proves he is the commander," Curio said. "You were right about him. He worried more about his treasures than his own men."

Varro summoned his two other raiders and pointed to the corpse at his feet.

"Cut off his head and don't lose it or your king will replace it with ours."

The raiders fell to the grizzly work while Varro and Curio remounted the stairs. A light shined in the distance down the formerly dark hall. Beyond, he heard nearer shouting and the stomping of feet. Above him, the ceiling thudded with men rushing in confusion.

The raiders returned with a sack that was already black with dripping blood. Without another word, everyone knowing their limited time, they retraced back to the slave room. The door hung open and all the slaves had escaped but for the one dead where he slept.

They filed out into the moonlight where shouted orders echoed through the yard and silver-lined outlines of men ran toward a dull orange blaze out of Varro's sight. Soldiers were climbing the very ladders they had used to descend the wall, too late to catch Falco and the others.

Curio led them to the rear of the fort, where the guards had all been drawn away to face the threat of fire in the stables and an approaching enemy to the front. The average soldier and officer would not realize what happened, and would guess the enemy had attempted to open the gates. Therefore, the guard was lightest at the quiet rear of the fort.

They did not hesitate, but made for the corner tower, finding its door unlocked. Varro kept his pugio ready as he swept open the door and led them inside. But the bottom floor was dark. Memories of Sparta filled his thoughts, bringing back fears of falling and hanging from walls. But he padded up the stairs, feeling like the black shadow he must appear as. The next floor had a lit lamp and straw beds, and the top floor was lit by moonlight from an opened door. Three men stood just outside of it, straining to see what was happening, but not daring to leave their posts.

Varro slammed the door behind them, and one of his men slid the bolt into place. The enemies outside shouted and banged on the door, but Varro and the team did not delay. They exited to the other wall and stopped just outside the door.

"This is horsehair rope," Curio said. "Stronger and thinner than the other stuff. I couldn't tie knots in this one and keep it long enough."

"No matter," Varro said. "You're the master of this art. I'll follow you now."

Curio gave a small smile as he produced an iron spike and iron-headed mallet. He dropped the thin coil of rope onto the wooden planks. It made such a weak thump that Varro wondered if it could hold them. But Curio had studied with masters from the palace who were learned in these ways. If they said this rope would hold them, he would not argue.

Working with practiced speed, Curio hammered in the spike and secured the rope. He flipped it over the side, then leaned out to check on it.

"I'll go first," he said. "It's not long enough to reach the ground, but hang a moment before dropping and you'll be fine."

With that, Curio disappeared over the ledge. Varro sent the other two before him while watching the tower door. The guards on the opposite side were bashing at the far door and a muffled crack of wood told they had breached it.

If they did, Varro was over the side before he found out. The rope was difficult to grip and he slipped a large way down, burning his hands. But soon he alighted on the hard earth underfoot. The four men smiled and clapped each other's shoulders before fleeing into the darkness and then looping around to where Baku had left their horses.

Whatever happened at the fortress, Varro never learned. He instead rode with his companions into the dark desert night with chilly winds assuaging the heat on his face. When he was far enough from danger, he laughed and felt as if he could ride forever through this silvery blue landscape and never tire.

∽

∽

THE FEAST KING Masinissa had hosted for them left Varro feeling more stuffed than he ever had before. While it was Numidian custom to eat mostly vegetables and little if any meat, the king had offered lamb and duck as well as fish and fine wine to his Roman guests. He sat at the head of his splendid table, in a plain white toga matched by all his guests, with Baku seated at his right hand. Being a cousin of the king already awarded him honor at court, but over the last year his esteem had risen with the successful raiding he and Varro had coordinated. He smiled, his halo of wild and frizzy hair nodding as he raised his cup.

"You have become a true ghost of the mountains," he said to Varro, as well as Falco and Curio who sat with him. "A year ago, I thought you would simply become a lost spirit wandering the mountains forever. But I was wrong."

They had already been toasted enough that night for Varro to wince in embarrassment. But Masinissa, full of drink and victory, joined his cup with Baku's and therefore all the gathered ministers and officers at the table once more put on their smiles and raised their silver cups.

It was the sweet date wine Varro had grown to love in his time in Numidia. Even though it had been first served to him by an enemy, he was willing to forgive anything for its delicious taste. He sipped it to savor its unique taste. Falco instead gulped it and feigned enjoyment. In private, he had called it too sweet and claimed he'd rather drink vinegar.

"I will never tire of hearing how you fooled the Carthaginians with straw men." King Masinissa had finished his cup and set it aside, smiling brightly and perhaps drunkenly. "That is the sort of trickery one would expect from the Greeks."

"I was long in that country, my king. So perhaps I had learned more from them than I thought." Varro had once refused to call Masinissa a king, as the idea of kingship was repugnant to him as it was to all Romans. But he had learned no other way to address him. Furthermore, he liked Masinissa and respected him as a modern leader and brave commander. So the title seemed the best way to honor him and keep himself out of trouble.

"I'll brook no credit to the Greeks for the good work Baku has done in teaching you how to fight like a mountain ghost." The king patted his cousin's shoulder, then left his hand resting on it. "Your consul sent you to learn these ways from us. And so you have."

Baku shook his head. "They have learned some things, my king. But not everything they could. There is still time yet, though. The best is yet to come."

While Baku laughed along with others seated around the table, Masinissa's expression fell and his hand slipped from Baku's shoulder. Unlike the usual sensitivity to a king's mood from his court, the toga-clad guests continued to laugh and enjoy their date wine. Varro looked to his friends for confirmation of what he had observed, but Falco was frowning as he forced down more wine and Curio was staring at one of the beautiful slave girls standing at the rear of the brightly lit chamber.

Only he seemed aware of the king's sudden melancholy. But

then that shadow passed and he was once more laughing with Baku, who had not caught the change in his king and kin's mood.

The night continued with retellings of King Masinissa's exploits, many of which were to Rome's embarrassment. Everyone was drunk, and rather than take offense Varro took it as a sign of trust in him. The king had a glorious past, and most of it had been as an enemy of Rome. But his loyalty as a Roman ally was not beyond doubt, as in a show of loyalty he had ordered his wife to suicide at Scipio's instigation. So Varro accepted the stories for what they were, tales to remind everyone Masinissa did not just sit on thrones and drink around banquet tables. He also rode to battle against his foes, bringing victory for his followers and allies and woeful defeat for his enemies.

Neither Falco nor Curio minded the stories. Indeed, none of them were of a high enough rank to express displeasure. As it was, Falco was glassy-eyed from drinking wine he disliked and Curio was distracted by the slave girl who had likewise noticed him. Neither was concerned with much else.

So the night ended when the king stood, thanked his guests, and thanked his Roman allies for settling what could've become a wildfire issue.

"Indeed, Carthage itself should thank you. For you spared them of a commander both corrupt and foolish, such a man no one wants leading his soldiers. I fear they will replace him with a better officer, one less greedy and more assured of himself. But I'd rather face trouble from him than the anger and outrage of my people."

The rest of the chamber stood after their king, and it was clear they would wait for him to leave before resigning the room themselves. So the guests raised their brows when the king announced otherwise.

"You may all leave now. The Romans must remain, and you as well, Baku. The rest of you, I thank for your company tonight."

Varro stood by, straightening his borrowed toga as he avoided looking at the other guests. While they had gathered to celebrate him with their king, he knew many were cautious of him as a foreigner, and several despised him for no better reason than that. So he tried to avoid the discomfort of fleeting glares and narrowing eyes. Certainly not everyone felt this way, but enough that he wished he were in the field fighting an enemy he could kill with a sword rather than with innuendo. Such was a king's court, and doubtless the Roman Senate would fare no better. Power begets such foolish jealousies, he told himself.

When at last the guests had retired, the king dismissed his servants. Curio sighed as the object of his admiration filed out the back door, never looking behind herself.

"She's not worth the danger," Falco said under his breath. "King's property and all."

"Was I so obvious?" Curio asked.

Of course he was, but Falco did not answer before King Masinissa again returned to his seat and gestured the others do as well.

"You have had a shift in moods tonight, my king. What has brought you trouble in victory?"

Masinissa gave a small smile. "Sorry to alarm you, cousin, for it is not grave news. Indeed, for some it might even be cause for rejoicing. But my mood has been clouded as this news reached me on this day. For I was just celebrating with my Roman allies and friends, and here I must bid them farewell before their appointed term has finished."

Varro leaned forward, as did Falco and Curio. Baku's halo of frizzy hair shook along with his head, but the king nodded in acknowledgement.

"The message arrived this morning." Masinissa pulled a papyrus scroll from where he sat. It was tied with a string and rolled lightly atop the table as he set it down.

Varro blinked at it, realizing his world was about to change again.

Masinissa pushed the scroll closer.

"You may read the message, as it is addressed to you three. But you must know what it contains already. There is trouble, and Rome needs you."

3

The parting at Cirta had been difficult for Varro. He had lived "leg to leg" with Baku, as he liked to say, for the last year. While parting with King Masinissa was a formality and did elicit regret at not learning more from this unique man, parting with Baku brought stinging tears to his eyes. That Baku would return to the men back at the camp without him felt strange and empty, as if he had dreamed.

But they stood at the stone bridge leading away from the impenetrable city of Cirta, framed in the cool light of a spring morning. Baku's hair waved in the wind as they gripped forearms in the Roman manner.

"Centurion Varro once more, eh? No longer the mountain ghost. The men will miss you, or at least they will pretend so."

Varro lowered his head to hide his smile. "They must march into the mountains every day, Baku. They can rest on the third day, then train with sword and javelin for another three days. Just keep that rotation and don't let them grow slack. I will find out, and I will return to issue punishments. I promise you."

"They will believe it if I tell them," Baku said, tugging on his arm. "But I will not tell them. The mountain ghosts will live on, even without me. With you gone, I expect another will inherit the command. It is good to have known you, Varro. Do not forget my lessons. You fight like a lion. Yet even lions will hide in the grass to catch their prey."

"I will not forget." He wanted to say more, but he felt as if something had caught in his throat. So he gave a hard shake, then clapped Baku's shoulder before turning aside to join the caravan headed to Russicada.

Both Falco and Curio made their farewells, but neither were as close to Baku as he.

Now, a day later, they stood on the deck of a fat-hulled trader and her escort ships heading north for Rome. From there, they would purchase ship transport to Luna, which was their appointed rally point. The sails above cracked and the masts creaked, while a drum beat the time of the oars as sailors labored at their benches. The sea air was crisp and fresh in his face, and while he was no great lover of ships, he was finding time on the sea to be less taxing to his nerves. He leaned on the rails and scanned the inscrutable horizon of dark waves and blue skies.

Behind him, Curio fretted in a low voice with Falco, wondering if his reading skills would be tested.

"It's the writing part that worries me," he said. "I can read fine, but I need to look at my letters when I write. What if they won't let me do that?"

"We're not presenting ourselves to a fucking tutor, Curio. We're joining the legion again. Have you ever heard of a writing test to join the army? What good would that do? You going to hand a letter to the enemy? No, you just need to kill whoever they say is an enemy, even if it's your mother."

"But it's required for promotion. I can't just be a ranker and be in Serv—"

"Shut up."

Varro heard Falco slap the rails and Curio cut himself short.

He was about to name Servus Capax, the organization that his great-grandfather had been part of and somehow his mother had managed to ensnare him in. Falco had sneered at the name, and indeed the name Useful Servants did sound harmless. In fact, he still understood very little of what he was doing in that service. He had dragged Falco and Curio into it, even though they followed him to Numidia of their own accord. They knew even less than he did.

Consul Flamininus, now a senator, had sent him to learn from Masinissa and practice guerrilla warfare. He had done so for a year, but wondered why such techniques would be of use if he were to be in active military service. The Roman army, and indeed most armies of the world, did not fight like that. It was the desperate tactics of outnumbered men, or so he supposed. However, he had learned to ride and fight from horseback, and now believed he could hold his own with any cavalryman. The consul had indicated both goals in his initial assignment, but again Varro could not discern the purpose. It was beyond him, and he just followed orders. In return, his life was taken care of and the enemies his father had made for him were kept at bay. Where his mother and sister were now, he did not care at all.

As Curio and Falco continued to mumble, Varro's mind carried back to the papyrus message sent from Rome. He withdrew it from his tunic and tried to hold it taut against the sea wind which swept over the decks as they sped north. He had lost the string, but was supposed to destroy the message in any case.

The letter was addressed to him, Falco, and Curio, and done in Flamininus's careful script. It occurred to him that he held a personal letter from a man history would remember. Suddenly the thought of tossing the papyrus into the sea felt wasteful, as if he might need one day to prove that he had in fact worked closely with Flamininus.

Yet equally likely, he might need to deny any association with him.

So he flattened the letter against the rails to read it a final time.

～

By necessity, our communications have been limited. I trust you have learned much and succeeded in all tasks assigned to you. I have utilized my own means to stay abreast of your progress. It is with some regret that I cannot allow for you to remain in Numidia any longer.

You are hereby summoned to report to Consul Marcus Porcius Cato at the port of Luna. A letter to the consul is attached, authorizing you to speak directly with him on my behalf. You must proceed with all haste, as you will be rejoining the legion in active duty and will be assigned responsibilities as Consul Cato sees fit. He will be aware of your complete service record and will certainly make use of your talents.

I must impress upon you to serve the consul as you have served me in the past. There is great peril to Rome's interests and the consul will resolve the issue, namely an uprising in Nearer Iberia. As such, you must do all within your power to ensure the consul's success, which is already assumed. But you must also do whatever is necessary to extinguish future uprisings and ensure those Iberian tribes allied to Rome remain firmly in hand.

You will find Consul Cato's camp to be quite different from my own, yet I'm certain you will make the adjustment. I will meet you in Rome upon your triumphant return from the campaign.

～

THE FINAL LINES were instructions on how to reach Luna and an order that he destroy the letter he now held in one hand over the rails. The wind tugged at it pinched between his fingers, as if the spirits of the air were eager to steal it. He watched the blank horizon, wondering what was beyond it and how sailors could know the difference between a horizon and the edge of the world.

The papyrus finally tore from his hand, spinning down the length of the hull to finally drop into the foam. An oar stroked over it and the letter was gone.

This was his first communication from Flamininus, though he had apparently been kept informed. While Varro wondered how he did this, it was not hard to imagine a spy in Masinissa's court passing information. Less dramatically, someone from Masinissa's court probably had a responsibility for sending updates to Rome. He shook his head, embarrassed at his overblown sense of importance. No one really cared what he did in the mountains of Numidia. Flamininus had probably received a single report to state something to the effect of "Varro is alive and following orders."

But there was something else in the letter that had caused him to read it twice more since Masinissa passed it to him. Though while once in Varro's hand the letter was safe, along the journey anyone could intercept and read it. How much more likely would that be for a man so recently famous as Flamininus? His enemies would be looking for whatever secrets they could drag to light. So he could not openly state his intentions, but had to stimulate Varro's interest to think deeper about what he meant.

Why did he mention differences in camps? There could not be any difference in a Roman camp anywhere in the world. They were of set design, operating with ferocious and tenacious precision. No detail was too small for standardization. Even the number of stakes per side of a marching camp were predetermined.

As he studied the sparkling waves that seemed to be racing alongside the ship, he realized Flamininus was warning him that Cato was a different personality. But more than this, he was likely warning him Cato was of an opposite faction to Flamininus's.

While he did not have the slightest idea of how the Roman Senate operated, he had learned much from Baku about court politics. Indeed, Baku himself had almost been left in enemy custody in hopes he would die simply for the envy of another member of the court. He understood politics as well as warfare and shared some thoughts with Varro.

It was important to belong to a faction, he had told him. Preferably the strongest faction, which was not always the one allied to the king or the most visible one. Varro could not imagine Baku betraying his own kin for politics, but then what did Varro know of such things? His friend had been honest and so he must believe him.

Of course, similar structures exist wherever men vied for glory and power, and there was no greater place in the world for this than the Senate.

So Cato might be of an opposing faction to Flamininus's, and therefore simply by association Varro and the others would be like uninvited guests to Cato.

"You've got that look," Falco said. He now leaned on the rail beside him, and Varro hadn't noticed.

"I was just wondering what it will be like to serve under Consul Cato."

Falco shrugged. "More of the same shit. You know, march all day. Guard duty. Drills. Working construction projects just to have something to do. Then go out and kill some enemies when we have a free moment. Why are you worried?"

Varro shook his head and smiled. He should not contaminate his friends with his own worries.

"I worry because everything is changing again. A new consul, a new land, a new people."

"You're getting a bit romantic, aren't you?" Falco's heavy brow rose as he faced Varro. "You're all poetic because Baku started calling us the mountain ghosts. Forget that, friend. Nothing is new.

It'll be the same as ever, no matter where we go. The army is a world of its own."

So they laughed off Varro's mood and settled into a journey of two days to cross the placid seas back to Rome.

The captain thanked them for the luck they brought, for he could not remember easier sailing. Falco was of the opinion that he'd have rather not used up good fortune on smooth sailing, but preserved it for Iberia. Then Curio pointed out they would never reach Iberia had their ship been lost in a storm.

But as it was, they spent a short night in Ostia before boarding their ship northwest to the rally point at Luna. The levity between the three of them diminished as they drew closer to their destination. All of them realized they were rejoining the legion and began to wonder what ranks they would be assigned. Surely once a centurion always a centurion?

Others traveling with them on the ship laughed off such thoughts. They all had stories of men who had not been invited back to their former ranks. Of course, fine men such as Varro and Falco would never experience that, they had said. Still, the thought left a stain on their moods. It would be a humiliation to be sent back to the ranks. Curio remained conspicuously quiet on this account.

With a score of doubts clouding his thoughts, Varro watched the approach to Luna with a tightness in his chest. Huge triremes sat at anchor like sea beasts waiting to be unleashed. Scores of smaller vessels dotted the waves and sped like water bugs between the giant ships. On the shore, a camp had been erected, full of billowing animal skin tents of the legionary contubernia.

"Just like old times," Curio said, leaning over the rails with the rest of them. "It feels like yesterday."

"Don't be so nostalgic," Falco said. "You'll be smelling some hairy-assed stranger's feet in your tent tonight."

"Well, they're not going to break us up, I hope." Curio's bright expression fell and he stepped back from the rails. "I mean we're all with Serv—"

"I'm going to break your teeth next time," Falco said as he clamped his hand to Curio's mouth.

"It's especially important not to say anything about it until we know what's going on," Varro said.

Falco held his hand firm and gave Curio a warning glare before he removed it.

"But it only makes sense that we stick together."

"I'll ask for that," Varro said. He now looked to the docks where soldiers met incoming recruits and ordered them into lines. "Just be patient with whatever happens. We're back in the army, and that means we're in danger."

Falco groaned in agreement. "That's right. Look at your superior the wrong way and he'll flog the skin off your back."

"I have a hunch Cato will be like that." Varro said.

They had little time for small talk with strangers along the way to Luna. But he had learned Consul Cato had made a name for himself recently as being opposed to repealing the Oppian Laws, which restricted women from just about anything. Varro himself had no opinion and did not care whether women should own property or wear jewelry. He was inclined to agree with Cato on principle, since these laws had been effective since he was a boy and he knew nothing else.

Cato's opposition had been described as particularly passionate, if ineffective, since the restrictive laws had been abolished. Based on that and the few things he heard about Cato from fellow travelers, Varro guessed he was a traditional man. As a consul, he would enforce traditional discipline.

They disembarked with the crew and carried all their gear down the gangplank. Enriched as they were, they had donned mail shirts. They carried shining bronze helmets, new scutii in bags over their backs, a bronze leg greave each, plus all their weapons and field gear. They looked ready for battle, and this drew skeptical stares from the soldiers sent to meet them.

"You boys got stakes for the camp in those packs?" One man with a narrow face, long nose, and amiable countenance met them first. He nodded to their gear. "That's infantry gear. Veterans, I see?"

"Centurion Varro, First Legion, Tenth Maniple Hastati. We have instructions here to meet with Consul Cato."

The smile remained unchanged on the man's face. "Of course, sir. You're returning to active service today. So I think you'll probably want to meet the tribunes first."

Varro thrust out another papyrus scroll, one Masinissa had given him after Flamininus's letter. It was their authorization on Flamininus's behalf to meet with Consul Cato immediately upon arrival in Luna.

"Don't tell me what I want. Take me to the consul or find someone who can."

The smile faltered, and he looked at the papyrus. "I don't read, sir. I'll have to take you to the optio."

Their exchange ended, and the soldier marched them through the busy docks to a desk set up under an awning where a man who looked like a child in his father's mail shirt accepted the letter and read it.

"How do I know this is real?" He looked up innocently.

"Do you feel it in your hands?" Falco said. "If you do, then it's real. If you don't, this is a fucking dream and you'll wake up sucking your mother's tit. But I'll give you a hint if you need one."

The optio blinked his bright blue eyes and stared between them, either unconvinced or trying to figure out if he was dreaming.

Varro sighed. "Would any man wishing to live forge a note to gain audience with the consul on the eve of his first campaign? If we are lying, it will be our broken bodies thrown out to sea and not yours. The letter is real, so take us to the consul."

"But what if you are trying to get close enough to kill him?"

"I'm close enough to kill you," Falco said. "But I haven't tried even though the idea makes my hands tingle. Just do your duty, Optio. They didn't assign you here for your big thoughts."

This seemed to be the logic the optio needed to hear. He rose from the desk and gave an imperious order to another bored-looking man to keep things under control while he was away. The man seated a desk away barely waved his hand in acknowledgement.

They set out through the camp just behind the optio. Falco leaned into Varro.

"Not a good showing for our future brothers in arms. The optio looks about ten years old and is about as smart."

"We looked young before the army got our faces cut up," Varro said. "He's just a recruit."

"If they put a recruit into an optio's rank, Jupiter protect us all."

As they proceeded through the camp, they found the legions were already assembled and officers assigned. Centurions screamed at their charges, messengers flitted down the main paths, and soldiers were already drilling in the parade ground.

"There's not going to be a command for us," Falco said. "We're too late."

"Don't worry about what hasn't happened," Varro said, but he shared the same fears. It seemed they had arrived with barely enough time to spare.

The optio led them to the headquarters tent, which was large and clean but lacking in any decoration. The guards before it seemed competent and read the letter the optio handed them. Then one disappeared into the tent while the other tried not to look at Varro while still sizing him up.

Expecting to be sent away, Varro had to conceal his surprise when the guard held the tent flap open.

"The consul will see you now."

All the poise and relaxation Varro had fought to maintain fled as he led their small party into the dim interior. He had built up Cato into a snarling beast ready to tear their heads off, even if there was no cause to believe so. But now passing under the tent flap he felt his hands grow cold.

Consul Cato sat at his desk. His mail armor and bronze helmet were set on a rack beside him as if ready for immediate action. He was bent over Flamininus's letter and shaking his balding head.

He looked up with clear, impatient eyes and frowned.

"What new worries do you three bring me?" He brandished the letter. "Nothing good if this one sent you."

Varro swallowed, realizing his fears had not been amiss.

4

The interior of Cato's command tent was lit mostly by the light penetrating the heavy cloth of his tent, creating a suffuse yellow light. On his plain desk, which bore the clear scars of use and travel, a single red clay lamp cast a brighter circle over Flamininus's letter, now flattened under Cato's fat-veined hand. There was a sour smell in the air even though a fresh sea breeze popped the wall of the tent.

Cato himself was unpleasant to behold. He stared accusingly at them with a frown that Varro suspected might never leave his face. In fact, it seemed a smile might never have visited his lips in his entire life. He was going bald and had shaved his hair down to bare stubble. It did little to conceal his age, as his face was a mass of folds and creases. Their arrangement caused an unbidden comparison to cabbage in Varro's mind, and in fact he realized the scent in the air was much like boiled cabbage but less appetizing.

The consul's knuckles rapped on the table.

"Well, boys, you look in fine kit," he said with a fake smile, perhaps the only kind he knew. But this blew away with the fury of a storm at sea. He slammed his fist down on the table. "But you are three undisciplined children! Where is your salute? How do you present yourself to your betters?"

Varro snapped upright, his face burning with shame, and gave a crisp salute. Falco and Curio did as well. He had been so wrapped up in his concerns he had forgotten himself.

He provided his name and rank, as did Falco and Curio, and then stood rigidly looking toward the dark rear of the tent, which had not even been paneled off like every other command tent he had been in. There were a few trunks and a simple field cot for his bed, the sheets neatly folded. A clean set of caligae sat ready to wear, and it reminded Varro of the deplorable state of his own. Jupiter save him if Cato inspected him now.

The consul sat back, mollified for the moment. He again straightened the papyrus letter, which had rolled up when he stood from the desk. His frown deepened.

"Let's see your marks, then." He looked up expectantly. At first Varro panicked, not knowing what he wanted, but the consul's gaze went to his hip.

"Here it is, sir." He slowly reached for the pugio, not wanting to appear threatening. Yet somehow he felt not even a charging elephant would intimidate Cato. He drew it and held the pommel forward. The others did likewise.

Cato leaned forward to confirm the stylized owl heads inlaid in silver on the pommels of their weapons. His eyebrows wiped up and down as he looked between the three. He then flicked his hand to indicate they should sheath them again.

He gave a long sigh, then slid his hand down his craggy face to settle over his thin-lipped mouth.

"Two centurions and one optio."

Varro stiffened. His mind was so clouded with nerves he had not listened to Curio promote himself. Instantly he understood this was some plot of his and Falco's. But now was not the time, as Cato seemed about to send them all back to the ranks in any case.

"In that regard, I cannot complain."

Varro looked to Cato in shock, but the glare he received in return set him back to staring forward.

"My legions are bare recruits, and my intelligence says the enemy outnumbers us."

"Is it the entirety of Nearer Iberia, sir?" Varro asked. "Or just a large tribe that rebels?"

Cato let his hand drop and gave a thin smile. He sat back in his plain wooden chair. For a moment, only the creaking of the time-worn wood made any sound. In the distance, he heard officers shouting commands while Cato remained frozen in thought.

This stretched out until Varro's heart began to throb. The consul stood from his chair, then clasped his hands behind his back.

"Marcus Varro," he said. "Your record shows you served with distinction in Macedonia. Your two prior consuls, that pro-Greek lot which must include you, speak glowingly of your service. You've two grass crowns and an armful of citations for bravery. You were promoted to centurion in only your first few years of your first campaign. Truly, I've not met many with such a record."

"Thank you, sir."

He hated the feebleness in his voice, and hated more his own inability to remain calm. He could not understand what about Cato unnerved him so.

Cato winced at the thanks, closing his eyes as if someone had spit in his face.

"Ah," was all he said, then stepped around his desk to become a blur in Varro's peripheral vision.

"Varro, you have recently come from Numidia."

"That is correct, sir."

Again another pause, and Varro at last realized his misstep, clenching his teeth shut against more words. The consul said nothing.

Varro thought he heard his breathing, but realized it was his own blood roaring in his ears.

Cato stood hovering at his side for what seemed forever until at last he stepped behind and continued speaking in measured tones.

"Thank you for confirming what I clearly already know. Do you imagine yourself an orator?"

Not knowing whether he should answer, he hesitated. But Cato was not allowing even a moment for it. He gave an exasperated sigh.

"You speak out of turn and don't answer a direct question. And yet here you show up in my tent, with letters commending you to me and the record of a hero. I cannot reconcile this."

The consul now stood directly behind him. Sweat began to bead on his forehead. He nearly expected a blade thrust between his shoulders. But the consul lingered in silence until Varro felt about ready to shout.

"I can only believe that you have come to think of yourself as a hero. As someone above normal protocols, and that you can treat with me as if we were old friends. Well, I'm not sure what that upstart Flamininus enforced, but I implore you to forget every moment of it. None of what you knew will be of any use in my legions."

At his sides, Varro could see Falco and Curio trembling. He felt it himself. The wrath of the consul was fiercer for its coolness. He did not seek to burn them down, but freeze their blood. Cato heaved a sigh, then paced behind each of them before returning to his desk. He tilted his head back, his face now even more like the boiled cabbage Varro smelled in the air.

"I am going to forgive your unruly behavior this one time. Once, Varro. This is my single indulgence to your glorious service record and the scars you carry upon your body in the service of Rome. But from this moment forward, you will meet every standard of a soldier and centurion in perfect detail. I enforce the rule of law, and I never select the more lenient end of the punishments accorded to them. Do you understand?"

"Yes, sir!"

Cato's thin lips formed that same false smile. He then narrowed his eyes at the others.

"Your companion has used up your chances. You'll have none, seeing how Varro has provided the example. Behave like the heroes you are supposed to be and demonstrate unflagging adherence to the rules and traditions of the legion, and we will have no problems."

Falco and Curio both straightened their shoulders and confirmed their understanding. Cato seemed to calm, then returned to his chair.

"Servus Capax."

He spoke the words so casually that Varro would've flinched had he not anticipated the consul's rage.

"What good are spies and assassins to me? I've a war to fight."

Unable to control himself, he looked at Cato. He sneered back at him, but did not rebuke him. Instead, he let his eyes fall back to the letter.

"Centurions Varro and Falco, the Second Legion needs veteran leaders. The gods know the hastati are in a poor state. Tenth Maniple, Ninth and Tenth Centuries. Seems you can have your old ranks back. I don't have to tell you I need strong leaders on my flanks. So you two will be honored to get those men in condition to keep it strong no matter how many barbarians come at you."

Now Cato paused and licked his lips, smirking at Curio.

"Now, you're not very clever, are you, Optio Curio? I just told you I reviewed your complete military record and found no reference to your promotion to optio. Such a lie should warrant a good flogging."

"Sir," Falco said. "I promoted him while in Numidia."

"I find it hard to consider you two were centurions in Numidia, much less that Curio was made optio." He narrowed his eyes. "Flamininus did not mention anything of the sort in his letter."

"Sir," Varro said, firming his voice. "Did Senator Flamininus say anything about any of our ranks while in Numidia?"

Cato leaned back, his eyes hooded and his mouth falling into his characteristic frown. "I suppose not. Do you vouch for this promotion as well?"

"Of course, sir." Varro gave a solemn nod to Falco and Curio. "We enforced as much military discipline on the locals as we could, including our command structure."

Waving his hand dismissively, he sat back in his chair. "Very well, we shall make it so. Your Tribune Galenus will be made aware. Which of you two will the good Optio Curio report to?"

"He reports to me, sir," Varro said before Falco could speak. "I think this is the best arrangement, if you agree, sir."

"I've wasted enough time on this," he said. "Present yourselves to Tribune Galenus, and he'll show you to your command. As for your Servus Capax roles, for now let us focus on the military. When I need a thief to stab an enemy in the back, I'll be sure to call on you. Now, dismissed."

They filed outside into the fresher sea air. Varro heard Falco inhaling and he grabbed his arm to warn him for silence. They collected their gear then stalked aimlessly past the tent guards, into the parade ground where triarii leaned on their spears while watching younger men spar.

At last they reached a point where none of the busy camp might overhear them. They drew together in a circle, Curio rubbing at his nose.

"Did you smell cabbage in there? I'm so hungry."

"Optio?" Varro asked, folding his arms. "Just a few days ago, you were wondering if you can read well enough for the role. When did you two decide on the promotion?"

Curio's youthful face turned red and he lowered his eyes. But Falco waved off the question.

"We need to stick together, and it won't do to have a ranker be in good with the centurion. I heard Cato was tough and figured he'd never allow it. Besides, Curio is ready for it."

"Except he still is not completely literate," Varro said, tightening his arms across his chest.

"Gods, Varro, you've seen some of the officers we've served with. I'm not no scholar myself. You only have to write strength reports and the like. It's just the same stuff all the time and he won't even be writing that. He might read written orders, and he's good enough at it."

"I won't let you down," Curio said.

Varro narrowed his eyes. "I won't let you down, *sir*. We're back in the legion, Optio. When we're in front of the men you'll address me properly and not question my orders. Frame your suggestions in an appropriate way, and I'll listen. Above all, I will see you practicing your reading and writing every day."

Curio straightened up and nodded.

Falco put his hands on his hips and looked back at the command tent.

"The Second Legion. We belong in the First, not the backup force."

"It doesn't matter," Varro said. "It sounds like we're going to be outnumbered enough that both legions will see plenty of action. What bothered me most was his thoughts about our other assignments."

"You mean Ser—"

Both Varro and Falco glared at Curio, who quickly clamped his hand over his mouth.

"Is it really that hard to learn not to say it aloud?" Falco asked, shaking his head. Then he looked back toward the command tent again. "He has a low opinion of what we do."

"Maybe he knows more about what we do than us. I'll kill Rome's enemies, but I'm not going to become a murderer." Varro thought back to his great-grandfather's frantic warnings and shivered. "In any case, he called us thieves. So I think we're safe to say he won't be much of an ally to us."

"He also seemed to hate Consul Flamininus," Curio said. "I wonder if we can change his mind about us."

"We won't," Varro said. "A man like Cato makes up his mind and there is no force in the mortal world that will change it. So let's hope for a warmer welcome from our tribune."

Once more hefting their packs and shields, they sought directions to Tribune Galenus and found him overseeing the drilling of the hastati. He stood dressed in his muscled bronze chest plate with arms folded and a vine cane usually carried by the centurion. Hundreds of his soldiers were sparring with wooden swords. The clack and cry of the exercise drowned out all other sound as Varro and the others crossed.

The tribune noticed their approach and unfolded his arms. Once Varro drew close, he immediately understood Galenus would be no friend of theirs even though a word had not been spoken between them. His angry face was a less-folded version of Cato's. His bronze helmet hid his hair, but Varro would not be surprised if he were as bald as the consul. Even their taut posture seemed to join them in Varro's mind.

Yet they reported to the tribune and repeated Cato's instructions. All the while Galenus gave shallow nods, and frowned when he learned Cato had agreed to name Curio as optio of the Tenth Century.

"The tenth already have an optio. I've been holding the centurion positions for you two to finally arrive."

While it was customary for centurions to have a voice in who would be their optiones, the tribune could override everything.

Varro did not answer the challenge and instead let his new commander consider his choices. At last, his frown deepened.

"I picked him myself. But if Consul Cato thinks this one is a better choice, then we will make the change. You're a veteran, Optio?"

"We all are, sir."

"I didn't ask about the others, did I? Next time answer my questions without any embellishment." He gave a tired look back to the men training. He handed the vine cane in his lean hands to Varro. "I'm glad to have experienced men to lead. Experience has been carved into your face, Centurion. You'll scare these men into shape. Take that vine and make them into soldiers. We've one day before we sail. You know what to do."

Galenus halted the training long enough to introduce the leadership changes and thank the acting optio for his service. This man, as youthful and clean-faced as any recruit, was clearly shocked to learn his role had been temporary. But upon seeing Curio now donning his war gear, the former optio's face reddened and he simply lowered his head in acknowledgement.

Varro and Falco spent their first hours assessing the men under their command. It did not bother him to have mostly seventeen-year-old men in his century. He was not old himself, compared to other centurions. What disturbed him was sailing to Iberia within a day. Just watching these men, he knew they were unprepared for combat. They had hardly formed any bonds between themselves, and did not know the danger facing them. Their weapon skill lacked.

The Iberian barbarian, as Varro had learned in conversations since returning from Numidia, was not to be underestimated. They were strong and brave and fought with swords just like his gladius. In fact, though he could not believe it, some said the gladius and pugio were introduced to the Roman army based on the Iberian barbarians' devastating use of such weapons against them.

When these green hastati faced the best weapons known being wielded by long-warring barbarian tribesmen, the bloodshed would be horrendous, and not all on the Iberian side. Many of these sweating, grim-faced young men were sailing off to their deaths.

He had a day to prepare them. It might be more effective to help them settle their wills and affairs at home than drill them any more in swordplay. There was no time to improve them.

Yet he did drill them. After the introduction and his and Falco's assessments, they set to work on the Tenth Maniple. Varro's cane slashed men into shape. He screamed in their ears, beat them on the shoulders, took the best aside and sparred with them so that each knew what defeat felt like. He had sixty men, as did Falco. One hundred twenty lives were entrusted to them. Varro knew Flamininus wanted him to learn how to spend his soldiers' lives in the service of a higher good. He could do that. But he would not spend the lives of men who had no chance.

So they drilled and practiced until men fell out in exhaustion. They remained training when other centuries retired, and this seemed to please Tribune Galenus. He left the Tenth Maniple to drill while others were already setting their cooking fires.

If the men did not hate him, Varro thought, then he was not doing his job. By the next day, he and Falco continued to focus on their weapon training in the same manner.

Then they climbed aboard their ships, exhausted and weary, hands calloused and bodies bruised. But they had no duties while shipboard except to recover their stamina. Throughout, Varro enforced gear inspections and other discipline to keep the men primed. The fleet stopped in another port on the journey, taking on more supplies and even more ships. The vast number of ships and all the attendant support vessels impressed Varro, causing him to wonder how such numbers could be exceeded by the enemy.

At last, the coast of Iberia rose out of the distance after several days at sea, with formations of triremes delivering the strength of Cato's legions into the waiting jaws of a province-wide rebellion.

Whatever hope of additional training Varro held vanished along with the morning mist.

The Iberians had captured a key fortress in this area, and Consul Cato was determined to wrest it back from them.

Their first battle was at hand.

5

The Tenth Maniple of Hastati, with Varro as the senior centurion to Falco, had been among the first ashore. Long lines of transport ships strung out behind them to the triremes offshore, delivering the men and machines that would make breaching the distant fortress more work than warfare. Varro could see the square peg of the structure rising in the distance. A morning mist hung over it as black dots of birds circled over its towers. It had been strategically set upon a tall hill that overlooked the shore as well as the interior. Not knowing the land, he could not judge the value of the location. Yet no one would expend the cost and effort to build in a worthless place. In any case, the consul wanted it recaptured.

The hastati under his command had chatted excitedly as the sailors ferried them to shore. But once they waded through the water onto the beach, Varro had shouted them to silence. They were part of the screening force to protect the landing parties from a surprise attack. He had sent men to scout for enemies, trusting those that claimed familiarity with woodlands actually had it. For his part, he hated forests and similar dark places.

To his left in the line, Falco stood facing his men who in turn presented their shields toward the dark tree line up the beach. He was a brooding, hulking figure. If Galenus thought Varro was frightening with his face scars, Falco's heavy brows and imposing shoulders made him even more menacing.

They all had set three black feathers into their helmets, something which renewed Varro's pride as a Roman soldier. While he missed his mountain ghosts, he was never really part of them. He had been tolerated and sometimes accepted, but they were not his people. Now, with the feathers in his helmet again and a proper century to command, he felt back at home.

The weather here was more humid than Numidia, and the dark and heavy trees to the front hinted at a land thick with vegetation. He had been long under the open sky and appreciated it more. But he smelled the leaves mixing with the salt of the ocean and his nose wrinkled.

His scouts had reported back finding enemy activity. They were shocked to have seen anyone dare to get so close, but they had fled on sight.

"Why so surprised?" Varro asked. "Wouldn't you want a look at the enemy, too? They're either going to abandon their fortress or else bar the gates, and I know which is the wiser of those choices. But we'll see how clearly these Iberians think soon enough."

The tedious disembarking of the troops lasted for hours. But no matter how he felt about it, he kept himself and his men poised and alert. Finally, Cato had arrived with his guards and messengers. He gave his orders and Varro listened for the notes sounded on the bucina. They formed up in marching ranks while scouts were sent to find the best paths to the fortress.

They assembled by the onager teams, whose machines would lob rocks at the walls or else into the interior. His men were fascinated by these even in their disassembled state, but he walked his line and straightened up their formation.

Before trekking into the forest, Consul Cato gathered his tribunes and centurions just off the beach and laid out his plans. Cato was dressed for battle, and Varro had to admit he looked at ease in his armor. Flamininus had always appeared more comfortable in a toga, and before him Galba was too old to seem a real fighter. But to Cato's credit, he seemed prepared to fight from the front like a centurion.

"It is a simple task," he said. "We offer one chance at surrender. If they refuse, we breach their fort, then kill all within it."

"Sir, I volunteer to lead the breaching team." One of the first legion centurions, a man with some gray in his hair and a barrel chest, had stepped forward to the admiring smiles of the tribunes.

While Cato smiled as well, he waved the centurion back.

"I applaud your eagerness, but I've another in mind." He turned his smile to Varro.

Stepping forward, Varro saluted. "Yes, sir!"

"You and Centurion Falco have extensive experience breaching fortresses during the Macedonian campaign. I would put that to good use today."

Others possessed the same experience. Varro had noted a few familiar faces among the passengers on his trireme, but never had a moment to reacquaint himself. It was a dangerous job, as the team would be subjected to fire and rocks dumped on them as they worked the ram. The mortality rate was high for the men in the team. While Varro's hastati wouldn't grasp this, he and Falco did. And he could not help but wonder if Cato counted on it.

"Thank you, sir!"

He could say nothing else, and Cato knew it. His nose seemed to widen with the smile in his craggy face.

"You will have every support if it should come to an assault. Once inside, you will secure a perimeter to protect the main body as they enter. Ensure the gatehouse is in hand, if it is not destroyed first. From there, I will command according to the situation."

The consul continued to elaborate on other points of the expected assault. It seemed he had no faith in the Iberians surrendering. The onager teams would do the preparatory attacks on the gates, hopefully shattering the defenses enough for Varro's men to work under minimal threat.

"We must complete the capture with haste," Cato said in conclusion. "This is not even a sliver of the enemy force, but we cannot allow an occupied fort to sit in our rear areas and become a strongpoint against us. Therefore, I expect this hill in our control by nightfall."

Cato dismissed his officers, then peered across the hazy sky toward his objective. Varro had to admire the determination in his expression, as if the capture of this one small fort would be the culmination of his life's dreams. Whatever his personal feelings for Cato, he seemed a dedicated man. The real test of his leadership would come when facing the main rebel army, but Varro was glad to be under a strong commander. He did not seem the type to indulge his tribunes in foolish games or politics.

"Good luck, Centurion."

Varro was about to turn after Falco, but a figure stepped out of the mass of dispersing officers.

He was the man who had volunteered for the breaching team. Up close, he was shorter and stockier than he had seemed, and tamed a beard so heavy that the stubble turned the lower half of his face gray. A light scar ran up from his lip almost to his left eye. It was thin and well hidden in his olive skin.

"We'll need it," Varro said. "It'll be the worst of whatever else happens today."

"No doubt," the centurion said. He smiled and extended his hand. "The name is Longinus."

Introducing himself, Varro clasped arms with Longinus. He nodded to the scar on his face. "You're a veteran as well. The infantry has a way of making a man handsomer every season."

Longinus laughed. "I've served in Iberia before, yes. But my mother gave me this scar. When I was just a child, she was holding a kitchen knife low and I bumped into it. Can't remember how, but I remember it hurt. Almost took my eye, too."

Varro shared the laugh. "Well, there'll be worse than your mother's kitchen knives today. Fortuna be with you."

They parted, and Falco stared quizzically after him.

"Making friends before we're sent to die in a fire?"

"It's never too late to make a friend."

They returned to their men, certain to drop any expression of levity. He and Falco had developed their own way of coping with danger, but he didn't want his men to misunderstand the dangers before them. As their leader, he had to balance between honesty and putting on a brave face for his soldiers.

They marched into the forest, following scouts from the First Legion. The paths were narrow and immediately Varro realized the onager wagons would not make it though. Yet this did not halt the infantry's progress. They would have to await the onager teams before attacking.

Varro never looked behind as he ducked under branches or pushed through bushes, and to his satisfaction he heard Curio at the rear shouting at the century for one reason or another. He struggled to keep the smirk off his face, for Curio was using an assumed voice. His own lacked real power and authority. Yet he had a sharp wit, and had learned enough from Falco to imitate him to good effect. He could keep recruits in order just fine.

The trek through the brief woodlands had left Varro with a bent helmet feather and dead leaves and branches caught in his mail. Without a doubt, these were the tangible remnants of the curses the forest spirits laid upon him for passing through their world. He had yet to spend any time in a forest and have good come of it. Spirits were easily trapped in the woods, even ones as small as this. He worried about what lay ahead of him.

More tedium ensued as they filed out to assemble in the fields at the base of the hill. It was a long slope up, studded with rocks and tree stumps that would break up large formations. But the manipular nature of the legions accommodated for these obstacles, rendering them useless for defense. Varro would lead his men around them without losing the integrity of their lines.

It took another full hour to array the legions so that they could envelop the fort if the defenders attempted escape. Cato wisely left them only one avenue, knowing cornered defenders were much fiercer. But this avenue could be cut off and the enemy destroyed. It was a clever illusion of options that did not exist for the Iberians. Again, Varro admired Cato's forethought.

All the while his men maintained their discipline. Their short time together had not afforded Varro a chance to demonstrate the punishments for disobedience. But sooner or later one of his boys would come up on a charge and serve as the unfortunate example. A sacrifice of one to the benefit of the many, or so Varro liked to think of it.

While they waited for Cato's messengers to return with a response, they stood at silent attention. All across the long line, centurions shouted at those who broke this solemn quiet. Varro overheard one of his second rank hastati whisper something about being bored.

"What's this? Someone is bored?" Varro whirled on the man, pointing to him. "You'll be in the lead with me. That'll provide some excitement today. You'll be praying for boredom when you're at those gates and realize you're standing in a puddle of your own piss and the blood of your friends. Now silence!"

They held without a sound thereafter. Varro stared into the glare hanging over the castle. The birds that had circled it had sensibly fled. As dull as the moment was, he understood some of the men behind him were taking in their last sights of the world. Maybe he was, too. There were no special rules for death, no grand moment of heroism for one who had survived as much as he had. He thought of Centurion Drusus. After a lifetime of campaigns in the most important war in Rome's history a pike from a nameless enemy pierced his skull and dumped his brains out in the mud. The same end might await him and come at any time. Even at an insignificant fort on the coast of Iberia.

He never saw the messengers returning. This surprised him, since they did not have the velite screen obscuring the front as they normally would. There was no need for skirmishers in a fort assault, and so they would watch from the flanks and carry away wounded or do whatever else was needed to keep the fight progressing. Yet the bucina sounded to begin the advance.

"Where are the onagers?" Falco shouted from across the line as they began the trudge up the slope.

"I'm sure they're in the rear."

Yet as they mounted the slope, Varro had a better view of the rear where Cato sat on a white horse to better observe the full battle. There were no war machines coming up, nor any covered battering ram.

They halted out of bow shot from the high gray stone walls. Varro held his men ready, with both heavy and light pila ready to cast as they had been taught. They would not need them now, but he believed correct discipline and habit saved soldiers in combat. So they waited on orders as they would in a standard battle, ready to charge and cast.

At last the battering ram was delivered up the slope to the right flank where Varro's maniple stood forward, with Falco to the rear.

His stomach went cold as he realized there would be no onager attack. They had not found a way around the woods, and Cato was impatient to see the hill fort taken. Worse still, the battering ram was uncovered. He had been expecting a covered wagon with a suspended ram.

In truth, the fort did not require such strength to take, and once inside it would collapse. But Varro wanted more protection, and now without onagers to scare defenders from the gate his men would be in even more danger.

"Testudo formation over the ram," Varro shouted. The men stared at him in shock. They had practiced this formation one time.

"You heard the centurion!" Curio began shoving men together from the rear of the line. "Get your shields up or I'll cut off your balls. Move!"

"We'll cover your sides," Falco said. "Once we're through, you push back whoever resists and I'll take the gatehouse. Should be fun."

Varro gave a bleak smile to Falco, who returned to his century to organize his own testudo. He then grabbed the man who had complained of boredom and put him on the front handle of the ram.

"This'll give you something to talk about tonight."

The soldier was pale and wide-eyed, but stammered his acknowledgement as he took the position.

The testudo formation utilized the massive shields they all carried. Varro likened it to a portable wall and so it was, covering from head to the middle of his shin. Even there he wore bronze greaves for protection. In his mail and helmet, he would be the unmovable plug at the center of their formation. The rest of his men were not as heavily armored. They wore bronze pectoral plates and helmets, but otherwise relied on their portable walls, the scutum of the Roman infantry.

Shield rims clacked together and darkness enveloped them. The ram team, made up of those who naturally selected one of the many handles, stood at the center. In the checkered darkness every sound echoed off the wood of the shields. Varro gave the order and they began to march, with him leading as he peered between the narrow gaps between shields.

As yet, they had not seen a single Iberian on the walls or elsewhere. As he trudged ahead, he wondered what they would be like. Why did they not taunt them from the safety of their walls, or shout insults like other barbarians? Even the Greeks had done this, and they were civilized. Could it be that Iberians kept the same silence protocols as Romans?

Yet as they mounted, the Romans behind cheered. They shouted war cries and banged their swords to their own shields. This naturally increased the century's pace, bolstering their sense of pride and giving them a kind of safety, knowing hundreds stood behind them.

As they marched, gaps kept opening between shields. Curio screamed every time a light flashed into the dark.

"What the fuck is so hard about locking shields? Are you getting tired so soon? Be a man, for the love of Jupiter! You're leaving a hole for the enemy to shoot through."

"The gods would have to guide their arrows to hit that gap from so far," said one labored voice.

"Are you questioning me?" Curio growled. "You don't need a good shot, you just need enough—"

Arrows slashed down with the suddenness of a winter storm. True to Curio's predictions, the shafts clattered into the gaps between shields. Screaming and cries of shock rebounded inside the dark confines of the testudo. The iron arrowheads scraped and rang out against the shields overhead, adding to the deafening storm.

"Keep formation! Forward at the double!" Varro's voice was deep and loud, yet still struggled against the continual stream of arrows.

A shaft shattered against the rim of his own shield, blasting wood splinters into his face. But the heavy doors were in view. A portcullis of wooden beams had been dropped before it as well.

The thought of having to break both drew fiery heat to Varro's face. He would have his revenge for it once inside.

He plunged ahead, but to his shock the darkness within the testudo brightened. He turned back and nearly fell over in surprise.

His formation had broken in half, with the rear of it lagging behind. The ram team was exposed. In that short glimpse back, Varro saw one man collapse with a shriek as an arrow stabbed through his cheek and popped out under his jaw.

"Optio! What is going on? Get them in formation or we'll die where we stand!"

Curio struggled to hold his own scutum up while dragging a man off the ground. No one had dared to flee, as even recruits knew that was certain death, but they had dispersed against their better interests. They had sidestepped the fallen and now the gaps in the formation left everyone exposed.

"Close up around the ram." Varro slowed the pace to let those holding formation close around the ram bearers. Curio would have to join who he could to the rear of the formation.

"You fucking idiots!" Varro shouted. "Stay in formation or you're good as dead."

He renewed the charge forward, relieved that the first volley of arrows had dropped to a trickle. Tramping down black-feathered shafts that now dotted the path ahead, he raced the team toward the portcullis.

"Ram bearers," he said as he sped forward with his men struggling alongside him. "We'll leave an opening. Charge that portcullis and get us through to the door. If anyone falls, the next man takes his place."

The screaming continued, but it was from Falco's equally disjointed testudo. For a moment Varro thought the Iberians had spent all their arrows. The ground was thick with the black feathered shafts and no more came.

But as they reached the wall, men grunting and cursing alongside him, another volley streaked down onto their shields. Varro felt the force pushing against his extended arms, which were already tiring. But his life depended on holding it up.

"There's the gate," he shouted. "Charge the ram and let the gods know our strength. For Rome!"

The hastati joined his cry and they charged at the dark, aged wood of the portcullis before them.

6

Arrows hissed all around, thumping into the soft grass or breaking in nerve-tingling cracks on their shields. With Varro's testudo now tightened, they were unbreakable. Only a lucky shaft might pierce the gaps, and then its force would be spent. He roared as he ran astride the ram, both arms raised to hold his shield overhead. His ears rang with the clatter of arrows and the shouts of his soldiers. The sour stench of fear and sweat filled the enclosed space.

The iron-headed ram, cleverly worked into an image of a real ram's head, now led the way. Varro ordered his men to let them through. His men leaned into it, threatening to race ahead of the formation.

The ram crashed into the wooden portcullis. To everyone's delight, bright yellow cracks splintered up from the impact. The sharp cracking noise drew cheers even beyond the confines of his testudo. The vague cheering reminded Varro he was not alone, but with a legion of soldiers behind him.

"Do not stop until you see the other side," Varro shouted. He looked up at his shield and found an arrowhead poking through the wood like an accusing finger pointing at his face.

The men on the ram heaved back, then slammed again. More wood splintered, and the squares now shifted out of alignment. More cheers went up both within and without the testudo.

He heard Curio shouting to the rear of the press, and so it seemed he had caught up the rest of the formation. Falco's voice was also clear above the roars. Few arrows could shoot straight down, and so the rain-like drumming of iron arrowheads had dwindled.

By the fourth ram, the portcullis was collapsing. Men shouted, excited for the impending breach.

"There's still the gate itself," Varro said. "Keep your shields up. Don't falter now."

Then something struck him so hard that he buckled and his shield momentarily collapsed.

A massive rock slid off it to thud into the earth at his feet.

"Jupiter's balls! They're dropping stones. Double up on the shields."

It was an order no one understood. Being in the moment, he forgot that his soldiers had not practiced to defend against this common threat. The men would press tighter and overlap shields to strengthen the roof overhead against large rocks.

But no one knew this, and so more stones began to punch through their testudo.

Most bounced off the ram or landed in the empty spaces. But soon the stones were breaking arms and crashing into shoulders, driving men out of formation to collapse in the grass.

"Draw together," he shouted. "Make a small target for them."

Even in desperation, the sweating, swearing men on the ram punched through the portcullis with a victorious cheer. The stones continued to fall, some small enough to bounce away and others crushing the unfortunate. Varro and others began pulling aside the shattered timbers, so the next strike had a better shot. It was a relief to lower his arms, and to see that the men behind him knew to cover this effort with their own shields.

They were learning, but too late to save those who had died needlessly.

The ram had to only strike four more times to crash through. The metallic notes of Cato sounding the advance were faint against the shouting and screaming men pressed about him.

Retrieving his pila from the strap on his back then facing his shield forward, he would lead them through the breach.

"Ready your pila. With me!"

Being the first Romans to step into the fort, Varro and those with him would face whatever defenses the enemy had prepared. He held his shield up, peering around the side.

Arrows laced into him and those following. The Iberians knew to clog the entrance with bodies of their foes.

An arrow skipped on the packed ground before him, bounced under his shield, and cut the inside of his thigh. It was a superficial wound but a reminder of what awaited him if he lingered.

"Cast pila!"

He faced a line of boxes, carts, hay bales, barrels, and anything else the Iberians could block the streets with. They crowded the front plaza by the gate, leaving the barest room for enemies to swarm. They had likely expected Varro would not bother with his pila, given the compressed ranges.

Varro cast his light and heavy pila one after the next. Even though the Iberians outnumbered his small force, all of them ducked behind the barriers.

That was all he wanted. It was the turning point in securing the front gate.

The Romans flowed through, with Varro racing after his cast to sprint into the defended positions. His shield kept him safe from the enemy on the ground, and the proximity to friends kept the Iberians on the wall above from shooting into the melee.

Whatever happened behind him, Varro could no longer see. He was pressed into the lines, leading by example and hoping his recruits followed. They were not bad men, just inexperienced. Each wanted to be a good soldier and support his brothers. So all around, more men leaped into the fight.

Stepping onto a bale, he momentarily felt as if he stood out to the world as a target. Indeed, a rock flew out of the crowd and cracked against his new bronze greaves. In times past, that would've broken his knee. Instead, it pinged away as he jumped behind the barrier.

At last, he beheld the Iberian defenders. He stood before a cluster of them, unimposing men for the most part in plain tunics and carrying round shields. He noted their swords, nearly exact copies of his gladius, or perhaps it was the other way around.

Their faces were full of fear, for behind Varro swarmed more of his men. A broken pilum lay between him and the group of defenders. They seemed to lean away in fear, as if to flee the main building at the center.

Then a strong man, a head taller than all of them, rushed around an overturned wagon. He wore a bronze helmet in the Roman style and carried an oblong shield. His muscular chest was bare, but he wore long pants of a blue and brown check pattern. He pointed his sword ahead and his men roared in answer.

Varro pointed out the leader, then charged.

Fortunately for him, his century had caught up and raced to fight alongside their commander.

Recognizing the challenge, the big Iberian shoved away all his companions that he should fight Varro in a duel.

They clashed together, slamming shield to shield in a contest of strength. Varro must have surprised his enemy, being a head shorter and less imposing than the Iberian. But both rebounded to square off again. The Iberian spit on the ground and began to circle, probing with his sword.

Varro knew this dance very well. He slipped along the ground, his freshly hobnailed sandals scraping the ground. The pale eyes of the Iberian studied him for an opening, but he was too intent and his shield side drooped.

Shooting in at the opening, Varro's gladius lanced for the exposed chest.

But it had been a feint and the Iberian gave a gusty laugh as he slammed his shield against Varro's side, knocking him to the ground while he was off balance.

He collapsed with his shield covering his side, eliciting horrific memories of Macedonia and huddling beneath his scutum as enemies trod across him. The Iberian, however, raised his foot to stamp on Varro's sword arm instead.

Rolling aside in perfect timing, he staggered to his feet. His shield was lost now; either he regained his footing or delayed to retrieve the shield. He used the moment the Iberian spent recovering from his miss to reposition himself.

The pale-eyed foe twisted deftly and crouched behind his shield, which he now wobbled as if to tease Varro for losing his own. He gave a predatory smile, then led off with it.

Varro jumped onto the shield, grabbing it with one arm and slicing down with his gladius in an inverted grip. The startled Iberian looked up in time for the blade to slice open his eyeball, then most of his nose, and part of his lip. He howled with agony as he spun back under Varro's weight.

Without delay, Varro lanced the gladius once more into his neck and again into his shoulder. The leader groaned and lay flat with blood rushing from a jagged cut across his neck.

Standing up, he dragged his scutum off the ground. The clash with the other Iberian defenders had ended and his men clustered around one of their fallen brothers.

"He's dead," Varro said. "We'll remember him later. Get in line. I need to reform the century before we scatter everywhere."

The disjointed attack had been his own doing. Despite years of training otherwise, he had picked up habits from the Numidians that did not mesh with the Roman way of fighting. Yet jumping atop the Iberian's shield had been something he learned in Numidia, where he had seen tribesmen overwhelm Carthaginian soldiers using such methods. Whether that was a true style of the Numidians or just the result of desperation, he didn't care. He had survived his fight.

In any case, his century had not proceeded in formation, but more like mountain raiders overtaking an unsuspecting caravan. Indeed, were it not for the surroundings he could have believed this battle was in Numidia.

The main force was through the gate. Looking across the low barriers to the walls, he saw Romans chasing Iberians who scrambled back down their ladders or toward their towers. They might be rallying at the main building of the fort, but more likely they were taking the offered escape route and would soon run into the force sent to cut them off.

With the entrance and gatehouse captured, there was no stopping Cato. However, Varro had to defend against a possible counterattack, and so rushed around finding his men and ordering them into position. He located Curio with a clutch of bloodied soldiers staggering alongside him.

"Optio, where is the rest of the century?"

Curio gave him a hard look, and Varro knew they were no more. By his estimate, he had lost almost one half of the sixty men assigned to him. Most of those were outside the walls. Rather than demand a reply, he looked away and started shouting orders to the soldiers left alive.

Falco waved from the top of the gatehouse and the men with him cheered. Varro wished he could be as happy as they seemed.

This had been a terrible assignment, no matter what kind of experience he and Falco had. What might have been a basic exercise with some minor casualties for veterans had been simple butchery for fresh-faced men.

Once more his opinion on Cato swung toward distaste, but he had other worries to attend to now.

In the end, the counterattack did not come. The Iberians had no stomach for a fight after their gate had been breached. Cato now entered on his white horse, his mouth drawn tight and eyes narrowed. The main force spread out into the small fort and Tribune Galenus ordered the Tenth Maniple to remain in reserve. He also sat upon a horse, like all the tribunes, though his was brown and less muscular than Cato's. He scanned the thin line of the maniple, then frowned.

"You've done enough for one day. Take your rest."

Varro would have liked a word of encouragement, not for himself but for the men who stood at attention despite being in utter shock at what had happened during the last half hour. Friends who had been merrily chatting on the deck of their transport were now staring empty-eyed at the sky, not seeing the dark birds circling in anticipation of a feast. The survivors had never experienced death on this scale before, and many would never be the same again.

"Thank you, sir." Varro saluted then turned to Curio who waited for a nod to order the men to stand down.

Varro asked for volunteers to help him find their dead and wounded. Every one of them turned back from their rest to join him. The bodies Varro found inside the walls bothered him less than those outside. Those inside had at least tested their swords and had come up lacking or else suffered back luck.

Outside the gate, he found the majority of his men strung along their path to the gate with black-feathered arrows jutting from their white flesh. These men died for lack of training and discipline. Varro had assailed mountain strongholds in the shelter of a testudo formation and had endured arrows, stones, and even rockslides without injury. Now as he lined up bodies by the gate, he felt a hot rage and self-loathing boiling up.

He should have not accepted that order, or at least tried harder to explain why the Tenth Maniple was not ready for the task. Certainly, he had assumed onagers in support and a better ram. But as he and Curio carried a sandy-haired man with arrows in his neck, legs, and chest to the row of casualties, he felt the immense weight of responsibility for his death. His crisp "Yes, sir" to Cato now sounded insipid and weak. His men had needed him to fight for them, and he had been too caught up in his own worries to realize it.

He found one of his soldiers trying not to weep over a body splayed out in the grass a few yards from the destroyed gate. Varro simply clapped his shoulder and squeezed it, looking down on the blood-soaked corpse.

"He fell and shouted for help. I said I'd get him up."

"Then you'd have been lying next to him," Varro said. "You'll go mad if you try to make sense of a battle. It's all in the hands of the gods and what they've decided for each man. Sometimes you step forward and it saves your life. Next time you do the same, and you get a pike through your skull. All the dead died as soldiers of Rome, in a great service to their city."

The man covered his mouth and nodded. Varro was about to leave him with his thoughts when he spoke again.

"What great service? This is no place, and these barbarians are no one."

Varro had heard this kind of talk before, and recalled how it led a man he once considered a friend to desertion. He grabbed the soldier by his shoulder again, harder and fiercer this time.

"Those aren't questions for us. Those are questions that lead to ruin. If you want to die, then throw yourself on an enemy sword to save your brothers. It's a better way to go than asking those poisonous questions. We serve Rome, and we do our duty to our city. There is pride in good service. Remember it and don't insult the memory of fallen with thoughts like those."

In the end, Varro counted nineteen casualties, including the soldier who had complained of boredom. He had made it into the fort but had been stabbed in the back. Varro hoped he had not been fleeing when it happened. But being out of formation had caused more unusual injuries than there should have been. Six more were injured enough to be out of duty for the foreseeable future. One had lost three fingers on his sword hand, and would be assigned to baggage train duty once he recovered. His active fighting days were over.

The onager teams did eventually arrive, their big wagons and horses appearing out of the trees at the far end of the field. Cato had been within the fort for a good hour before emerging to declare victory. Shouts went up into the afternoon sky, momentarily scattering the circling birds. Even the onager teams cheered.

"And what've they got to shout about?" Falco folded his arms and glared at them. "They took a stroll in the woods while we bled and died for it."

He, Varro, and Curio now stood aside from the rest of the maniple. Falco's optio watched from a distance, but seemed to understand he was not part of their circle. So instead he made a nuisance of himself to the men trying to rest in the grass.

"We didn't have it as bad as you," Falco said. "That was a rough job for boys just arrived from their farms."

"Nearly half of them aren't going to see those farms ever again."

Falco hissed through his teeth. Curio shook his head.

"It's my fault, sir. I let the formation break up. You should put me on a charge, really."

"I'm sure I should for something," Varro said. "But not this. I'm the leader and I'll answer for it."

"And speaking of which, I think you're going to need that answer soon. Messenger incoming."

Varro and Curio both faced the approaching onager teams, and did not see the runner coming from the fort until they turned to follow Falco's gaze. The young velite dashed up from behind and saluted them.

"Centurions Falco and Varro, the consul commands your attendance immediately. Please come with me, sirs."

The energetic young man set a difficult pace for Varro and Falco in their heavy armor. Their weary limbs had still not recovered from battle. He delivered them to Cato, who stood outside the gate with hands on his hips as if surveying his handiwork. They introduced themselves with crisp salutes and clear voices, then stood to attention.

Cato had other messengers running back and forth from where he stood. A groom handled his horse and two older men served as his bodyguards. They offered grim nods to Varro and Falco, even as Cato ignored them for the moment.

The looting had begun, with everything of value being carried out in a long line of soldiers leading back into the walls. Captives that surprisingly included women and children were also led out of the walls. The aid station, set up under a white canopy, was not busy. The bodies collected there mostly belonged to Varro's century and other injuries seemed superficial. After a brief resistance, the Iberians had collapsed.

All of this transpired in his field of vision as he stared straight ahead awaiting the consul's indulgence. He at last turned, a genuine smile on a face that reminded Varro of a cabbage.

"Well done," he said. "The Iberians have quit their fort and will be rounded up shortly. Your men are to be congratulated."

"Thank you, sir."

Cato's smile did not shift.

"Of course, you haven't very many men remaining, do you? In fact, Centurion Varro, were it not for the bravery of your men, you would have lost all of them. What exactly was that disordered run to the gate? Something like a testudo formation comes to mind, but that couldn't have been what you were doing. What happened once you entered? There was hardly any resistance, but you seemed to have suffered casualties as if there had been."

"Sir, we advanced beyond the enemy barrier and engaged the barbarians."

"The correct decision," he said. "But I wonder if you would have been better served advancing behind a solid wall of shields rather than running around in disorder like a bunch of desert tribesmen?"

"Sir, I judged speed of attack more important. Of course, I see your logic and I regret the losses for my decision. But it was my decision to make, sir, and had we tried to draw up ranks while pushing through that ruined gate we would have died there and blocked your advance."

"Certainly," Cato said, now turning back to gaze at the fort. "You completed your task successfully, if sloppily. It seems your time in Numidia has unduly affected you. As a veteran of Macedonia, and one with such glowing praise from his commanders, I expected more. Now I see I must judge your worth for myself."

He now faced them, glancing to Falco and then back to Varro.

"Your century is already under-strength and I'm not even a day ashore. We can pull from the baggage train to fill your ranks. In all honesty, I'm not sure what to do with you. I'll have to assess your future."

Cato raised an expectant eyebrow over the deep folds of his sour face. It seemed the glee expressed was not in his victory but in somehow jabbing at Varro. It struck him as small minded, with him being the consul and Varro a simple centurion. He had a dozen rebuttals swarming to escape his thoughts, but in the end he straightened his back.

"Yes, sir!"

"In the meantime," Cato said. "I've no men to garrison this fort and we cannot leave it for the enemy to repopulate. Therefore, the onagers will be set up to level this place. In the meantime, I want your centuries to fire the buildings. It only seems fitting that those who gave the most to capture this fort should have the honor of burning it to the ground. Both of you begin assembling what you need to start the blaze. I'll order you in once we've secured the prisoners and goods."

After being dismissed then crossing back to their centuries, Falco muttered next to him.

"What does he mean by evaluating our positions? He wants to demote us?"

"He said my position, not yours. And I don't know what he means. I didn't do anything deserving of a demotion. But he can do as he pleases."

"This old fucker is going to be a problem for us."

Varro shrugged. It was true, and both were powerless to help themselves.

7

Black birds continued to circle above the fort. Varro stared up into the flat glare of the gray sky, listening to them chirp in anticipation. They must have scented the blood that dried in wide pools by the smashed gate. He gave a thin smile as he considered the patient creatures would ultimately be denied their prize. He wondered if birds could feel bitterness like he did.

He and Falco oversaw the work of their centuries, with both of their optiones going deeper into the fort to direct the men placing bundles of dried kindling inside the buildings.

"What a shame," Falco said. "Seems like we should've made something out of this place rather than just burn it down."

"The consul has a good reason," Varro said weakly. "Better to tear it down than have to return to capture it again."

Falco remained shaking his head until he caught sight of some men resting where they thought they might be unseen.

"Why don't you go lie down in the fort where it's quieter," he shouted. "Then we can have the pleasure of burning it down while you sleep!"

He continued to shout at the idling men, and Varro turned to the matter at hand. While he had razed plenty of buildings during his term in Macedonia, he had never had to plan it. He had been like these men, simply following orders. So he had them carry kindling into the fort and once all was prepared they'd light the fires in stages, letting them back out as they went. Of course, fire was unpredictable and trying to impose order on the process was madness. Fortunately, the wind was a mere breeze today.

Curio arrived back with a deep frown, but he saluted and made a formal report that everything was ready.

"What's the face for?" Varro asked, as they were apart from the men. Curio relaxed, becoming more of his old self.

"Just some of the men giving me shit."

"I hope you straightened them up."

"Of course I did. But some of them think I'm too small to lead them. What has that ever had to do with anything?"

"I'd tell you to punch them in the balls and let them know being low to the ground has its advantages."

Curio laughed. "Good idea, sir. But something is bothering you, isn't it? I know that expression. Maybe we can speak later?"

Varro nodded, and they shifted to their plans. Falco ordered the signal be made to alert the consul. Once the bucina sounded, they all took flaming brands from an iron brazier set by the gate.

"Curio and I will take teams into the fort. Falco, your men can begin firing the surrounding areas once we give the signal. Then we just back out, setting alight the kindling we've set. No one will get burned, I hope."

"No one will," Falco said, narrowing his eyes at the men he had just threatened. "We all want to get out and watch the onagers smash the place to bits while sparks fly into the air."

Cato had made short work of stripping supplies and valuables from the fort. As he entered and climbed the stairs up, he thought back to the Carthaginian fort and its priceless treasures. As harrowing as it was, he had fond memories of it. He had been in charge to plan and execute as he wished, and he had done what few believed possible. Now he tramped up creaking stairs with a burning stick, following strict orders.

For all the years he had wished for less responsibility, he found himself wishing for more.

They set fires in the top floors, ensuring it would collapse on the bottom levels. The onagers would mostly focus on the walls and towers, but the fort would be left mostly to burn and collapse on its own.

Descending the stairs, he escaped the smoke spreading along the ceiling of ransacked chambers. On the main floor, he and his team again set fires to the stacked kindling and anything that seemed flammable. These fires caught swiftly, and his group had to escape the fort coughing and choking on the smoke.

Outside, Falco had seen the smoke from the roof, and had begun his work on the surrounding buildings.

Other than stinging eyes and a raw throat, his plan had worked. The heat of the burning fort pushed all of them into the yard. The stone of course did not burn, but all the enclosing timbers did, and as Varro retreated with his team, the fort was already engulfed in fire. Bright orange flames licked out of the top floor windows. The birds above now fled with indignant screams and drew a laugh from Varro.

"The sun is still in the sky, Centurion Varro. Don't waste time!" Falco shouted across the open parade ground, and Varro returned to the work at hand.

"Just a few more buildings," he said. "Then we'll be done."

The men cheered for the destruction. It seemed a good exercise to work out whatever anger they felt.

But as Varro's team moved off toward the next zone, he heard two thin, shrieking voices coming from the fort.

He would have just kept following his men to the bundled

kindling, pretending he did not hear, but Curio turned with a raised brow.

"I heard it," he said in answer to the unspoken question.

The screaming continued, young voices crying out in abject terror.

"Well, that's going to haunt my nightmares," Curio said, then began to turn aside.

"Mine as well." Varro imagined two children burning to death. "And my dreams are haunted enough. Keep the men occupied. Don't let them see this or the consul will have me flogged."

He did not look back for Curio's response, but now rushed toward the screaming. Fortunately, the cries did not come from above, where he would be helpless to do anything. Instead, he followed the voices around to the rear of the fort where he found a small entrance for slaves and servants. The wooden door was closed, but streamers of smoke fluttered from the top of the frame.

With one foot he smashed on the wood, cracking the weak planks and collapsing them into the smoke beyond. A second kick broke the door in, and he put his hand through to pull out the bar.

The screaming was louder now, and clearly it was two children trapped in whatever hiding place had otherwise protected them. Varro called out to them, but they did not seem to hear.

The door led to a short flight of wooden steps into a basement. A dull light shined below as ceiling beams burned with rolling flames.

"Come out," he shouted. "The way is clear still."

But the screaming continued, and Varro ducked under the door. The stairs threatened to break under his weight, sagging and groaning, but he leaped down to the earthen floor, bending low and keeping away from the burning timbers.

"Come out," he shouted again. Now the shrieking stopped. The area was filled with cobwebbed crates and barrels, all empty and some smashed. Assorted junk littered the small area to indicate this area had been long out of use. Two small heads popped up from behind dry, old crates in one corner.

And they screamed louder now, ducking back into their corner. Of course, being a Roman soldier Varro supposed he must seem like a nightmare to them. So he growled and padded over to their hiding place, pulling aside the crates.

Two children, perhaps about ten years old, one boy and one girl, dressed in dirty brown tunics looked up to him. Their eyes reflected the burning timbers as tears streaked their faces.

"Screaming won't help you," he said. "Come with me if you want to live."

But the children recoiled in horrified shrieking. In the next moment, the ceiling above groaned and sagged, then something cracked and flaming debris fell into the crawl space.

Cursing, Varro seized both by their arms. He hauled them out of hiding and dragged them toward the stairs. They resisted and squirmed, and Varro let out an exasperated shout.

"What do you brats want? Don't fight me!"

Now more flaming debris collapsed through the hole and the heat and smoke began to choke all three of them. But Varro had gained the stairs and bounded up and out of the fort.

Dragging the children behind, Varro ran headlong into Curio and his team.

They stared at him in amazement, but Curio began slapping at Varro's helmet.

"Your feathers!"

They had caught fire, and for a moment all Varro saw was Curio's arms frantically batting at his helmet. Together they threw it aside, letting it thump to the ground while the feathers burned up.

The children recoiled from the surrounding Romans. It seemed that if they could flee, they would.

"Are we taking them prisoner, sir?" one of the men asked while staring as if he had never seen children before.

"Of course," he said while collecting his helmet now that the feathers had burned up. "Get away from here, you fools. The fort is collapsing."

To reinforce his statement, a bright crash echoed out of the broken door behind them. They all turned and fled, even Curio. But Varro instead grabbed the children and kneeled to meet their eyes. He pointed at the south gate where the defenders had fled from. The children would have to thread around a burning building, but he trusted to their youthful agility.

"Go that way. Run and be free."

The children's eyes were wide with madness. The creaking and snapping from the fort, plus the intense heat of the fire rattled their senses. Varro shoved them toward the gate and gestured they should run. At last, he donned his helmet, then fled after his own men. He had done all he could for the children. In a final glimpse back, he saw them running the way he pointed.

"Where are the captives, sir?" Curio asked, but his expression indicated he knew what happened.

"The girl bit my hand," he said. "They fled into the fire. We've got to move now."

The men did not require any encouragement to run. Falco's team had already gone ahead, and most of the fort was ablaze. They skipped the remaining zones, and instead ran out the gates to where Falco and the others waited.

"What happened to you?" he asked, looking Varro up and down.

"I fell," Varro said. "It's nothing. I'll explain later. Let's get away from here."

Coughing and rubbing at his eyes, Varro sped away from the gates toward their lines. The centuries assembled as if on parade. But they were being granted the spectacle of the fort's destruction.

When Varro and the others had crossed halfway back to their position within the lines, the onagers began snapping off rocks that were piled beside them.

"Sir?" Curio approached him while they were still in open formation. "Why?"

"I don't know," Varro said, his throat raw from the smoke. "I risked so much for them, just to make them slaves? Honestly, I thought about what Consul Cato would want me to do, and did the opposite."

Curio gave a grin. "Fuck that old bastard."

"The men saw it. It won't do to make them think I care what they report, or else they'll just use it against me. So don't make it an issue. I doubt the consul will ask for the details."

But Varro was not sure. Cato had an eye for detail, and he so far seemed willing to get far more involved with the daily life of a soldier than any other consul Varro had served under. He might find out. In any case, he felt good about what he did. It was foolish and the children would probably perish on their own or become slaves to an enemy tribe. But he would sleep easier for having not walked away from their cries.

Upon rejoining the line, they were treated to one hour of onager bombardment, which elicited cheers for each volley. The fires Varro had planned were overly effective, creating such a massive conflagration that had there been a wind the flames might reach and burn down the forest. As the bombardment broke open the fort, more air fed the flames and caused them to shoot up into the evening sky.

Though they had enjoyed the spectacle, they were soon ordered to form a camp for the night. The next dawn they would embark on the triremes again and head for their objective, which was a mystery to Varro.

"Probably a place just like this," Falco had opined. "But with more cowardly rebels to kill. Suits me. I'm already signed up for the campaign."

"I hate forests," Varro said, eyeing the deepening dark of the tree lines surrounding them. "This whole land seems like nothing but forests."

The site selected for their camp was just on the other side of the woods where the onagers had passed. The clouds above the fort now glowed orange with the light of a fire that would burn well into the night.

Varro set his century to working on the ditch and spikes that would surround the perimeter. Teams were sent to fetch water from a local stream, and Varro watched them enviously. The soot and blood on his skin made him feel awful, but he would probably get nothing better than a bowl of water to basically clean himself.

"Fall in the ocean when we board," Falco suggested. "Just make sure you leave off your mail."

They stood together and supervised the men at work until Tribune Galenus arrived. He looked as if he held vinegar under his tongue.

"All right, you two get in there and dig," he said, his voice mild and strangely weak.

"Sir?" Varro cocked his head. "Is this a change to procedure?"

"It's my order, Centurion Varro. So I'll be pleased if I needn't repeat it." Varro noticed the tribune held a soldier's trenching shovel in a white-knuckled grip.

"Of course, sir," Varro said. Falco shrugged, and both retrieved their shovels. Tribune Galenus also joined them, looking as if he had forgotten this most basic aspect of a soldier's duty.

"You can begin over there, sir," Varro said. "Fewer rocks that way."

"Ah, yes," he said. Then wandered over to the spot and joined the other men of the century in digging.

Varro could not help but wonder why he was again trenching,

but he had no hesitation to follow the order. Other than hunger and exhaustion from the battle, he was fit for the task. But he stole glances at the tribune, who despite being in fighting condition was clearly unaccustomed to trenching. His shovel pecked at the earth like a bird eating seeds.

Putting his head back down, Varro dug alongside his men until he worked up to Curio. They shared a brief smile, Curio shaking his head.

"I guess we missed a few changes while we were away," Varro said.

But Curio simply nodded across to the trench line at a right angle to theirs.

Varro did not know what he was supposed to see, finding soldiers bent to their work either trenching or setting in their spikes. Then he saw the bald head and craggy profile of Consul Cato.

"Is the consul digging a trench?" Varro raised his brow to Curio.

"Looks like he's serious about being a soldier, sir. No task too menial for him. He expects the same from his officers, too. I have to say, that will buy him goodwill with the men. Honestly, it does even with me."

"Me as well," Varro said, narrowing his eyes at the consul before returning to work. "And I'd rather not hold those opinions of him. I don't think he's an ally of ours."

"Doesn't seem like it, sir."

For all that had transpired that day, it ended in good cheer for most of the army. Moods were high after seeing centurions and tribunes taken down a notch to labor with the common soldier. Some, like Varro and Falco, thought nothing more of it, but others let it show they were not happy to do work they felt belonged with a lower rank. This was particularly true for Tribune Galenus, who left for his tent with an even angrier expression than usual.

The next day Varro had permission to lead his men to the local stream to clean up, and therefore draw water collection duty as well. They loaded up barrels and casks, nothing near enough for what two legions would require. Later, he learned this was for the cavalry horses still aboard the transports. He had a softer spot now for horses than he used to, and remembered the loyalty and friendship of his mount, Thunder, left back in Numidia. He wondered if the horse missed him as well, but given how clumsy he was compared to the Numidians he was more than likely relieved to be rid of his Roman burden.

They boarded their transport ships once more and set sail south along the Iberian coast. Tribune Galenus conceded that the depleted Tenth Maniple could rest, even while other centuries exercised and drilled on deck. It was a full day of sailing to wherever they headed. As Falco had said, they were going to a similar place to fight the same enemies once more.

That place turned out to be a city of Greeks, who welcomed them with open arms. Varro had long been gone from Greece, but was immediately heartened to hear the familiar tones of the language and see the familiar mannerisms. He would've preferred a Roman city, but this was better than what he expected.

They sat at anchor for most of that day while Cato's emissaries worked out details of their arrival. For Varro and Falco, this meant leaning with their men on the rails of their transport ship and awaiting orders.

These finally came, and a long and arduous process of disembarking two full consular legions began. This time he was not first ashore. There were no enemies or other dangers present. So the consul and the cavalry went first. At last, he stepped ashore and assembled his men into the larger formation of the second legion.

The recruits gasped when at the end of the day the navy transports left. Varro had to smile, for he remembered the feeling of being abandoned when he had disembarked at Apollonia so many years ago.

"That's right," he said to them all in their ranks. "You won't see them return for another year. If you see them earlier, it's bad luck for you since then you've had your balls cut off and you're being sent back to Rome. So wave goodbye to the navy. The campaign is just beginning."

Two more days passed as the legions marched inland near this city called Emporiae and established their permanent camp. Throughout, Varro had been so busy with his duties, even with a reduced force, that he had largely forgotten the razing of the fort.

But on the morning of the third day, he received a messenger summoning him to Cato's command tent. The young man had interrupted a tent inspection he and Falco were conducting. He stared down the row of hide tents still waiting for his review and the expectant looks of the hastati standing outside with their gear ready.

"Did he say what it's about?"

"No, sir, only that you, Centurion Falco, and Optio Curio should report to him immediately. Please follow me, sir."

After gathering Falco and Curio, and leaving Falco's optio to finish the inspection, they shared silent glances as they followed the messenger across the camp. Falco still did not know about the children Varro had let free. But it seemed like this did not spare him from the consul's ire. Where one of them was involved, it seemed all of them would face his wrath.

Varro gritted his teeth and followed the messenger into Cato's tent.

8

The familiar scent of cabbage, intermingled now with the odors of sweat and lamp oil, hung heavy inside Cato's tent. He wore a simple tunic and sat at his desk behind a fortification of wax tablets. As Varro stood to attention with Falco and Curio at his sides, the consul held up his left hand that they should wait while he furiously read the tablet before him.

He held it close to the lamp so that shadow would fill in the impressed words. His bald head reflected sweat, as if his reading had exerted him. Indeed, it seemed from the number of reports stacked beside him that it might be so. Setting the wooden slate down with a soft clack, he looked up.

His heavily creased face gave no hint of his mood. His eyes passed across Varro to the others, then back again. Then he stood up from the desk, but kept them at attention. He straightened the hem of the tunic over his muscular legs.

"I've given more thought to the depletion of your maniple. I've also been considering your expanded skills." He paused to spread his hands wide, as if to give an estimate of how expanded he believed their skills were. To Varro's eyes, this did not seem much. He then folded his arms and leaned against the desk.

"I remain critical of your approach at Rhoda."

This was the first Varro had heard of the fort's name, which had until that moment been a simple objective. Giving it a name now made it seem more important that it was.

"However, you did as commanded and with less support than you expected. I have to respect that, even if I doubt what you people are really about. Servus Capax. Since when did we need secret groups and secret signs for men to serve Rome?"

He raised his chin to Varro, as if daring him to answer. But of course, Varro stared at the back of the sparse command tent and once more to Cato's fastidiously neat field cot.

"Well, I'll tell you when that started. It started when some senators wanted more power than they already had. So now we've got these little spies crawling all over, and who knows how many and what they're spying on. All of them sworn to serve Rome but yet somehow taking orders from one senator or another."

Varro blinked. He hadn't considered this. While Cato had a point, it made no difference to him. His family problems were solved and his future secured, not to mention he was wealthier than even Cato himself might suspect. So he continued to stare ahead, choosing not to let the consul's jabs draw any blood from him.

"If you want to serve Rome, then do as soldiers do. Do as farmers do. You three seemed on the right path, good farming families and good soldiers. But then someone corrupted you, and I know who it was. The Greek faction. Oh yes, I see that surprise in your eyes, Centurion Varro. But believe it when I say there are those wishing to see Roman ways corrupted by what they think are better systems. But what do the Greeks have? You were there. You saw it yourself, but you will dare tell me that was better than Rome? Ha!"

Cato wiped the back of his wrist across his mouth as if he had just been punched and was ready to counterattack. But instead, he shook his round, bald head.

"Well, what is done is done. You have your secret signs and secret masters, and one day that will send you three to early graves. I'm not certain if I will be sorry for you. But I am sorry Rome has lost the service of good soldiers and good farmers, without which there would be no city at all."

The urge to speak out burned in Varro's chest. It took all his effort to remain staring ahead, at rigid attention. He was glad Falco and Curio did as well, for he knew how much they felt the sting of having all their sacrifices denigrated.

Cato let out a long sigh, then pushed off the side of his desk.

"I suppose if I've been granted access to you three, then I'm not using you to your fullest by training my recruits. Any other veteran could do that. For the time being, I'm going to assign the three of you to my staff, at your current ranks, of course. It's a better thing that I keep you near than let you get too far out of view. The Tenth Maniple will be reorganized and filled with what men I can spare, which are already too few. You three will move your tent into the headquarters area and remain accessible to me at all times. I promise to keep your days busy. Do you have any questions?"

Varro had no questions that he would not be flogged for asking.

"No, sir!"

Falco and Curio both gave the same answer, but he could hear the anger in their voices. If Cato noticed, he gave no sign as he settled back in his chair.

"I will inform Tribune Galenus of the change. He will no doubt be upset, but what does not upset that man? You may inform your men that new leadership will be assigned before the evening meal. In the meantime, you should speak to the camp prefect to have your tent lot assigned. Dismissed."

Outside the tent, the three once more proceeded back toward the intersection of the main camp roads in silence. Yet the pulse raging in Varro's ears drowned out any other sound. His face could have warmed his evening puls with the heat it threw, and it worsened when he considered Cato must have realized how enraged he had become.

"This way," Falco said, stopping them at the main crossroads and pointing toward the edge of camp. Per camp standards, two hundred feet of empty space between the tent lines and trenches kept soldiers out of enemy missile range while they slept and gave an area to assemble to march out. This also served as a private area for them to speak while ostensibly still heading for their centuries.

The moment they stepped into the middle of the cleared edge, all three began shouting curses and complaints. None of them listened to the other, but instead vomited out everything they had held inside. Finally, Varro shouted for calm while raising both hands.

"We're just drawing attention to ourselves."

"Let them listen," Falco said, his heavy brow drawn into a V shape. "I don't care if Cato knows we hate him. Did you hear what he said? He grouped us with murderers and thieves? None of what we've done in service to Rome counts? Look at my shoulder, Varro, look at that burn scar. That was for Rome, and I won't let some cabbage-faced politician tell me it means nothing."

"His face reminds you of cabbage, too?" Varro looked between him and Curio.

"He smells like cabbage," Curio said. "I suppose he does look like cabbage."

Falco growled and shook his head. "Don't try to distract me. I've a mind to boil him just like a head of cabbage."

"All right, don't shout stuff like that," Varro said and resumed their walk back to their centuries. "Don't give the old man an excuse to discipline us. We need to think about this differently. He doesn't know us and really doesn't understand what we're about."

"I don't even know what we're about," Falco said. "But it's surely not stabbing people in the back because those are my orders. Flamininus sent us to become guerrilla cavalrymen. If he wanted killers, he'd have just had back-alley scum in Rome teach us."

Varro held his silence. If Flamininus had ordered them to kill a rival, what choice would they have? He had considered Servus Capax as a secret military brotherhood. But Cato had him second-guessing what Servus Capax could become, and in some ways his dire accusations were not implausible.

"For the love of Jupiter, Varro, you've got that look again. Like you're thinking about how to be nice. I hate that look. It makes me want to punch your face in like I used to when we were kids."

"You wouldn't try that now," Varro said. "I've given up my oath of nonviolence."

"Exactly," Falco said, stretching both hands before himself as if displaying the answer to their problems. "No matter what you say, you're still a man of peace at heart. How can the consul accuse you of being a murderer?"

"Because he doesn't understand us," Varro said. "But he'll get to know us better when we serve him directly. Listen, the both of you, we'll drive ourselves mad if we nurse our anger. I'm as enraged as both of you. But let's see if we can't win this battle just like we do on the field. It's a different kind of fight for us, but one we shouldn't surrender without testing ourselves in combat."

"I'm going to have to write for him," Curio said. "I can't write. I can read a little. But what's going to happen when I have to take notes or something? I'm in trouble."

"We'll cover for you," Falco said. "And besides, he's not pulling us off the line to take notes. That's fucking ridiculous. He's got servants and slaves for that. I'm sure he's pulling us off the line to somehow ensure we get in trouble. I don't like him."

"None of us are going to like him," Varro said as they arrived at their tent line. "But we can work within his framework and find a peaceful balance. We share the same ideals about soldiering. So let's build from there."

Falco shook his head and muttered something about beating his face inside out. Varro pretended not to hear it, while Curio was wrapped up in his terror of note-taking.

The rest of the afternoon sped past in a blur of activity. Varro was surprised at the outpouring from his men when informed of the change. He had to order them to silence. Even a single experience of combat had forged a bond between them. They told him he had led the charge, and they wished to be as brave as he was. Varro did not know about that. He never felt especially brave, but rather more often he felt foolhardy. Still, even after they were dismissed, men tarried to express their hope to serve under him again one day.

As refreshing as it was to hear this, he couldn't savor the feeling too long. He pivoted to setting up a new tent assignment. So he volunteered to speak with the camp prefect for all three of them, who would share a single tent. It was a straightforward affair. The prefect had been apprised of the change, and had the lot selected before Varro arrived.

While returning along the road, just outside of headquarters, someone called to him from behind. He turned to find Centurion Longinus hailing him. The late afternoon light hit him squarely, cutting a stocky figure. As he approached, Varro noted the thin scar on his face that he had got in a childhood accident. It made him smile to think of how the centurion might have played up that scar over the years.

"Centurion Varro," he said, catching up. "I wanted to congratulate you on breaching the fort in Rhoda. Your men did an admirable job, and as I hear it you led a charge right into the enemy defenses. That is what this legion needs, a real hero to set the example."

"You flatter me, Centurion Longinus." Varro inclined his head with a smile. "But you also surprise me for learning of my actions inside the fort."

His chest tightened, wondering if Longinus had found out he had freed captives in defiance of orders, and was now about to blackmail him. Why must these kinds of people dog his every step, he thought. But Longinus shook his head with a smile.

"Well, I had volunteered for that task. So of course I wanted to know how well you did. Besides, your men have been bragging to all the other hastati. After all, by now they're the most experienced soldiers of this year's recruits."

Varro shook his head. "I wish there were more of them left."

Longinus nodded and stroked the thick black stubble on his chin. It seemed no blade would ever fully tame his beard.

"It was a mistake to send your men in. The consul should have let my boys take the gate, or at least a better experienced team. I don't mean any offense. Your men did well with the little training they had, and you certainly set an example for them."

"No offense taken." Varro raised a brow to Longinus. "And who are your boys? Forgive me if I'm not as familiar with you as you are with me."

"Forgive me, I should've explained myself. I'm First Spear."

Varro straightened up. "Sorry, sir. I had no idea."

Longinus waved his hands. "Well, you wouldn't unless we were introduced, or you saw me at an assembly. We're not even in the same legion. In any case, I won't keep you. I just wanted to congratulate you, and let you know that I admire what you did and hope to see more of it. If you need help with your boys, let me know how I can assist."

"That won't be a problem any longer, sir. I'm being assigned to Consul Cato's staff."

The statement turned Longinus's head so that he regarded him as if they had just met, and he did not trust him. The sudden shift in his attitude took Varro aback. It was not such an unusual assignment that it should warrant any suspicion. But Longinus seemed suddenly distant.

"That's too bad. You're better off in the field, in my opinion. Well, best of luck to you, Centurion Varro."

They parted, with Longinus headed into the headquarters area and Varro following the road back to his century. The interaction was strange, and he could not account for the shift in the attitude. Cato seemed fairly well loved by all for his willingness to dig a trench. But perhaps that love was not so universal, or his trench-digging was a ploy that more experienced men saw through. In the end, he could not make sense of Longinus's attitude and left the thought behind him.

The remainder of the day and the next were a blur of transitional activity. Tribune Galenus was indeed as unhappy to see Varro and the rest go as he was to have had them assigned in the first place. Their new arrangements set them outside of Cato's tent, much more like servants than special duty officers. Their first assignments were in organizing scouting and foraging teams and creating patrol schedules. It was tedious work and every tribune wanted special treatment of some sort. Having never seen this up close before, Varro was amazed at how so many acted as if they were the only officer in the legion. It felt like an entirely different army to him.

To Cato's credit, he straightened out any tribune who thought himself better than the rest. He took their names and soon thereafter they had no more special requests.

It seemed such tedium would be their lot forever, as the Iberian host had not been located yet. Varro felt pressure for the scouts returning with little to no intelligence. In a morning meeting with Cato and his staff in the command tent, he slapped his desk with his gnarled hand.

"Then we shall have to get direct with these Iberians. If no one seems to know where to find an army that is said to outnumber us four to one, then I smell a lie." Cato's eyes narrowed as he looked into the distance, then he turned to Varro and the others.

"Cancel the remaining scouting activities. From now on, I want captives from the local populations. We will have it out of them one way or the other. If these barbarians think to trifle with Rome, then they will learn their lessons in broken limbs and torn flesh!"

"Sir, you want captives for interrogation?" Varro knew restating the order would draw ire, but he loathed what this meant for civilians.

"That is exactly correct, Centurion. I want them tonight, and every night until we ascertain where these rebels are hiding in their untold masses. I would expect interrogations to be a specialty of yours."

The other staff in the room, some officers and others just adjutants, looked quizzically at Varro.

"Sir, I'm no better at it than another, and probably worse."

Cato hissed in disgust. "Order captives taken and I'll have real interrogators work on them. And don't bring me just the men. Women and children see and know things as well, and won't hold out as long as a man. We must act with haste or else the barbarians will sneak upon us unprepared."

Varro could only salute. He again thought of the two children he spared. Were the gods toying with him now, exchanging those two for scores of others?

It seemed Cato drew a breath to conclude his morning brief, but a messenger was granted urgent access. He presented himself to the consul.

"Sir, there are three emissaries from the Ilegertes tribe to see you. They have an urgent request."

"Send them away," Cato said, waving off the messenger with a wax tablet he had just selected off the pile on his desk.

"Sir, they come from the king of that tribe and one is a prince."

Cato glared at the messenger, who lowered his head expecting a rebuke. But the consul sighed.

"Very well. I will see them in that case. We have precious few allies here, and it would not do to insult their barbarian pride." Cato dispatched the messenger and the rest of his staff, but he held Varro and the others back.

"I need witnesses, and you three will do. Optio Curio, take notes. I need an accurate document of what we discuss."

9

Varro, Falco, and Curio were provided seats to Cato's right side. Servants rushed in and out of the tent to prepare for the emissaries with chairs and a table laid out with wines and salted meats. For all his austerity, Cato knew how to play the role of a powerful host. He sat in stony silence, much like the guards he now had posted inside his tent. Besides the working servants, no one else made a sound. Only the shaking of Curio's stylus against the blank wax slate gripped in his bloodless fingers made any sound.

Curio stared wild-eyed at the square of light streaming in from the entrance. Servants set out clay cups for all of them while one overseer fussed about the placement of wine decanters. This happened right before Curio, but he did not move or blink.

Varro pressed back a smirk. Taking pleasure in Curio's distress was wrong, he knew, but he and Falco had concocted this lie. So now he would be found out, and with possibly terrifying consequences. Cato was a disciplinarian on his best days, and a true tyrant in his foul moods.

Yet the humor remained because Falco had also swiped a wax

tablet from the consul's desk. He lacked a stylus, but had somehow acquired a twig that would serve in its place. Being that they all sat behind the consul, he would take the notes and give them to Curio before the end. Varro took extra enjoyment from the glistening sweat on Falco's brow. Maybe this would finally teach both of them that Curio needed to become properly literate.

At last, the servants cleared out and there was a dramatic pause. Cato shifted impatiently on his chair and scratched furiously at the gray stubble wrapping his bald head. The same messenger from earlier entered the tent, and this time dark shadows blocked the light of the entrance behind him.

"Consul Cato, I present emissaries from Bilistages, King of the Ilegertes, led by his son, Albus."

The consul waved them on as if he were calling home children who had been outside too late.

The messenger vanished as three men entered, and there was no doubt which of them was the prince.

Albus stood a head taller than the other men, and probably a head taller than Falco himself. He was broad-shouldered with an improbably thin waist cinched by a heavy belt. He wore a coat of fine mail and a cloak of some exotic black fur. He carried no weapons, obviously surrendering these before entering the camp, but it did nothing to diminish his stature. Most striking was his long, pale hair and beard. Varro had never seen the likes of it, being almost washed of any color.

"Great Consul of Rome," he said, bowing. "I am Albus, son of Bilistages, and I am honored to be allowed your company."

The prince spoke with fluid, if accented words, something Varro had grown accustomed to hearing from his time in Numidia. But the accent seemed to grate on Cato's ears, for his chin sank into his neck and his nostrils flared as if he had caught wind of a foul smell.

"Be seated, friends." For all his appearance of disgust, Cato spoke cordially and extended a hand toward the table. "I've prepared refreshments for you after your journey."

The two others with Albus, also imposing men with blue tattoos crawling up their necks from beneath their mail coats, waited for their prince to take the center seat, then settled beside him. They wore heavy beards like their prince, but their hair and eyes were much darker and more wary than Albus's. The prince seemed completely at ease, even folding his hands serenely on the table. Varro noted blue tattoos on the backs of his hands that looked like eagle talons.

A servant stepped out of the corner and poured wine for the guests. Varro had only eaten some bread dipped in vinegary wine for his breakfast. The strips of salted meats drew water to his mouth.

"Let us begin," Cato said, glancing to Curio to indicate he should begin documentation. He snapped up his slate and stylus with such violence that Varro thought he might fly out of his seat.

Albus had extended his hand for his freshly filled cup, but withdrew at the consul's words. The other emissaries set their cups down when their prince did not drink.

"My father was gladdened to learn of your arrival, a Roman host to put down the madness that burns through the land like a wildfire."

"That is fully my intent," Cato said. "You would not know where the rebels have secreted themselves or who leads them?"

"There is no leader," Albus said as he considered his wine cup. At length, he reached for it and his two companions followed. "Every tribe has drawn together in some madness that compels them against Rome. I cannot say how the fire started, but it burns brightly. The tribes are all proud people, as you must know, and it takes nothing at all to bring them to violence in a common cause. There must be a dozen kings and chiefs who have gone upon this rampage with little thought to how it might end. If you ask who leads them, even their answers will be at odds."

"But the Ilegertes remain loyal to Rome." Whether Cato asked or stated this was not clear, but Albus drank deeply from his cup before answering. He set it down with a clack and tilted his head.

"Many will not drink Roman wine. They say its flavor is too sour. But I have developed a taste for it, as has my father."

"Can you not give a clearer answer?" Cato glanced once more to Curio hunched over his slate and crushing the stylus in a white-fingered hand.

"The Ilegertes are ever loyal to Rome," Albus said. "We are the few who have not betrayed our promises."

"But you have in the past," Cato said.

Albus gave an easy laugh. "Great Consul, I was a mere child in those days. Let us not cast our thoughts back so far, but think only of today. For today, the Ilegertes stand by Rome, and my father sends me, his only son, directly to you as soon as we learned of your presence."

"But not without urgent purpose, and I assume you will at last relieve me of the mystery of your arrival here?"

"Great Consul, the Ilegertes, having chosen to remain loyal and true to Rome, now share a common enemy. We would add our swords to yours, but we are in turn besieged. Our farms have been trampled and overrun and we are held within the walls of our own stronghold. We three have escaped at great peril to come to you, our ally and friend, and ask for relief."

"You seek military assistance?" Cato looked to Curio once more, and he doubled over his slate and scratched into the wax in response.

Albus watched that exchange with hooded eyes, but inclined his head to Cato.

"I have beheld the greatness of your camp and the vastness of your force. If you could but send three thousand of your soldiers, then our enemies would not stand against us and flee back to the safety of their homes. It must be a small thing for you, with so many at your command."

Cato had begun shaking his head halfway through Albus's request, but it did not deter the prince or seem to cause him any dismay. The two others with him, however, looked anxiously at each other across the back of their prince.

"I cannot divide my force when I've not yet learned where my enemy is, or his strength, or even his intentions. I expect now that my arrival is well known, an attack must come soon. I will need every available man, for the only thing I do know is that the rebels outnumber us by a large margin."

"Certainly, it is said one Roman soldier is worth ten of any other." Albus smiled as he held his cup out for a servant to refill.

"Then you must seek thirty thousand other allies instead of my soldiers. You have my deepest sympathies and respect. I admire your personal bravery in seeking me here. But I must ask your father to hold out longer. Once we have shattered the main rebellion, if your enemy still dares challenge you, I shall destroy them."

Albus held the wine in his mouth a second longer than he should, then swallowed. He set the cup down and folded his hands once more.

"My father has told his people Rome is a fair and good friend of the Ilegertes, and that our faithfulness will be rewarded. It is not an easy thing to keep some men from rethinking their alliances."

"Is this a threat, Prince Albus?" Cato's voice hardened. Both Falco and Curio bent over their slates to capture the moment. But Varro simply observed, feeling sorry for Albus. He was never going to be granted what he needed. Cato was a stubborn man.

"It is the truth. If it is inconvenient to hear, I am sorry. We Ilegertes value truth and honesty in our dealings, as I know Rome does as well. But if our people benefit nothing at all from aligning with you, or it appears so to them, then the flames of this rebellion might begin to burn within my father's hall. I hope it will be otherwise."

"You'll benefit by being spared the punishments visited on those who aided this rebellion once it is crushed. Do not doubt that I will see this fire completely extinguished."

"Is that also not a threat, Great Consul? Friends should not cross swords like this when it is in their mutual interest to fight side by side."

Cato's eyes narrowed and Varro again bit his lip against smiling. This Albus was fearless and had a brutal but appealing honesty. Moreover, he was a natural orator, and if he had been Roman, he might have had a place in the Senate. Yet Cato continued to shake his head.

"Take it as you will. Deliver my regrets to your father, but also impress on him that he needs to hold in place for only a short while. When the rebellion is shattered, he will reap his earned rewards. In the meantime, you may remain here as my guests and rest before departing tomorrow."

"We will hold out as long as we can," Albus said with a sigh. "But Rome may find her ally no better than a corpse upon the battlefield before then. Please take the night to consider our plea, and understand that the Ilegertes pay a heavy price for loyalty."

Varro was sad to see the prince led out of the tent to be shown to his campsite for the night. Though he stood tall and with his shoulders back, nonetheless the weight of his people's hopes seemed to press on them. Varro could sense despair even if he would not openly show it. But more than that, he had enjoyed the way Albus spoke and comported himself before Cato. A barbarian prince he may be, but there was something even more civilized in him than Varro had seen in fellow Romans.

"Optio, hand me your notes."

Cato stared after the departing prince, but extended his hand for Curio's slate. Varro did not catch the planned deceit, but did see Falco stuffing something under the hem of his mail coat. Curio dutifully placed the slate in the consul's palm. He then looked it over with an ever-deepening frown.

"Good enough for me to enhance with my own thoughts later," he said. As he was about to set the slate down, he pulled it closer, then tilted it side to side. He then pinched something out of the wax and held it up to his eyes.

"Is this bark?"

He flicked the sliver away, then turned over the slate to check the wood. In the meantime, both Curio and Falco took on a waxy pallor of their own.

"Sorry, sir," Curio said. "I had inspected the forage teams last night, and a piece of bark must've stuck to my hands."

"It stuck all this time?" Cato set the slate aside and shook his head in dismissal.

"Very well, Servus Capax, what do you make of our allies?"

Varro blinked, surprised that Cato would hear their opinion. He looked expectantly to them and seemed irritated with the delay.

"He's a good-looking man, sir," Falco said.

"By the gods," Cato muttered. "This cannot be what you would tell me."

"I mean, he doesn't look like he suffered much on the way here, sir." Falco sat up straighter. Of course, Varro knew Falco had meant what he originally said, and his mind did not work in metaphors.

Cato inclined his head in agreement. "So you think he overstates his needs? It is possible."

Varro now considered Flamininus's message, which instructed him to not only help defeat the rebellion but also preserve the tribal alliances still in place.

"Sir, it might also be that Albus skillfully avoided his enemies.

He seemed a competent man, and he is the only son of their king. There must be some real need if he risked sending him with only two guards."

"Perhaps they could not spare the men for a suitable escort," Cato said. He no longer seemed irritated but in deep thought, staring into nothing and tapping his finger against his bulbous nose.

Varro tried to break into those thoughts. "Sir, they are an allied tribe, and we have too few who still stand with us. Even when we put down the rebellion, it may flare up again in time. If we do not aid our allies today, we might not have them when we need them. And who else will ally with us if our promises mean nothing?"

Cato snapped up from thought, his face a sour grimace.

"They ally with us because their other choice is to fight against us, and they will see what that earns them. Rome does not recognize defeat. And I did not say I would do nothing, but merely delay handling their problems until the larger issues in the province are solved." Cato shook his head and waved them off. "I've heard enough. You're dismissed to your duties. Bring me captives tonight."

Once outside again and away from the tent, both Curio and Falco began laughing.

"You two think you are so clever," Varro said. "But this can't last forever. It will be even worse if Cato learns you're deceiving him. Isn't it better, Curio, that you actually learn to write?"

"I'm trying," he said through his laughter. "I can copy words, but can't write them out of my head. I don't have time to study enough."

"Then you should find the time, or else one day you will be found out."

But Falco groaned at Varro's warning.

"So he had to take notes once. This is the first time we've ever had to do anything like taking notes. It'll be ten years before that happens again."

"You got bark in my notes," Curio said. "Next time you should have a proper stylus."

"Well, you're picky for someone whose skin I just saved."

A full day lay ahead, and Varro and the others set about revising their plan and issuing new orders. Villages were selected and teams assembled. They would work by moonlight to avoid any detection by enemy scouts. No one had any idea of the enemy's position, and Varro did not want their teams cut off and destroyed.

He tried not to think of what he was organizing, which was the systematic torture of innocent villagers for what they knew of the enemy, which might be nothing at all. Yet, if they did hide knowledge of the rebels, then they had chosen their side in this war. He consoled himself with this excuse and was glad his rank as centurion excluded him from the actual raids and subsequent torments.

The Ilegertes emissaries had been settled near headquarters, but Varro had no chance to see Albus and his men again. They had pitched a modest tent of animal hide near the consul's. While this showed trust and respect, they also had two guards assigned to them as well. Trust went only so far, Varro mused.

During the night, the captives were dragged into the camp and thrust into the hands of the interrogators. These were regular infantrymen who had been selected mostly on the basis of how large and frightening they appeared. Varro did see women dragged in, but fortunately no children. But this was only one night of what must be days of this to come.

He and Falco had to wait outside for the intelligence the interrogators had gleaned. Curio had begged off to study writing. The screaming of both interrogator and victim echoed through the camp. The beatings thudded wet and meaty until gore-soaked bodies were flung out of the tents like so much waste and new victims herded inside.

This horrid cycle carried on as more parties returned with their captives. If any were left alive after interrogation, they would become slaves. But it seemed most did not leave the tents breathing.

At last, the final party returned and the last interrogation ended. Varro and Falco, who had passed the night in silence, debriefed. The interrogators, three brutes who were well suited to their roles, were splattered with blood. Their leather-wrapped hands were red, and one carried a cudgel that dripped onto the trampled grass.

They had tormented twenty locals that night, and eight of them had survived. These had yielded some measure of information. Varro and Falco both recorded what they had learned to present to Cato at the morning brief. The reports conflicted, but they gave a general direction of the rebellion's heart.

They returned to their tent and found Curio asleep with no indication that he had been writing. Varro shook his head at Falco, who rolled his eyes as he prepared for sleep.

The next morning at the brief, Cato was pleased with at least an estimate of strength and location. He consulted a crude map scrawled on vellum. It seemed nothing that Cato would've created himself, but he now found the blank spot in their scouting patterns.

"I want this area thoroughly scouted," he said, setting a stone to keep the vellum opened on his desk. "Good work, you three."

The simple statement filled Varro with pride. Cato was miserly with his praise, and even such a tepid compliment normally had to be eked out of him.

The others in the room raised their brows as well, and nodded to the crude vellum map as if it contained all their answers. To

Varro, it was a bunch of symbols scratched in charcoal that made little sense.

The rest of the briefing concerned plans for further interrogation of the locals and other minutiae of camp administration. But once more, on the cusp of the conclusion, the guard outside the camp presented the Ilegertes emissaries.

Albus looked happy and refreshed, as if he had not spent a night lying on cold earth and listening to tribesmen scream as they were beaten to death. Instead, his two companions seemed to have taken on the physical burdens of their lord. Both had dark circles under their eyes and their hair was disheveled as if just risen from sleep. It seemed their faces might slide to the hard-packed dirt floor of Cato's tent.

After an exchange of formalities, Albus again presented his request for aid.

Varro looked away, embarrassed by the rejection he surmised from Cato's long pause.

"I have considered your needs," he said, leaning on his desk as the pale-haired prince of the Ilegertes tilted his head back as if anticipating a slap. "I am not unsympathetic to your plight. We are allies, after all, and if I would call upon you and expect your aid, then I must honor the same in return. You shall have your three thousand men."

Varro looked to Cato, who still held both hands against his desk like a man hoping not to be thrown overboard during a storm as sea. Even Albus widened his eyes and lowered them at the consul.

"You will spare three thousand of your soldiers to aid my people against our common enemy?"

"I have said so." Cato released the desk, apparently leaving those stormy seas that raged in his mind. "And so it will be."

The two other emissaries bowed and thanked Cato, their

words a jumble of rough accents. But Albus once more resumed his cool demeanor.

"I cannot thank you enough, Great Consul. I will lead these men to my homeland, yes?"

"No," Cato said. "I will send them by sea to disembark on your shores. I cannot chance rebel spies noting the passage of so much of my strength from camp. It might encourage an attack before I reorganize."

Albus nodded gravely, but he then seemed to reconsider.

"I shall see these three thousand men board their ships."

Cato hovered over his desk and his eyes paled and nostrils flared. But he slowly nodded.

"Yes, you may supervise the embarking of the men. And I have a further benefit for you."

Cato paused and a small smile touched his face. Albus raised his brows.

"I grant you the services of my aides, Centurions Varro and Falco, and Optio Curio. They will accompany you and serve as advisors to King Bilistages. Centurion Varro is the senior. So, let your king direct all his questions of Rome to him."

Varro blinked in astonishment, and it took a moment for him to realize that Consul Cato grinned at him, waiting for his acknowledgment.

"Yes, sir!"

10

The Ilegertes exited the tent in high spirits, with Albus appearing the calmest of them. Consul Cato watched them leave, then dismissed everyone but his three aides. The morning sun shone through the tent roof as a brilliant yellow spot, lighting up behind Cato like a faint halo. He grinned, the folds of his cabbage face catching the shadows.

"You are not surprised, are you? I have three officers without men to lead. So I have decided you could do some good managing relations with our ally."

"Of course, sir," Varro said, looking to both Curio and Falco who displayed equal astonishment. "But you invested much power in us. Are we leading the three thousand men?"

"I said no such thing," Cato said, resuming his seat behind his desk. "Tribune Galenus will lead the men. By the chain of command, you will report to him. But I want someone to stay close to these Ilegertes and ensure they remain loyal. That is what you Servus Capax people can do for me. In fact, those are my express orders to you. You will ensure the Ilegertes remain loyal to Rome, and you have no special authorizations to promise them wealth, territory, or anything of the sort. You'll have to use whatever techniques your masters taught you to keep their loyalty."

Varro stared into those pale eyes and he found something he did not trust within them. But he could not directly state his discomfort. Once more, his opinion of the consul swayed from positive to negative, and he doubted it would ever change again.

"Yes, sir. Tribune Galenus will lead the men in battle, and we will support this King Bilistages with whatever he needs."

"Yes, yes," Cato said, ducking his bald head. "Isn't that what you did in Numidia? Serve some foreign king? Well, do it again, and make sure this one doesn't join the rebellion. You will remain with him until I recall you to my service. Until then, you three prepare to march. Draw whatever you need from the quartermasters. If they have any complaints, send them to me."

They saluted and were prepared to be dismissed. But Cato narrowed his eyes and lowered his voice.

"Now, I have one more thing." Though seated, Cato seemed like a lion ready to pounce. His hand sought something beneath the vellum map. "Just as I was beginning to think differently about the three of you, I instead confirmed my suspicions."

"I'm not sure what you mean, sir?" Varro and the others exchanged confused glances. But Cato remained poised and snarling.

Then he ripped out something from beneath the vellum and held it forward like it was the spear of Mars himself.

"This! Look, it is a twig and one I found on the floor right beside my desk after the three of you left yesterday."

The straight twig with a raw yellow point trembled in Cato's gnarled fingers. A burning ember felt as if it had dropped into Varro's belly. He resisted the urge to glare at Falco.

"And what should I find on its tip? Wax." He brandished the twig so all three could see, but he held it before Curio.

"One of your friends wrote those notes for you. You never

made a mark on your slate, but just set it back on my desk. In the wrong place, too. There is an order to everything here, but you three are too pleased with your own cleverness to notice."

He flicked the twig into Curio's bright red face and he winced. Cato laughed.

"You were not even smart enough to use a stylus, and arrogant enough to drop that twig under my feet. Do you not see how I maintain this tent? Order, men, order. I know the position of each speck of dust in this tent."

Cato paused, leaning back in his chair and smiling.

"When you return, Optio Curio, you will write your confession to this deception while I watch. If you write well, I will rethink my feelings on this matter, and depending on your success with the Ilegertes might even forget it completely. But if you misspell a single word, fumble through your writing, or compose your thoughts like a child, I will demote you and have you flogged raw. If you survive it, you'll be sent to a different unit and legion from your accomplices."

Curio withered under the consul's glare and gave a feeble acknowledgment. But Cato had already rounded on Falco and Varro.

"And as you two aided in deceiving me, you will share the same punishment for Curio's failure. I might not be able to strip you of those special pugiones on your harnesses, but I can strip you of both rank and skin."

At last the tension in his limbs released and he smirked, satisfied.

"Dismissed. Fortuna go with you."

Outside the tent, Falco and Curio both began to splutter excuses. But Varro's head throbbed with wooly rage. Rather than tear into his friends, he simply held up his hand and left them in the middle of the parade ground. Nothing but a brawl could come of this now. He needed a distraction from this completely avoidable trap the consul had set for them. If he thought even one more minute on it, he would likely cause irreparable damage to his friendships.

So he plodded off to find Albus at his tent, where his two advisors and he stood outside while congratulating each other with shoulder and back slaps. Varro forced a smile and approached Albus.

Remembering his experiences at court in Numidia, he realized even barbarian royalty expected deference to their status. He liked what he had seen of Albus so far, but it did not mean he would indulge any familiarity.

"Prince Albus," he said when they noticed his approach. "If you have a moment, I wish to introduce myself."

"Excellent!" Albus clapped his hands together. The eagle talons tattooed there seemed to clutch all his fingers between them. "I have noticed you in these audiences with your consul. You have the eyes of one who has seen much, and who might see more than he speaks."

The abrupt assessment of his personality left him wordless, and this seemed to please Albus, who tilted his head back with a laugh.

"I am Centurion Varro, sir." Not knowing how to respond, he simply continued as planned. "I hoped to meet you and learn more about the enemy we face."

Albus continued to laugh, and his tattooed guards shared his mirth. He was one of the tallest men Varro had ever seen, and his long pale hair was bright against the black fur cloak he wore over battle-scarred mail. For all his imposing appearance, his laughter was easy and welcoming. He did not seem to laugh at Varro, but rather out of joy.

"Well, you are direct as most Romans are," he said at last. "Where are the other two?"

He had just been forgetting his anger at them, and it flared again at their mention.

"They're procuring supplies for our assignment, sir."

"I'm not your superior officer," Albus said. "But neither am I your lord or prince. Since we will travel together, you may call me Albus. But my father is a king, and so I warn you to name me as a prince before him. And of course, you must call him king."

"It might be easier if I always call you prince," Varro said, smiling even when he did not feel it. "But I appreciate your offer. Now, three thousand infantry is a large force. How many enemies will we face, Prince Albus, and what kind of enemy?"

"An old enemy." Albus's face darkened and his jovial mood vanished, and the same for his two companions. "His name is King Diorix. His tribe and ours have been at odds since the days of my great-grandfather, but we've had peace in recent years. Until the rebellion happened."

"So Diorix used your alliance with Rome as an excuse to attack?"

"Just so," Albus said, staring beyond the camp as if he could see his enemy through the rolling blue hills. "But my father is wise and knew to prepare for the storm. He recalled his folk to our stronghold and stockpiled grain and wine and fortified the walls. Diorix came and burned what he could. Stole what he could. Then bolted us up behind our walls. He might have a thousand or more men, but he could call on allies. Only his greed keeps him from doing so now, or else he would have to share the spoils."

The other two emissaries lowered their heads, exposing more of the blue tattoos encircling their necks, and Albus's eyes narrowed. There was more to what he feared, but it seemed he was not ready to speak it aloud. They stood in awkward silence until Varro cleared his throat.

"You are not fully surrounded, though, or else you could not have escaped so easily."

Now Albus turned fierce blue eyes on him and he seemed more like the eagle whose talons were drawn on his hands.

"Easily? We stole away by night, with what provisions we could carry, and fought Diorix's scouts. We must do the same once more to return with our news. I had hoped to lead your men back, which would make returning to my father's side a simple thing. But now six men instead of three must steal through Diorix's lines."

"We will succeed," Varro said with flat confidence. "In this, I may possess more experience than you."

Albus nodded, but looked down from his great height with hooded eyes.

"And what technique will have us pass unseen through enemies and through our own walls?"

"I must see the landscape and the enemy, and then I will know how to get around them. But you are correct. It will probably come to a fight and mad run to your gates."

"Honesty!" Albus's fair mood returned, and he clapped one of his companions on the shoulder. "Better than sweet words to please me. So, have your blade sharpened, Centurion Varro. Though I have wondered, should we await the landing of your men and proceed with them?"

Varro considered this.

"It is a possibility. We would need to camp near to their landing spot, which only the ship captains will determine when they see the coast. All the while, we would be avoiding capture by Diorix. What would happen if you were to become Diorix's hostage?"

"That could happen even if we fight our way back inside."

Again, Varro nodded in acceptance. "We don't need to worry about this. I expect our forces will have landed ahead of us. If they depart today, we should be able to meet them on the march inland. There will be no issue returning to your father in victory."

Albus accepted this, and they discussed other details of their journey back. They needed provisions, which Varro could requisition on their behalf. Since they had to escape in secret, they had traveled on foot rather than by horse. Albus hinted that he might enjoy a loaned horse, but Varro also hinted that was out of the question. Having concluded their discussions, they agreed to meet again to watch the troops board their transports.

Varro avoided Falco and Curio after his meeting with the prince. Rather than return to their tent, he went to the quartermaster. He requisitioned the supplies he needed and rations to support a three-day march. The quartermaster, being an old triarius, had plenty of curiosity about where he was going. He found Varro's explanation fascinating.

"I never got any special assignments like that in all my years in the legion. This is my last term, too. Best of luck to you, son. Sounds like an adventure."

The quartermaster handed him some of what he had requested and promised delivery of the rest. Varro took up the pack and gave his thanks.

"There is one other thing I need. How much vellum can you spare? As well as ink?"

The quartermaster frowned. "How many reports are you going to write? I've got lamb skin vellum in good enough supply. But that's for the consul's use, mostly."

"I'll take all that you can spare. Our optio is going to be doing a lot of important writing."

Varro found other excuses to remain away while he cooled off. He had never felt such anger at either of them before, not even at Falco for bullying him in their youth. But he could not avoid them all day and eventually returned to the tent with the partial supplies he had requisitioned.

Both Falco and Curio were packing in stony silence. They paused when Varro entered the tent, then turned back to their work. Varro lingered a moment before sliding into the cool interior. He set his pack down, then began to gather his own things.

The shuffling and sliding of their gear disturbed the otherwise unbearable silence. While Curio studiously avoided looking up, Varro knew Falco stole looks at him constantly. It was not in their nature to remain quiet with each other when angered. So this sudden shift seemed to worry him.

At last, Varro dropped his bag and sighed.

"I've requisitioned as much vellum as the quartermaster could give. You're going to write that confession letter until you can do it in your sleep. Falco and I will correct you. But you are going to make this your highest priority, Curio."

"Yes, sir."

"Thank the gods you can speak again." Falco dropped his pack and also sighed. But Varro narrowed his eyes at him.

"You just left the twig on the floor? You can't see how ordered and neat Cato is?"

"I thought it was in my tunic, but it must have fallen out. I realized it later, and just hoped it wasn't in that tent."

Falco's voice was soft, and he lowered his head in shame. Varro glared at him a moment longer, then picked up his bag again.

"All right, that's done with. Curio is going to learn to write. And not just that damn confession letter. If I understand Cato, he'll switch the topic at the last moment. So practice the confession letter, but you'll learn to write anything. Even if you have to practice during combat. Pin a vellum sheet to the back of your scutum."

This made Curio laugh, though Varro had been deadly serious. Falco took it up, acting out what fighting and composing a letter at the same time might be like. He ended up dancing around on one foot and it was so ridiculous that Varro went from smirking to outright laughter.

And when they were finished, the tension dissipated. Varro's chest felt lighter and his head clearer. It was just one more obstacle in the way, and they would get through it as a team.

By the early afternoon, Cato had assembled three thousand men at the shore. Tribune Galenus, lean-faced and frowning, stood before them. The men had their shields hanging in bags from their backs, their bronze helmets reflecting the sun as they waited for orders to board the ships that would take them to the triremes waiting in the offshore mist.

Albus and his companions arrived to watch, and Cato gave the sign for the men to embark.

Varro, who stood back with Albus, seldom had the opportunity to observe from the outside. He was usually among those boarding. It was an impressive sight, with ordered ranks receiving the commands of their centurions to board, then crisply proceeding to their boats. These shoved off and carried over the gentle waves while white gulls called down to them.

Neither Albus nor Cato moved during the entire process of embarking, but each one stood watching the soldiers climbing the rope ladders onto the triremes. When at last Tribune Galenus was ready to board the final transport, he presented a salute to Consul Cato, who returned it with less ardor.

"Prince Albus," Cato said, at last acknowledging the Ilegertes emissaries. "Here are your three thousand men. Are you satisfied to see them aboard ships?"

"I am, Great Consul." Albus smiled then bowed low to Cato, which must have shocked the other emissaries, though they bowed alongside their prince.

"Travel in peace and safety," Cato said. Then he looked to Varro and the others. "Serve our allies well, and know you represent Rome in all you do."

Varro stood to attention and saluted. Cato left with his now smaller staff and the camp returned to its normal functioning.

All the planning of patrols, interrogations, and administration was no longer important. All that mattered now was linking up with Tribune Galenus and chasing off this King Diorix from Ilegertes' territory. Keeping the Ilegertes happy after that would be a simple matter of patrolling territory and discouraging further attacks.

They set out on the march shortly after the men boarded their transport. The Ilegertes emissaries would lead the way, as they were chosen to accompany Albus not only for their fighting prowess but also for their woodland skills. Albus claimed they were as good as hounds at sniffing out danger. Before they crested a small rise that would take them out of sight of the Roman camp, Varro looked back.

The top masts of the triremes were still in place. They would need time to organize the troops and assign rowers, which would be reduced to accommodate the extra men. The delay provided them a head start to rendezvous in two more days.

A sense of both freedom and sadness pressed on him at leaving his companions, particularly the men of his century. They might no longer be under his command, but he would feel a responsibility toward them for as long as they served. He hoped they would have good leaders so that they could become veterans rather than casualties. The legion only produced those two outcomes for those who served.

They found Albus enjoyed light conversation, and by the evening campfire on the first night he retold stories of ancient Ilegertes heroes. But his fellows debated his translations and they fell into playful arguments. Varro never learned the outcomes of the stories the prince had begun. But he did find himself enjoying his company even more.

"Better than looking at Cato's sour face," Falco observed the first night as they prepared for sleep. "At least White Hair likes to laugh."

"You should be more respectful than that," Varro said. "I know you like assigning nicknames, but you might let it slip at the wrong time."

Curio had volunteered to take the first watch of the night, possibly to avoid writing practice. But both Falco and Varro agreed he wouldn't get away with that the next day.

So they passed their travels lightly until noon of the second day when Albus suspected Diorix might have his scouts in the area. From that point forward, they spoke only when needed and then only in whispers. Albus pulled up his fur cloak, revealing a hood which had been hidden against its blackness. He stuffed his long, pale hair into it.

"We mustn't make it easy for them to find us," he said with a smile.

Diorix's scouts did not find them, though Albus's had reported signs of their passage in the area. Varro and the others had carried all their standard weapons, including a light and heavy pilum each. Albus worried about the shine of their bronze helmets and greaves, but in the end it made no difference. They arrived close to the shores where the triremes would disembark three thousand infantry.

Only, they found no one there.

The gray sea rolled calmly under a hazy sun on the third day. The cove Albus suspected the triremes would use remained empty, dotted with trees and black rocks rounded by wind and water of untold ages. While gulls perched there, staring at the new arrivals out of the tree line.

"Is there another landing place?" Varro asked while squinting into the sun.

Albus's lips had become thin and tight, and he stared into nothing a moment before answering.

"It would be far to the south. There is a thin beach north of here. It could be put ashore there, not realizing this would be a better place."

Varro looked north along the rolling waves. It made no sense. The triremes could not have passed this cove, especially since they would be watching for such a place to make their landing. Therefore, he reasoned they could have only disembarked back the way they had come. Yet they had traveled close to shore, and should have encountered Tribune Galenus's scouts by now.

"This doesn't feel right," Falco said, leaning close to his shoulder and whispering.

Curio also stood with arms folded, staring hard into the glare. He shrugged.

"It has been hazy these days. Maybe they were lost? Or they just disembarked them earlier because the captains were spooked."

"That's a good point," Falco said. "You know those navy bastards, always worried about stuff no one else can see."

But Albus broke into their conversation, stepping up to join them. His pale hair now flew freely over his broad shoulders.

"What say you? The ships could not have missed this perfect landing. So they can only be where you are looking. Did we miss them?"

"It seems so," Varro said, still staring down the misty beach. He prayed that the dark shapes of the trireme masts would show through the gauzy haze. But nothing did. "Let's follow the beach north again. I'm sure we will pick up their trail, which will be unmistakable."

Albus gave a good-natured laugh. "Three thousand men cannot hide themselves on a beach. Let's go find them!"

But Varro did not share his mirth, and suspected something far worse that he refused to think upon. Still, he gave a weak smile.

"Yes, I'm sure they're only a short distance away."

11

The salty air was sharp and fresh in Varro's nose, but the sea was dead and gray. In his anxiousness, he led the group north along a strand of grass that hemmed the beach down a long slope. The sand became the barest sliver at points and other times it spread out as if giant waves had forced it toward the trees. He rushed now, his strong legs capable of putting up speeds that the Ilegertes were pressed to match. Seagulls mocked him from above, following the strung-out line until losing interest and gliding away.

Curio was right behind him, and Falco hung back to make sure the Ilegertes did not lag too badly.

"This is too far," Curio said.

"Too far, sir," Varro corrected. His eyes fought the glare of the water, finding nothing but dark and rolling waves that were getting bigger with the arrival of high tide.

"Of course, sir." Curio's voice was thin against the breaking waves down the slope, but the sarcasm was clear. "We've undone a half-day of travel and found nothing. They did not land here."

"Then where did they land?"

The answer, Varro knew, was obvious but unspeakable. It was too much even for a master politician like Cato.

"Sir, I'm going to stop everyone here. Keep searching ahead if you like. But it's a waste."

Varro stopped and unslung his shield bag from his back and dropped his pack. Sweat trickled down his chest, leaving a dark wedge of dampness on his collar. The breeze immediately cooled him. Curio came to his side, and Falco rushed up shortly thereafter.

"I can't believe that old shit," he said, stomping the final distance to draw to them. "He didn't send the ships!"

Varro snapped up at hearing his fears spoken from Falco's mouth. Behind him, the giant form of Albus in his black fur cloak and his two men staggered up the shore. They had become winded and lagged far behind.

"Don't let them hear that," he said, knowing the Ilegertes were out of hearing.

Falco chuckled. "Do you think they're that stupid? It's obvious. When three thousand infantry come ashore, they leave a mess behind. We've not seen as much as a footprint this whole way. We're practically going back to camp at this point."

"Could they have sailed past that cove?"

Neither Falco nor Curio answered. Of course, the question was formed out of desperation. Unless every navigator was staring out to sea at the same time, they would've seen it. And they would have monitored the coast for hazards in unfamiliar waters. They could not have missed the cove.

"We're already ahead of them," Falco said, pointing his thumb back at the lumbering Ilegertes. "We can outrun them. Let's get back to camp and just say the prince changed his mind and didn't want us. If we stay, I think we're going to end up in a fight, and I don't want to kill the prince of our ally. What a fucking mess."

"A mess, I'll agree," Varro said, now watching Albus slow to a walk. He waved and Varro raised his hand in answer. "But we can't go back until Cato orders us."

"Right," Curio said. "Or you know what he'll do."

He began to mimic a beating motion with a heavy club, pounding an unseen victim into mash. That would be their fates for directly disobeying an order.

"He wants them to blame us," Varro said, more to himself than the others. "That's why the Ilegertes king is to direct all his questions of Rome to us. We are to take the blame."

"He staged three thousand men and didn't send them," Falco said, putting his hands on his head. "Just to trap us?"

"Not just for us," Varro said. "We were a convenient addition to his plan. He just wanted to send the Ilegertes away and leave them wondering when help would arrive. It keeps them hopeful while he deals with the main rebellion, and then he can come to their aid later."

"I didn't think Cato was such a gambler," Falco said. "He doesn't even know where the enemy is right now."

"Albus is getting closer," Curio said. "What are we going to tell him?"

"The truth," Varro said, causing the other two to snap around with wide eyes. "We don't know what happened, only that the promised infantry didn't come. Do we actually know anything else? Maybe Cato received news of the enemy position right after we left and recalled the men to fight."

They did not have time to corroborate their story, as Albus now jogged the short distance and his two followers struggled behind. When he arrived, his face was flush and pale hair matted to his temples to reveal a narrow skull. He gave a brief smile.

"They say you Romans can run like wolves. Now I know it's true."

Their laughter was strained and soon they fell to silence and let the rumbling waves fill it. The other two Ilegertes at last caught up, and they labored to even stand upright. One doubled over with his hands on his knees, cursing in his own tongue.

"We've no sign of the landing," Varro said, trying to sound as matter-of-fact as he could. "I can't believe they missed that cove, and we've definitely searched beyond any reasonable distance for another landing site. At this point, Prince Albus, I think we should return to your father. We can await their arrival from the safety of your stronghold."

Albus's easy smile turned to confusion. He wiped his brow with the back of his hands, then shielded his eyes against the glare to scan the surging tide.

"Where did they go? There was no storm to blow them off course and no fog to blind them. What could have happened?"

"I can only guess," Varro said, imagining Cato's self-congratulatory smile at their predicament. "But the most likely cause is they were recalled to face a greater threat. The consul has an idea of the enemy's hiding spot and has increased efforts to pinpoint it. Perhaps his scouts were discovered and the enemy has decided to strike while there is still a possibility of surprise."

Albus considered this, then shook his head.

"They were aboard their ships and ready to sail. If they were recalled to fight, then it must be soon after we left. We would have heard such an attack. At the least, we would have seen the dust of battle in the air later that night. But we saw nothing of the sort."

Varro shrugged. "I did not say they went to battle right away, but only that Consul Cato recalled them before they set sail. He would only do that if there was a dire need."

Albus seemed satisfied, but then one of his men whispered something in his own language. This caused Albus to straighten his back once more.

"He would not send a messenger after us, but leave us to think we had been deceived?"

"Prince, we have taken care to not leave signs of our passage.

Perhaps the messenger is lost. Also, we do not know the situation that caused the consul to recall his soldiers. It could have been urgent and confused, and by the time he thought to inform us it might have been too late. I think he will send a party to deliver a message directly to your father."

"But they would have to fight Diorix to even reach our gates, which we would not open to anyone we did not expect."

"I trust the consul would send capable men aware of the challenges."

Varro was even beginning to convince himself, and perhaps he had been too rash in judging Cato. Albus seemed likewise convinced, shrugging and pinching his nose in thought.

"It now comes to the original question, Centurion Varro. How do we rejoin my father in his hall while Diorix's warriors watch our gates? I had hoped to return with an army at my back."

"You are too shrewd for that to be your only plan," Varro said. "You must have considered the consul might send you away with nothing."

Albus shrugged and looked at his companions.

"Yes, I thought of it. The lookouts will know me and will open the gates as long as I do not bring Diorix's men in pursuit. My father was clear in his command. He would not risk all his people for even his own son."

While Varro wondered at that statement, he simply nodded.

They rested in the thin grass by the edge of the woods. Strangely, Varro had not minded his days of traveling between these trees. He was in the company of peoples native to this place and the spirits seemed forgiving of their passage for it. But as they rested, portioning out their final marching rations in case they needed another day, Varro now stared into the purple darkness. Somehow the woods had become less welcoming, and he wondered if the spirits haunting its darkness had been happy to lure him deeper inside to an even grimmer fate.

He hated forests, and so twisted aside to face the gray sea.

They continued to follow the shoreline, confident that Diorix had not sent his scouts this far out. But soon the Ilegertes led them into the woods, following game trails and pathways Varro would not have found on his own. As they drew closer to their destination, the two scouts began to look back with impatient frowns. At least a dozen times they stopped to glare then place a finger across their lips.

"Let's see them sneak around with all this armor and kit," Falco muttered. "We're doing the best we can."

Varro grunted in agreement. "Apparently Diorix's men are the most alert of any I've ever known."

Of all of them, Curio seemed the most adroit at not drawing the ire of their scouts. To Varro's eyes, he seemed to be crashing into the same bushes and scratching against the same trunks as he and Falco, except he managed to pass in silence. Falco noticed this too, rolling his eyes and shaking his head.

By late afternoon, they paused and crouched in a circle with Albus while awaiting the reports from the scouts probing ahead.

The prince once more pulled up the hood of his black fur cloak and hid his white hair. He noticed Varro staring at him as he did and smiled. He then leaned closer to whisper.

"It is a gift from my mother, who you shall soon meet. Friend and enemy alike can always find me on the battlefield, but it is a poor gift for secret work like today's."

"I've not seen anything like it outside of Rome," Falco said.

Albus lowered his head and smiled. "I would like to see Rome one day. But I fear I will never know that great city."

Varro was about to ask why, then realized the burdens Albus carried. But Curio did not and asked in a bare whisper.

"Why not? It's a few days by ship if the weather is good and you sail straight."

"I belong to my tribe," Albus said. "And even while my father rules, I am not free to travel far from his side. My tutor described it to me, and it seems a wondrous city. Maybe overly so, for some of his claims are too grand to be real."

Before Varro could ask for examples, the two scouts returned to push their way into the circle. Both exchanged grave looks, and one nodded for the other to begin the report.

"Diorix has strengthened his line around our gates." He spoke in thick Latin, but Varro was grateful to hear the undiluted report. "South gate is our best chance."

Albus turned to Varro. "Well, you are experienced? What should our plan be?"

"A diversion is best," Varro said.

"There are six of us and a thousand of them." Albus looked past Varro as if the enemy were right behind him. "How can we divert so many?"

"Fire," Varro said. "What is more terrifying? Do they have horses?"

The scouts exchanged confirmation and confirmed a limited number of horses and mules.

"Set the horses free to create more chaos, and then we run for the gates."

Albus and his scouts debated the plan, falling into their own language. It seemed one of the scouts supported the idea and the other did not. Varro simply waited while both Falco and Curio rubbed their faces and tried to be patient. At last, the prince turned back to Varro.

"There were gaps in their encampment we exploited when we first escaped. But now these have been closed. I fear by attempting to sneak though their lines we would be discovered before reaching the gates. Only a week ago, Diorix was far less vigilant, but must've learned that we evaded him. We cannot risk the same approach we used the first time. They will see us."

"Then we will make them look elsewhere," Varro said, folding his arms. "If we are caught halfway to the gate, slings and arrows would make short work of us if we are discovered too soon. It is better they not look at us at all."

With their plan settled, they waited for nightfall before moving out. During their wait, Varro and the others smeared dirt and mud over their bronze to dull its shine. Albus smiled approvingly. "But your consul would punish you for such a dirty appearance."

"The consul isn't here to see," Falco said, replacing his mud-smeared helmet. "And I'd rather avoid an enemy slinger than pass an inspection."

The exact details of the plan could not be determined until they saw the actual circumstances, but Varro would use the enemy campfires to start a distraction. Bright, wild flames in the dark were certain to create panic, as he well knew from his own experience.

They approached the fort under the darkness of velvety clouds, with nothing but the vaguest starlight to lead them. Every cracking twig or rustling branch made Varro's chest tighten. If forest spirts planned mischief for him, he thought, then now was their moment. For between the trees he spied the low orange light of campfires.

Now they had limited communications to hand signals. The two scouts indicated they should loop around the camp to the south. Without any knowledge of the land or clear sky to see, Varro assumed they approached from the west. As described, the fluttering campfires stretched as innumerable dots in a wide arc around the fort. The fort itself was simply a black plug atop a cleared hill. Yellow points of lights flickered sporadically where men watched by torchlight from the ramparts. But other details of its construction were blanketed in darkness.

As they looped around the perimeter of the enemy camp, Varro noted the details. Hide tents were scattered like leaves blown by a wind. The campfires burned unattended but for shadowy figures that moved from one to the next in a lazy semicircle. There was no plan to the layout, which would only enhance the confusion once they set fires.

They found a position exactly opposite the south gate, which Varro could see by the cluster of torches glowing above it. From this distance, he was uncertain if the walls were of stone or wood. But the gate itself was heavy wood with huge beams to reinforce it. The bottom vanished to shadow.

Protected as they were among the trees, they still tightened into a huddle to plan their attack. Their heads nearly touched as they leaned in, with only Curio sitting back to watch for danger.

"Falco, Curio, and me will light brands in the campfires and spread the flame off to this side." Varro pointed in the direction they had approached from. "I do not see any horses here, but we will release any we can find. Prince Albus, watch for the moment your enemies move toward the fires. You then cross the camp and run for the gate."

"What of you three?" Albus asked.

"We will already be headed for it. A fire does not need much encouragement from us, though a strong wind tonight would have been better. We'll meet you by the gate."

"It is not a complicated plan," Albus said. "I expected something more elaborate after your earlier claims."

Varro grinned. "A basic plan is better, and will become complicated once we touch flame to the first tent. Depend upon that, Prince."

They handed their burdens to Albus and his men, who only needed to run for the fort. Varro and the others would likely fight and could not do so burdened with their packs. But they did remove their shields from their carrying cases and set them on their arms.

With a quick nod from each man, they separated to their tasks. Curio had found them each a dried branch to serve as brands.

Varro snaked around a tent to the closest of low-burning campfires. The men in the tent snored as he slid along its edge. He kept his shield to its wall, disguising his shadow if one should see it from the inside.

He crouched low by a campfire and held his breath as his branch caught flame. Farther down the camp he saw the shadows of Curio and Falco hovering over fires.

Once his branch sprouted flames, he then turned to the tent he had just passed. It was as good as any to set aflame. The heavy hide would not catch easily, but when it did, he moved onto the next. The fire was a thin ribbon running along the top of the tent. He did the same to the next and then skipped to another. Falco and Curio did likewise. Soon this entire section would be ablaze.

With the branch swiftly burning down toward his hand, he thought to set one more fire away from this one. The first tent was already shooting up flames into the night. It seemed odd that no panicked cries grew with it.

But as he stepped out from behind his tent, a figure leaped out at him from his right side and seized his torch hand in an iron grip.

Varro tugged around, surprised and off-balance as the ambusher yanked him back, cursing at him.

Alarm horns sounded and screams from where Curio and Falco worked now shattered the night's calm.

The chaos had begun.

12

The hand gripping Varro's wrist tightened as his shadowy attacker hauled him back. He was cursing in a language Varro did not understand and seemed unaware of his danger.

Varro spun on the ball of his foot as he plowed his scutum into the man's side. The heavy wood and iron boss clobbered the Iberian to the ground. Varro stepped back, then flung his brand into the man's face, causing him to scramble and scream to avoid the fire. It broke over him in a bright but fleeting shower of flaming ash.

In that time, Varro drew his gladius in a fluid motion, then struck down to impale the man in his guts. He folded up with a scream, but Varro did not linger to confirm the kill. He already sprinted toward the front of the enemy camp.

Horns blared and now fires brightened the night. Men scrambled out of their tents, falling over each other and swiveling their heads toward the obvious fires. Whether Albus and the others were joining him in his rush to reach the safety of the gate, he could not say. The emptiness up the long hill was considerable, and they would need a head start to beat the enemy inside.

The encampment was not deep, as it seemed Diorix stretched his men to keep watch of the fort from all sides rather than defend in depth. The front of the camp was a tangle of logs and stones as well as heaps of thorns and other debris. But all this faced away from him, and the exits were easily seen from the rear. Yet this did channel him in the wrong direction.

He joined with Falco, who rushed to the same exit. He was painted on both sides with orange light from the spreading fire. The center was black with shadow, but his grin was clear.

"Great idea," he shouted. "This will keep them busy."

They both pushed ahead and Curio was already awaiting them on the other side of the barrier. The alarms repeated down the row of the camp and silhouetted figures sprinted in different directions to answer the flames. Some men were trapped in their burning tents, their horrified shrieking filling the night.

But they cleared the barriers and had remained ignored while the fires drew strength from the crisp night breeze.

Now they turned to rush up the hill toward the gate. More torches on the walls joined with others already set, appearing like a cluster of fireflies hovering in the dark. But Varro did not see Albus or the others.

"They're in black cloaks, after all," Falco said as he ran beside him. But Varro had said nothing, and realized Falco worried as he did that Albus was not yet out of the camp.

Halfway to the gates, Varro realized this was the truth.

Albus's white hair had spilled out of his hood, marking him even in the low light. He and his companions had only just passed through the barriers and lumbered ahead to the base of the hill. They leaned forward under the heavy packs that Varro and the others had shouldered without complaint. Their own shields and packs, as well as their mail, further bent them.

Varro and the others had stopped. They could not approach the gates without Albus, nor would they want to. The fires were blazing in some sections and dying in others. It was clear to Varro it would not spread any farther. The Iberians were already shouting across the barriers to blame the Ilegertes.

Behind Albus and his struggling group, torches began to gather at the barrier.

"They're coming out," Varro said, already running back. Falco and Curio joined them.

"Drop the packs," Varro shouted as he closed on the prince. "Run to the gate. We will defend the rear."

The prince looked up but his face was lost in darkness. He shook his head, and continued to plod ahead under a weight too much for him, even at his impressive height and strength. It took a different kind of conditioning to bear such loads, and certainly the Iberian warrior class never trained for this.

Yet the prince seemed too proud to surrender a feat of strength.

"Form a line behind them," Varro shouted to the others.

They broke around the group as they labored up the hill, then reformed to lock their shields together.

It came none too soon, for the first sling stone cracked on the edge of Varro's scutum. It sent a violent shock down into his head, and Falco yelped in surprise.

"That'd have broken his skull. Good fucking shots, these bastards."

Two more stones cracked against their shields and more thudded into the grass. They backed up the hill to cover the prince, but this could not hold. The dark shapes that had discovered them were now calling out their location.

"Prince Albus, drop the packs and run or we will be caught!"

"I can carry it," he shouted back, his voice quivering with indignation. "I am the strongest of my tribe!"

Falco groaned. "You'll soon be the deadest of your tribe. Drop the packs!"

The packs thumped to the ground, and Varro heard footfalls thudding up the hill. But their enemies had only paused long enough to sling one volley of stones, and now ran for them.

"We've got to flee," Falco said. "Now!"

"Take the packs," Varro said. But Falco and Curio had already begun sprinting away.

Varro now looked at three heavy packs like gray stones in the flattened grass. Their kits could be replaced, but there was ink and vellum in one. A wry smile came to his face that he should be worried about Curio's instruction while fleeing from enemies. He could only grab one, and he hoped he had found his own. Its weight tugged against his arm as he snatched it while chasing after the others.

The Iberians were lighter and driven by anger that sent them flying across the ground. Varro could hear them closing and chanced a glance back.

Six men pursued him, now close enough for their enraged faces to show gray in the weak light. Enemies painted in orange light from burning tents now pushed out of the barriers behind them.

Varro turned back, then sprawled forward, landing hard atop the pack and dropping his shield. He grunted and cursed, and flipped immediately to his left, pinning his shield but freeing his right side to reach for his pugio.

The first man reached him and raised his short sword over Varro. The edge blinked with yellow light.

He rolled back to kick up with both feet, but the Iberian fell away screaming even without Varro connecting.

Arrows zipped overhead, and one had caught his attacker in the armpit. He kneeled where he had stood, and blood that looked like ink in the darkness streamed over his chest. The other pursuers had crouched back behind their shields.

Varro only had time to grab his own. With his free hand now grasping his pugio, he had to leave the pack behind.

Ahead, the gates had opened and Prince Albus's white hair revealed him leaning out as he urged on his Roman friends. Curio had raced past Falco, and would be the first inside. Varro chased after both of them, with Albus shouting for him to go faster.

Reaching the gate, Albus hauled him behind it, while guards dragged it shut. They had reached safety, at least for now.

"What happened?" Falco asked, examining him with fear-brightened eyes. "That was too close."

"Wasn't it obvious?" Varro's face grew warm and he looked at the dirt underfoot. "I tripped."

"Then the arrows were not wasted," Albus said, his voice filled with relief. "And your plan worked as good as you promised. Excellent work, Centurion Varro."

The prince slapped his back, then ushered him from the gates. Ilegertes tribesmen in gray wool cloaks drew a heavy bolt across the door, one as nearly thick as an old tree and needing two men to move.

All six of them now smiled at each other. Their skin gleamed with sweat and the two scouts leaned on their knees. Falco and Curio just seemed happy enough to have escaped.

They stood in a large clearing. Stone walls had been built up around the top of this hill, and these had been heightened with woodwork above them. Towers overlooked the gates, and the guards on duty there seemed torn between watching for Diorix's men and the arrival of their prince.

Tents which were clearly temporary dwellings sprawled out everywhere in what must have been parade grounds or even small garden plots. Varro noted a large well and a cistern close to it. The main fort was constructed from stone, but was hidden in the darkness. For the moment, they stood in a globe of light from the torches of the men come to their rescue.

"My father is abed," Albus said. "And I would rather he slept, for his burden is heavy. For now, perhaps you shall be happy enough to find a place to camp and sleep before meeting the king."

Varro looked to the gate. "Thank you, Prince Albus. But all except our weaponry now sits outside the walls in the grass."

Albus's pale face reddened and he swiftly gathered Varro and Falco under his arms.

"Of course it would be rude of me to ask you to camp here. We shall find a place for you within the fort. My father is a generous man, and you represent his greatest ally. I was thoughtless to suggest otherwise."

The skirmish at the walls seemed over, as bowmen withdrew and waved to each other.

"I don't suppose someone could be sent to recover our packs?" Varro realized more than vellum had been lost. But all the gear to maintain their armor and weapons as well as their pila had been left on the hill. It would be a fat prize to anyone, for the Iberians used weapons similar to their own.

Albus tilted his head. "Those packs were dropped closer to Diorix's camp than I'd dare send anyone tonight. It is why I wanted to carry them, Centurion Varro. But you had been so insistent."

Falco matched the tilt of Albus's head. "Well, you were too—"

"Thank you, Prince," Varro said, cutting off Falco. "You did as I asked and I accept the loss."

"I can replace whatever you need, if it is in my power to do so." Albus squeezed Varro's shoulder. "Now let me take you inside where you may find rest."

The hill fort had roused from sleep in the tent areas. But whenever sleepy-eyed faces appeared, Albus or one of the

Ilegertes warriors who now accompanied him shunted them back into their tents.

Varro had expected the prince's arrival would be greeted with celebrations. But it seemed Albus was more intent on finding his own bed.

Once they came to the fort, a bland stone edifice that was more functional than aesthetic, Albus assigned one of the two who had traveled with them to see to their arrangements. He then went off to his own business.

It did not take long to clear away a storage room to serve as their quarters. Blankets and feather-stuffed pillows were provided, which was a great luxury. They would be sleeping shoulder to shoulder that night. A single clay lamp threw weak light over them. Fortunately, their gear was settled in the room next to theirs.

"A night without sleeping in armor," Curio said, stretching as he arranged his makeshift bed.

"And feather pillows." Falco fluffed the small white pillow. "I can stand this assignment for longer than I thought.

"I wonder at the hospitality after we talk to the king tomorrow." Varro settled his own space, which butted up against a wall.

"Don't worry about tomorrow," Falco said, stretching his long body out on his blanket. "Maybe it won't come. Just enjoy your bed. This pillow is amazing."

Both he and Curio laughed at Falco's grim warning. Before Varro joined the legion, such a statement would've been met with wards against bad luck and hostility. But that grim outlook was the best way he knew to deal with the uncertainties of enlisted life. Tomorrow was never guaranteed. He had seen too many friends worry for a tomorrow that never arrived. Their lives would've been better lived if they had just enjoyed their moment.

So Varro stretched out beside Falco and Curio extinguished the lamp to drop them into darkness.

"Optio, did you practice writing today?"

The pause lengthened into the dark, but Varro waited in the comfort of the feather pillow.

"Yes, sir, during our afternoon rest. I wrote a few words about the plan for tonight. But they're in my pack."

"How convenient," Falco said. "I thought you went foraging for hazelnuts?"

"Well, sir, I wrote about how brave Centurion Falco was going to lead us to victory in a single day. If you find my pack, you can read about it."

"Should I flog him, Varro?"

"Curio, starting from tomorrow I'm going to review everything you've written. And if you haven't anything to show, then I will watch you write. I don't care if you have to write in blood. Every day, Optio."

"Yes, sir."

The dejection in Curio's voice could not have been more distinct. Fortunately, no one could see Varro holding back his laugher in the dark. With this settled, he drifted off to sleep, exhausted from days of hard marching and the night's tension. Tomorrow's worries were for tomorrow, if it came at all.

He fell into a blank sleep and awakened feeling remarkably refreshed. The blankets had eased the harshness of the wood floor and the feathered pillow had been as if his head had been held in the lap of a goddess. When the cockerels crowed beyond the walls of the fort, he struggled to stand.

They were shortly visited by servants who brought them a wood basin of water and towels. They stared at this in surprise, but Curio was the first to help himself to the amenities.

Falco scrubbed his face after Curio was finished, splashing water on the wood floor.

"Not bad for barbarians," he said. "I wonder if we can get razors from them? I'll be growing a beard otherwise."

"We'll keep our pugiones sharp," Varro said. "I don't think we can ask for more."

The servants sent to look after them did not speak Latin, but they were nonetheless able to indicate they should wait in their rooms. This made sense to Varro, as Albus would likely meet his father first before introducing them. In the meantime, they were given a rich rice gruel that Varro found plain but filling.

"It's not like they're under siege," Curio said as he finished the last of his meal.

Falco nodded, lifting the bowl to slurp the last of it before offering his thoughts. "I think they're treating us nicely until they see what their king thinks."

They were soon to discover the king's thoughts, for one of their traveling companions arrived to ask them to join the king in his hall. Albus would be awaiting them there.

So they brushed their fingers through their hair and straightened their tunics before they were led through narrow hallways to the main chamber.

Albus was unmistakable, standing taller than anyone with his long, pale hair splashing over the black fur of his cloak. He stood with his wide shoulders squared and held back, and one tattooed hand resting on the grip of his sword.

King Bilistages sat on an oversized wooden chair beside him. His hair had once been black, which now showed only as streaks in the thin locks that flowed to his shoulder. His beard was shockingly white and tied in a braid. He had a thick gold braid clamped around his neck that shined with the light of dozens hanging lamps.

Varro hung back as his guide introduced them, bowing low before the king. While the rambling introduction continued, Varro decided he would not bow even if commanded. Since they represented Rome, it would be a disgrace to humble themselves before the Ilegertes king.

He went ahead of Falco and Curio, who were always glad to let him speak for the group. Despite his duty to represent Rome, he felt a little deference could not go wrong. He inclined his head to the king.

"I am Centurion Marcus Varro, here by special appointment from Consul Cato. With me are Centurion Falco and Optio Curio."

Bilistages and Albus shared the same wry expression and even if their complexions and hair colors did not match, they were unmistakably father and son. The king's eyes were dark, but one was cloudy and so he titled his head to use the other to fix on Varro.

"Three Romans come when I have asked for three thousand. You cannot imagine my frustration." Bilistages spoke with the same accented fluency as Albus, but he had none of the jovial tone of his son. "I had pledged myself to Rome, and my people have suffered for it. We are now the most hated among all the tribes, and as you have seen, we are surrounded by enemies. I now wonder at my decision."

"The consul has promised three thousand men," Varro said, lowering his head. "I have seen those men board their transports, as did Prince Albus and his companions. They will come."

"You guarantee this?" Bilistages raised one wild, gray brow. "My son says you have been given authority to represent your consul. Do you say this in his name, or is it your own opinion?"

"Both."

Albus, standing at his father's right side, raised his brow but otherwise betrayed no other thought. The king sat back on his chair.

The wide hall was filled with attendants and men whose purpose and rank were unclear to Varro. They held a remarkable silence for so many, particularly since most would not understand the words. But they watched their king with keen intensity and their moods would shift with his.

"Then where are they?" Bilistages looked to his son as if he might answer, but the tall prince only deflected the gaze to Varro.

"I do not know, your highness. There was no sign of a landing or a shipwreck. Therefore, I believe the consul recalled them for an immediate need and that a messenger will soon arrive to explain the circumstances."

Bilistages rose from his chair and his aged but strong body unfolded to a height just short of his son's. His cloudy eye darkened under his drawn brows.

"The Ilegertes were promised three thousand men! Diorix and his dogs press us from every side. They have destroyed our farms and stolen our livestock. They have driven my people to other lands or behind these walls. Children have lost their parents, and parents their children. All of this suffering because we are the only remaining friends of Rome. And you say there is a more pressing need?"

Varro straightened his back, feeling the weight of his great city on his shoulders.

"Your Highness, you will have your promised men. However, the consul did not promise when he could send them. He makes decisions for the good of Rome and her citizens before all else. The soldiers were ready to sail when we left. But if he has not sent them yet, then there is indeed a higher need than yours."

King Bilistages's mouth fell open and Albus closed his eyes. The hall now murmured around Varro, like bees still in their hive but readying for an attack.

"You dare! Would you say this to the mothers of slain children?"

The king turned to yell at Albus in their language, causing him to step back and press his eagle-taloned hands to his chest while shaking his head. The king then shouted to those gathered at the sides of his hall, and they began to moan.

"Uh, maybe I'll talk next time," Falco whispered from behind. "You're doing a shitty job."

"I spoke the truth," Varro hissed, trying not to turn around while the king carped on in his native tongue. "He knows we represent Rome. He has to be more careful with us than we of him."

Falco sucked his teeth, but said no more. At last, the king ended his tirade and stabbed his wizened finger at Varro.

"You'll be my prisoners until we decide if our alliance has been misguided from the start. Maybe I will send your heads back to your consul and tell him Rome can burn!"

The hall filled with lusty cheers as sword-armed men emerged from behind their king. Albus looked aside, his head down and face bright red.

"Looks like I'm growing a beard," Falco said.

Then the guards seized them by their arms, then prodded their swords against their backs to lead them from the hall.

13

"As far as prisons go, this has to be the best."

Falco stretched out on the floor, patting his feathered pillow. His legs rubbed up against Varro's who sat next to him. The sweat and hair were gritty on his flesh, and he tried to pull back but could not. Their room was too small.

It was also unlit, with only faint light slipping under the barred door. After two days in confinement, pressed against both his friends, even the slightest touch aggravated him. It did not seem to bother the others much, but each had their complaints. They were allowed into the hallway once a day to relieve themselves in a wood bucket and under guard. Falco was correct in that this was reasonable treatment and not some barbaric imprisonment. But it could not continue before the stress of hunger, darkness, and confinement set them all at each other's throats.

"I'm hungry," Curio said. "That gruel would be great now."

"It's too soon for them to deliver bread again. Or so it feels to me," Varro said. "If Bilistages wanted to kill us, it'd be done by now. I think he's just teaching us a lesson."

"Fine by me," Falco said. "This isn't so bad, except when you fart, Varro. You know you've been doing that a lot? Are you nervous or something?"

Curio laughed, but Varro kicked out at Falco's leg.

"I appreciate you two keeping your heads, but even if the king releases us, we could be in a lot of trouble. What if he sends us back? Cato hasn't ordered us to return and we're charged with keeping this alliance alive by both him and Flamininus."

Falco groaned. "Servus Capax. I'm not sure I even care anymore. So we got to ride around Numidia on horses for a while and make trouble for Carthage. That amounted to nothing. Honestly, what are the three of us going to do for Rome, anyway? It's a waste of time."

"Waste or not," Varro said, kicking Falco again. "We're sworn to it for life, or whenever they'll let us go."

"Which is when we die."

Falco and Varro engaged in a weak battle of kicks in the tight confines before both lost interest and fell to silence. Varro heard scratching on wood from Curio's side and asked after it.

"I've found an old nail and am scratching my name here. Writing practice, sir."

"What good is that if you can't see it?" Falco asked.

"I can see enough. It's something to do."

"Well, I'll correct it for you," Falco said. "A man has to spell his own name right, after all."

Whether hours or days passed after that, Varro was not sure. He had reckoned they had already been captive for two days based on the deliveries of water and stale bread, not to mention the stubble growth making his jaw itchy. But it seemed the activity now happening outside the door was too soon for another delivery. The bar trembled against the door, then lifted away.

Bright yellow light spilled through the opened door to blind him. He shielded his eyes with his arm and saw Albus's huge shape in the doorway.

"You're free today," he said, his voice restrained but happy. "My father has a temper, and it is especially bad in our current situation. Don't hold it against him. He would never do the terrible things he said. At least not to Romans. To me, quite likely."

Albus extended his hand, which Curio accepted, then pulled him into the hall. Varro was last out of the room and found Albus accompanied by a spearman. They shuffled down the narrow passage to a wider room where they could speak more comfortably.

"I am to attend to you," Albus said. He spread his hands wide, revealing the talon tattoos from beneath the long sleeves of a green shirt. Even out of his war gear he was an imposing sight who stood half a head over Falco. "But you will report to my father."

"What took so long to decide you weren't going to cut off our balls?" Falco asked while he dusted down his tunic.

"We waited two days in good faith for this messenger to come." He paused to give Varro a long-suffering look. "But strangely, there has not even been a hint of an attempt to contact us."

"Maybe the messengers were captured," Varro said, hoping he sounded more convincing than he felt.

"Perhaps," Albus said. "But if that was true, by now Diorix would be waving the messenger's head at our gates. So I think your consul has not been truthful with us. He cannot have forgotten us for so long. Therefore, he never intended to launch those ships. I was a fool to not have insisted I sail with them."

"I cannot say what happened." Varro's throat constricted and his gaze faltered. This caused Albus to laugh.

"You will never be a senator, Centurion Varro. You are a poor liar."

"You would not have been allowed aboard military transport in any case," Falco said. "So, your father knows nothing is coming from Cato. What does he expect from us?"

"Well, you are advisors, yes? If you are what your consul sends to us for aid, then we must accept it." Albus tapped Varro's shoulder. "Your ruse to get us inside these walls was a great success. Perhaps you have another plan like it to defeat Diorix?"

Varro scratched the back of his neck while Falco smirked at him.

"First, I would have to understand your situation better. But throughout history, as far as my limited knowledge goes, sieges are only defeated when the attacker is worn down or the defenders are relieved by an outside force."

Now Albus smirked. "Well, we have learned there will be no outside force to relieve us. We cannot go into harvest season with Diorix collecting it all and leaving our people to starve. So we require a faster solution. I suppose you must come up with a new way."

Varro nodded, but wished he would've been sent back to Cato instead. It seemed an easier problem to solve.

"Do not be sad, Centurion." Albus again clapped his shoulder. "By your own words, you will now do something never achieved in history. You'll be a hero remembered for all ages."

"Maybe," Falco said. "But I wonder what he'll be remembered for. What happens if the great Centurion Varro doesn't have a brilliant idea never tried in history? Because I think you might expect too much."

"Ah, well, you will share our fate, of course." Albus now shifted his huge hand to Falco's shoulder. "But you will more likely be blamed for our hardships, and the mob will tear you to pieces first."

"Succeed or die," Falco said. "The usual choices, I suppose."

"That's the spirit," Albus said. "And since I have stood by you three, I will also share that fate. It doesn't matter that I'm a prince. Many people are saying I'm too Roman. Even my father has wondered if my curiosity about Rome has led me to forget who I am."

"That's not an insult," Curio said. "I'm Roman and proud of it."

"You were born Roman. I have chosen to study Rome, something my people consider a waste and even a betrayal. Look at my size. I am to be their warrior king one day, not their senator."

"Great allies," Falco said, shaking his head. But Albus laughed again and squeezed Falco by his shoulders.

"You will learn about the tribes in time. We were once free to kill each other as we wished, to steal land and livestock from each other, and to vie to become the high king of all the world. But ever since Carthage came, we have had to unite and fight against outsiders. After Carthage, it became Rome. No one wants to be ruled by foreigners. We want to fight among ourselves, as Diorix does now against us."

"You don't seem convinced of those old ways," Varro said. "You understand what Rome brings."

Albus shrugged. "I see more of what Rome takes, which is pulled up from the earth as iron and silver. But, yes, the old ways made us weak so that Carthage could lay claim to us. Rome is stronger than Carthage, and I see where the strength of the world gathers. I've heard news that you have won a victory in Greece. Soon, all the world will be yours and I'd rather we Ilegertes stand with rather than against you."

"No matter what happens with Diorix," Varro said, "Consul Cato will destroy the rebellion."

"We shall see," Albus said. "He faces all the tribes. It is not so easy to crush the wills of so many."

Varro smiled. "It is far easier than you believe. I've seen it done. But enough of this. We've got to make history if we're to live long enough to see that rebellion defeated."

Albus escorted them around the fort interior and outside where tents pressed against outbuildings. Refugees from the countryside were now a burden on food supplies, which were expected to last only another month. But after seeing the state of the granaries, Varro wondered if they had calculated correctly.

"How much are you rationing? It seems this can't be enough for so many extra people."

"Rationing? I am not sure of this word. Do you mean are the people restricted in the grain they can draw? No, we do not do that. People are wise enough to only take according to their need."

Falco snorted, which drew a frown from Albus. But Varro shook his head.

"Maybe because they expected quick relief from Rome. But it is unwise to count on anything until it is in hand."

"So I have learned," Albus said coolly, leading them back toward the fort.

"The king must establish rationing. To do that, someone needs to calculate how many people versus the amount of food stores. I don't suppose you keep records?"

"That is not our way." Albus stiffened and sped his pace.

"Then I will have Optio Curio lead the effort," Varro said, keeping up. "I'll need a written report on all of this. Fighting strength, rations, weaponry, a full picture of what we're working with. Can you do this, Optio?"

"Yes, sir." His crisp answer faded as he elaborated. "But I've nothing to write with."

"Get him charcoal and animal skins, Prince Albus. This report is vital."

The prince's face reddened, shining bright against his pale hair.

"Take care not to order me like one of your men, Centurion. And anything you want to do must have my father's permission first."

"Then let's get it," Varro said, ignoring the prince's hurt pride. "Because dying of starvation will be more horrible than falling to Diorix."

"You've not met him," Albus said. "He is more vile than a snake. But we shall see my father soon."

"Will we see him after we eat?" Curio patted his stomach. "I'm starting down that road to starvation already."

"Well, now that Centurion Varro wants to limit what we eat, perhaps we should ask him."

While the others chuckled, Varro considered. He also felt hunger pangs, and it clouded his mind. "We need to eat enough to regain our strength. But from then on, we should all be rationing our food."

They ate gruel with bits of meat and salt, something akin to puls which was the legionaries' standard meal. But after bread and water, it tasted finer than anything Varro could remember. They were then shown to new quarters that contained all their gear, including weapons. Despite all Albus had warned them about, this was a show of trust he appreciated.

After settling their living arrangement, Albus disappeared for an hour only to return with a summons to meet King Bilistages.

They joined him in the same hall they had been dragged from two days earlier. The king still sat on his throne with his white-bearded chin resting in his palm and golden torc gleaming at his throat. But now he was attended only by two guards and three older men dressed in plain tunics. They were tanned and strong, and their necks and arms showed aged, smudgy tattoos. All three were balding and frowned at their arrival.

Prince Albus addressed his father in their native language, but shifted to Latin when he stepped aside for Varro to present himself.

"Thank you for the trust you've shown us, your highness."

"Do not make me regret it," he said, his voice tired and low. "My son said your consul placed great responsibility on you and named you three as his favorites. So for that much, I am grateful."

Varro wondered at what Albus had heard, but he would not dissuade the king of the idea.

"Albus says you have ideas already. What are they?"

Varro glanced at the prince, who gave a barely perceptible nod, then to the gleaming, beady eyes of the king's advisors. They seemed already predisposed to detest him. The king himself tilted his head back and ran gnarled fingers through his gray hair. He was a handsome man, but time and worry had drawn down his features.

"We must begin by rationing the supplies on hand." Varro paused, expecting an outburst. But he realized no one understood the word. Once he elaborated in simpler terms, the advisors recoiled as if he had indeed passed gas as Falco had accused him.

"Absolutely not," Bilistages said with calm finality. "A king who steals food from his people cannot remain king."

"Your highness, I mean only to limit what people take. For now, they may well take only according to their need. But surely you know that every man will define his need differently, and increase it as the food supply decreases. You will have fights among your own people. It is better that you dissatisfy them today, rather than drive them mad tomorrow."

Bilistages rolled his neck and groaned.

"You are right."

His advisors shouted protests to him in their language, but now Albus stepped toward them and growled something that caused them to cease.

"Thank you, your highness. I will ask Optio Curio to compile a report and recommendation on how much we should ration."

"Are all your ideas going to anger my people?"

"If your people want to return to their farms for the harvest, then they must swallow that anger. We all survive or perish together."

Bilistages waved Varro on to his next request. But as he assembled his thoughts on how to resist Diorix, the door at the far end of the hall burst open.

Varro whirled around at the sudden noise and found a young man in a plain tunic rushing over the wooden floor to then kneel before the king. He spoke in a breathless rush. The advisors' eyes widened and Bilistages's left eye twitched.

"It is Diorix," Albus said, stepping back to translate. "His men are gathering for battle."

"Just so," King Bilistages said, rising to his full height. "Albus must attend to his men. You Romans prepare yourself for war and meet us at the north gate."

Albus led them halfway back to their rooms, then went to summon his men. All the time Varro donned his armor and war gear, he could hear shouting outside the walls. From the wooden roof above, he heard footfalls rushing back and forth. He thought he heard women crying, and he wondered if servants were quartered there.

They stumbled out of the fort, still unfamiliar with its layout. But once under the pale blue sky, it was easy enough to follow the flow of men toward the north walls. The women and noncombatants all flowed in the opposite direction.

With their shields on their arms, Varro and the rest cut through the flow to reach the main gates. Two square towers of stone flanked it and the heavy doors were as sturdy as those to the south.

Men were climbing to the parapets from ladders set on the sides. King Bilistages, now dressed in polished mail, and his honor guard stood just behind the doors in a tight knot, poised to lead the men in battle if his gates were breached.

Albus was already atop the gatehouse, and the king pointed them up to join his son.

"It seems Diorix is coming forward to speak," Albus said as he met Varro at the door from the gate tower. He pointed over the walls. "But his men stand back. It would seem he intends to make an offer."

Albus had again donned his impressive war gear, only now he wore a plain bronze helmet. He had twelve men with him, all tall and strong like their prince. Their grim faces stared out across the walls, not acknowledging the Romans among them.

Varro joined them in looking across the long slope to where Diorix had gathered his men. He had massed them in blocks at the base of the hill. A crude battering ram housing had been built with a massive log suspended in it.

"He's got better gear than we had," Falco mumbled beside him.

"Something about these lines doesn't seem right," Varro said. "But what is it?"

Both Falco and Curio leaned forward to study the line. But Albus pulled Varro to him and pointed.

"There he is, Diorix."

From the distance, Varro could only see his standard, which was a wolf head mounted on a long pole and a red banner trailing after it. A cluster of warriors bore it up the hill, but none stuck out to Varro as an obvious leader. They all wore mail shirts under heavy fur cloaks. They strapped short swords like gladii to their hips and carried plain wooden shields.

"Not impressive, really," Varro said. "Our men appear in better shape."

"We are for now," Albus said, rubbing the white stubble on his chin. "But once we begin to ration, we will look like them."

"Fighting men draw better rations," Varro said, then offered a smile. "And that alone encourages more to take up arms against the enemy."

At last, the group of Iberians stopped out of arrow range and set their banner. One man came forward from the rest, Diorix, or so Varro assumed from the hiss that escaped Albus's clenched teeth.

Having expected a giant brute to be the leader, Varro raised his brows at the average man who now stood at the fore. He was not weak, but average for these Iberians. He had dark hair and dark eyes that the distance smeared into a nondescript countenance.

But when he shouted up to the wall, Varro understood the source of his charisma. His voice was deep and booming, so out of place for such an average man that it seemed as if another must be voicing his words.

"Bilistages, you cannot hide behind these walls forever!"

"Latin?" Varro turned to Albus who also cocked his head, but nonetheless shouted down to the small figures.

"Go back to your farms, you filth! You will find only death here."

Diorix turned to his companions and waved two men forward. They dropped three leather packs onto the grass before him. He then turned back to the walls with a sneer.

"I'll find three Romans here, I suspect. And I will make a dear trade with you for them. What say you, Albus? Give me the Romans and I will give you grain that you must need."

14

Diorix repeated his offer in his native tongue. Varro knew this from the stares of Albus's men. But Albus himself roared back defiance, raising his fist to his enemy.

"Are those the Romans?" Diorix pointed to Varro, Falco, and Curio lined up against the stone wall of the gatehouse. He waved at them. "I have found your packs. Look inside, see?"

Diorix spilled one over, dumping all of Varro's kit to the ground along with the sheets of vellum. He then kicked at the spilled contents, laughing as he did.

Falco balled his fist on the edge of the wall. "He'll regret that. I'll stuff that vellum down his throat."

"No," Varro said, glaring at Diorix as he kicked Varro's gear across the grass. "Curio needs it for writing practice. But he'll refill my ink pots with his own blood."

While Diorix and his henchmen laughed at the destruction of the pack, Albus had already begun to argue with his men. They kept looking toward Varro and the others, and he knew they debated the offer. He inserted himself into their group.

"They cannot be serious. It is some sort of ruse to get you to open the gates, or else they will take us and give nothing in return. Worse still, they may send poisoned food. There is no reason for Diorix to aid you."

Albus shook his head and growled. "Of course there isn't. But do you think everyone who heard his offer understands this? If we ration food per your plan, think of what the people will do."

They stared at each other in stony silence, neither one needing to articulate what a desperate mob could achieve.

Falco broke into their silence. "What does he want with us?"

"Ransom, of course." Albus now looked back over the wall. "Your consul will pay for your lives."

Laughing, Falco patted Albus's back. "No, he won't. Maybe if I were a tribune, and even then I'd have to be a famous one. We're expected to fight to the death. If we get caught, it's up to the gods if we are to be freed again."

"We will not explain that to him now." Albus pointed back over the walls.

Diorix had finished his sport and now drew his short sword to point it at the walls. He made demands of Albus, who seemed to curse him. The battering ram now trundled up the long hill behind him. He once more repeated his offer in Latin.

"Romans, if you have any mercy you would surrender yourselves to me. I will break these gates then kill all the men and give the women to my warriors. But if you come down now, I will spare them for a time, and even feed them."

"Do not answer," Albus said, grabbing Varro by his arm just as he drew breath to shout. "My father must make the final determination. I have sent a messenger to him now."

They turned to the yard before the gate where King Bilistages stood with his warriors. The messenger ran from the gatehouse tower to him and delivered his message. He looked up and his one milky eye caught the sheen of the diffuse sunlight. It seemed he stared at Varro for a long moment, but then he slowly shook his head.

"Good," Albus said. "We will fight as we should."

Being in charge of the wall defenses, Albus shouted commands that repeated down the line. If his men disagreed with rejecting Diorix's offer, Varro could see no sign of it. They took up bows, slings, and javelins. The defenders had collected piles of stone at the top of the gate, ready to drop on the ram.

"What role do you wish us to play?" Varro asked.

Albus raised a brow and paused in shouting his orders. "Well, kill anyone who gets over the wall."

He left Varro at the gatehouse and went to address the men in the towers.

"I guess we can drop rocks on them," Falco said, prodding the pile with the edge of his scutum. "Not much work for infantrymen up here for now."

Curio remained staring at the dark line of warriors. He seemed caught up in his thoughts, and Varro had learned to leave him alone at these moments. He was trying to work out something that might help them.

Diorix had retreated to his lines while the ram and a covering party pressed ahead. The primary force shouted insults and war cries that were too thin from this distance to sound intimidating. They inched forward a respectful distance behind the battering ram.

"Are they all drunk?" Falco asked, nodding to the encroaching line. "They seem to mass to one side of the ram, not around it to support a break through like they should."

Varro scratched his jaw, oddly wishing for a moment to shave while he studied the formation. He shrugged. "We've not seen Iberians fight. They may have weapons like ours, but that is the end of similarities. They might have no practical experience of taking a fortified location."

"Lucky for us, then. We'll die of starvation instead of a sword wound."

"Don't be so pessimistic. Something is off and we're about to find out what." Varro pointed with his chin at Curio, who seemed even more wrapped up in his thoughts as he leaned farther over the wall.

Both waited for him to share what had captured his interest. Varro knew something was off in Diorix's approach, and he was confident Curio would reveal it.

"There he goes."

Curio stabbed his finger forward like shoving a gladius into an enemy's heart. Both Varro and Falco crowded to his side to follow his line of sight.

At first all Varro could see was a long but thin line of Diorix's men keeping pace behind the ram, which was now coming into bow range. Falco murmured something about being blind, a sentiment Varro shared. He could not see as far as Curio could. But then he caught the blurry black dot that raced away toward a copse of trees.

"Diorix?" Varro asked, sensing what Curio must be seeing.

"But his standard is right behind the ram," Falco said. "And I still see nothing."

"It's him," Curio said. "I've been watching the line. There's not much to them. They're spread out down there, and I can see they're only a single rank in place. I've done some counting. This can't be more than half Diorix's numbers."

"Not enough to take the gate," Varro said, putting the rest of the enemy's plans together. "This is a ruse. The actual attack is coming to the south. He's drawn everyone here."

Falco struck his scutum to the wall. "And he distracted everyone with that business about trading food for us. A sly one, this barbarian."

Albus had not returned to the gatehouse, but his men

remained. They now drew their bows and were ready to take aim at the ram.

"Who speaks Latin?" Varro shouted among them, but only received irritated stares. "I don't know where Albus went. But we need to shift men to the south. I'm sure Diorix has a horse hidden in those trees and will ride to the south side. He'll be awaiting a signal. Probably when he hears the attack on the gates begin."

The ram rolled closer now, passing over their scattered gear. Varro took the others down the towers back to King Bilistages. He fixed Varro with his clear, angry eye.

"You must support my son on the gate."

"Your highness, this is not the actual attack. We've seen Diorix heading for some trees. He's going to bring the main attack to the south walls."

The king whirled around as if the attack had already begun. "How do you know this? He can't bring a second ram without being spotted."

"He'll rush the walls and scale with ladders," Varro said. "It will be easier with only token lookouts back there. Unless you act now, he will be inside your walls. Give me fifty men and I will foil his plans."

"Fifty?" Bilistages looked over the defenders and frowned. Then he turned to his personal guard.

"Take these thirty. They are as good as sixty men. Hurry, Centurion. If you are right, we have no time to lose."

They rushed back across the fortress, pressing through terrified people huddled into tents or in the eaves of buildings. Several of the king's guards understood Latin well enough to translate Varro's orders.

Upon reaching the south walls, he ordered the men to take ladders up to the ramparts, but then kick them away to prevent Diorix from exploiting them. That they consigned themselves to a fight to the death was forgone.

A deep thud echoed behind them, and Varro knew the ram had begun its assault. He had guessed the reason Diorix had massed his men on one side was so they could slip away to join the real attack coming here.

They clambered up the ladders, a thin force of thirty men who joined half of their number already watching from the walls.

When Varro reached the rampart, he looked out at the long slope tumbling down to where Diorix made his camp. We're it not for the heavy thudding and shouts from the north gate, it would've been a quiet and empty view. For no one was here.

Before he could curse his ill luck, an alarm came from the west wall.

"We're out of position," Varro said under his breath. He had guessed Diorix's plan, but not the location.

Worse still, at his orders his small company had thrown back their ladders to prepare for a last stand. These warriors now whirled in confusion to face the new alarm, then looked to Varro.

He did not hesitate and ran along the parapet to the west wall. The others ahead of him did the same. But they would have to pass single-file down the narrow planking, and a misstep could plunge them to their deaths. Varro and the others, with their huge shields, had an even worse time gaining speed.

Already the tops of ladders appeared and the minimal defenders were shooting frantically down the side.

"How did he come up unseen?" Falco pressed behind Varro as they drew close to the corner tower that led to the west wall.

"We'll find out. He's been misdirecting us all along."

Enemy ladders popped up the length of the west wall, and the beleaguered defenders had to choose between their bows or pushing back the ladders. Before stepping into the tower, Varro saw most seemed intent on shooting. It was a panicked reaction and the worst choice.

"Focus on the ladders," Varro yelled, knowing they would not understand him even if they heard him.

It seemed to take hours to traverse the distance to the west wall, but he found most ladders had not yet yielded the first enemies. As more of his warriors spread out along the wall, Varro realized they could not cover enough of it in time. Diorix's men would reach the top no matter what they did.

He left Falco and Curio to organize the defenses closest to the tower. If the enemy were to capture it, they'd have easy access to the ground level and the fort would be lost. He continued to where the defenders thinned.

Looking over the wall, he saw deep ranks of enemies pressing into lines to mount the ladders. Slingers stood back and aimed at the defenders, and Varro made a fine target.

A stone exploded against the edge of the wall beside his left cheek. Shards of it stung his face and pinged against his helmet. He pulled back and continued until he found a ladder where the first enemy was already pulling over the wall.

His scutum was like a battering ram as he rushed forward. He could not see the enemy, but felt his weight bounce off the shield, then heard his scream as he plunged from the walls.

But another came behind him, and Varro found an enemy at his back. He could not turn easily with his shield, but wrenched aside in time to avoid a strike that grazed across his mail shirt.

He punched down this enemy, sprawling him onto the parapet and causing him to drop his short sword off the wall. But then a new foe stepped off the ladder and Varro knew the enemy had secured it, cutting him off from the other defenders except for the few men at his back.

So he retreated, intent on preventing the rest of the wall from being overrun.

From the tower on the opposite end, Albus strode out. Then a cry came up from below and scores of Ilegertes warriors rushed to the walls to bring their own ladders to the parapet. Others raced up rickety wooden stairs set along the length to reach the fight.

Now Varro raised a war cry to join Albus's.

Diorix's advantage had been ephemeral. Now the parapet shook with the stomping feet of the defenders and a true battle began.

Sling stones and arrows cracked and shattered on the walls, but also striking defenders and drawing blood and shrieks. Protected behind his scutum, Varro did not fear. It created a barrier that no enemy could pass. Down the wall, Falco and Curio did likewise.

They created zones to trap their enemies. But this likewise trapped the defenders. It fell onto the Romans to become plugs that kept the enemy from gaining more of the wall.

Varro struggled to push to a ladder, where he could stopper all enemy progress. He kicked bodies off the parapet, some still alive, as he slowly worked against those resisting him. His gladius darted out from the side of the scutum to drive into exposed flesh. In turn, nothing reached him. The scutum was a more fearsome weapon than his sword in this circumstance.

Greaves protected his legs, a helmet his head, and what passed his shield was turned by iron mail. The Iberians shouted in frustration.

The sling stone clattered like hail on the wall. The thrum of the defenders' bows vibrated in concert. Everywhere, men screamed to their gods as they died. Behind Varro, Albus led a battle song as he and his men cleared the ladders.

It was butchery, and most of it suffered by Diorix. He had been too clever, and without the full weight of his attackers they could not mount the walls. Varro slid in blood flowing along the boards, being more dangerous than the enemies still struggling to mount their ladders.

His shoulders now burned with the stress of continual battle.

His ears rang. His nose was filled with the foul stench of death. His foot slipped on dismembered fingers and he had to throw himself against the wall or else fall back into the yard below.

He could not see much of the battle's progress hidden behind his shield. But he sensed the shift in the attackers' spirits. The sling stones slowed, now becoming random cracks across the length of the wall.

"We've cleared the ladders." Albus's voice was loud at his back, and Varro glanced over his shoulder. Someone still struggled against his shield, possibly two men. But he still managed to speak as he forced them away.

"They can replace them. Be alert."

"I'm not so foolish, Centurion. Diorix's men have lost heart. They are running."

Varro smiled as he leaned into his shield. Sweat ran into his eyes and mouth. An iron point jabbed under the scutum, but his bronze greaves spared him injury.

"Help me dislodge these enemies!"

Albus threw his weight behind Varro, and they slid forward. The enemies pressed back, but one fell to the yard. The other collapsed to the parapet. Varro stamped on his neck as he stumbled forward. The hobnails of his sandals were not just for grip, but also a weapon in their own right. They could crush the bones of prone enemies. Varro again drove his heel under the enemy's jaw, driving his head back so his neck snapped.

That final crack matched the horns signaling retreat from below.

Varro shouted in victory, then at last set down his shield atop the slain enemy to look once more over the walls. The scene had changed. The ladders lifted away, and some were abandoned where they fell. Piles of dead and dying were heaped at the foot of the walls. Some still cried out, clutching at shafts in their bodies.

The Ilegertes defenders let out a cheer, led by Albus at Varro's side. He raised his sword beside the prince's.

"We have won!" Albus's pale hair was stained with blood, and a heavy cut to his biceps steadily leaked blood. But he held both sword and shield overhead with ease and rotated to face the men on both sides of the walls.

Varro cheered as well, glad to have avoided what could have been a disaster. Down the line, Falco leaned against the wall and stared at the retreating enemy. Beyond him, Curio was embracing one of the Ilegertes warriors in celebration.

"Your quick thinking saved us, Centurion Varro." Albus lowered his arms and turned to watch Diorix's force vanish back to their distant camp. "I was certain they planned to breach the north gate."

"It was you who saved us, Prince. Thirty men would not have held long. You were wise enough not to take the bait offered you."

Albus tilted his head and paused. "I saw what you did and followed. I have never endured anything like this before, and so I trust your experience. It did not fail me, and I am glad you were here or we might have had enemies among us now."

Varro accepted the praise and watched as the last of Diorix's force retreated into the distance.

"It is vital you take prisoners for interrogation. Do not kill all your enemies. We must learn more about Diorix's actual condition. I suspect he is not as strong as you believe."

"Why so?" Albus waved a hand over the dead bodies below them. "There are always more willing to join a chance at easy victory. He will replace these losses."

Varro gave a wry smile.

"Get me prisoners, and I will confirm what I already suspect. We might be closer to breaking the siege than you believe."

15

The aftermath of a battle was no less painful for the victors as the defeated, or so Varro felt. Wounded men still rolled on their backs, crying out for relief or else mumbling as their grip on life faded. In the wide yards surrounding the main fort, Bilistages supervised the treatment of the wounded. Varro and the others attended him along with Albus. It was grim work, for many had fallen from the parapets and suffered grizzly wounds.

Women and young children bent over the injured stretched out beneath a gray sky. They worked with purpose, but were overwhelmed by the numbers. Varro had never seen such disorganized handling, where the women flitted between whoever cried loudest at the moment. In an organized military, there were always doctors and their aides ready to deal with any sort of wound. But Bilistages's people practiced folk medicine that to his untrained eye seemed ineffective.

The king visited the wounded who lay in long rows waiting for attention and spoke words of encouragement to all he met. Following in silence, Varro admired this compassion in the king.

In his experience, consuls rarely visited the injured. But here was the king of a tribe of thousands bending over to pat the shoulder of a young man whose leg and knee had been shattered in a fall.

Yet even more surprising, he learned that both the queen and Bilistages's second daughter tended the casualties. Both were graceful and demure, and the source of Albus's pale hair was apparent in his mother's long locks. The daughter seemed just short of marriageable age, but she worked with the focus of an older woman.

Varro had a new appreciation for these Ilegertes. He could never imagine such egalitarian behavior from Roman leaders, though if Consul Cato was sincere, he came closest to this ideal.

When their inspection of the injured concluded, Bilistages had reports of the numbers lost and other damages. These came from his own men, who made their statements in their own language. They stood outside the fort as the breeze carried the scent of blood to them. Both he and Albus frowned, but said nothing in response. However, the crows sitting patiently atop the fort roof seemed to understand, cawing and flapping their wings as if expecting a sumptuous feast.

"I am grateful for your leadership," Bilistages said to his three Roman advisors. His milky eye no longer seemed as stern, and his face seemed to have aged since the morning. "My son said you fought bravely and would've given your lives in that attack. I see you are better than advisors, but true warriors at heart."

"We are Romans," Varro said. "As well as allies. So we would stand shoulder to shoulder with you, even to the death. That is the Roman way."

Bilistages gave a bleak smile. "Perhaps for you three. You are young and idealistic yet. But your consul's definition of an alliance seems much different."

Varro winced at the stinging truth. He knew his words were stilted and almost patronizing. But he had not forgotten his duty to preserve this alliance. If he earned any praise from the Ilegertes, he hoped to reflect it on Rome overall. Being a diplomat was far beyond his reach or training and he did not know what else to do.

"Which brings me to the sad news." The king looked down, idly fingering his gold torc. Varro wondered if it served as the Iberian's version of a crown, and if the king was debating its weight as he tapped the braided gold.

"This victory cost me three hundred men."

"That cannot be," Varro said, turning to look at the dead and injured across the yard.

"It is," Albus said for his father. "You forget the men at the front gate. Diorix still pressed his attack there."

"They are not all slain," Bilistages explained. "In fact, most are just wounded. But they cannot fight, at least for now, and so I must subtract them from my strength but carry them for rations. This was a victory that cost too much."

Varro rubbed the back of his neck, trying to comprehend how this battle cost so many lives.

"Which means I must repeat my call for aid to Consul Cato." Bilistages squared up to Varro. "You must deliver that request."

"Your highness, the consul commanded me to remain as your advisor until recalled to my century."

"I am king here," he said, his voice even but firm. "You obey me while within my walls. We need relief now more than ever and so I would send you back now while Diorix is occupied with his own dead."

Varro noted both Falco and Curio shrank back, happy to leave him to make excuses. Both Bilistages and Albus squinted at him against the glare of the overcast sky.

"Consul Cato would not see us, but have us arrested."

"Then I shall send my own messenger." Bilistages waved dismissively at Varro's face. "And you can send a letter to him with the same request. What good will your advice do me if I've no men to act on it?"

"I can write a letter." Varro looked to Curio, who did not seem to understand he would have that responsibility as he stared off at the wounded in the distance.

"Have it readied for me. I cannot delay while we have this opening. Then I would have you advise me."

Yet the manner of his voice said he thought little of the advice. He left with a muttered command to his servants and vanished up into the fort. Albus remained behind and gave Varro a chiding look.

"You cannot wound my father's pride like that, or you will achieve nothing."

"So I should lie to him?"

Albus bit his lip in thought and all of them stared off in silence until he at last spoke again.

"Lies don't help either. But you must be more sensitive. You cannot deny him so flatly. Now, you must write a letter that will convince your consul to send help."

"He will not send help until he is ready." Varro met Albus's pale eyes and hoped his doubts were not obvious. Cato would not be ready until he defeated the main rebel force, and no one could say when that might happen.

"Then you will not keep the Ilegertes in hand."

"A threat?" Varro raised his brow, matched by Albus.

"The truth. There, do you now see how it feels to my father?"

Varro's face warmed and he gave an embarrassed smile. "I will choose my words with care from now on. Curio, you will write the letter. Falco, review it before I hand it to the king."

"But he needs it immediately," Curio said. "I'll be too slow."

"Falco, ensure the optio's full concentration. Use your vine cane if necessary. I want a clean, ready copy for the king's messenger within the hour."

Curio shrank under Falco's eager grin.

"Come on, Curio. Don't fear a bit of ink."

Varro waited for them to return to the fort, and Albus chuckled.

"The short one looks like he's going to his death."

"He may well be. Falco isn't known for restraint with corporal punishments. Now, I need to interrogate captives if I'm to advise your father on anything."

Teams had recovered wounded from both sides who had fallen outside the walls. They left the enemy wounded in the shade of the north wall, unattended but for a group of spearmen guards. The captives were all in terrible condition, or else they would have fled. Albus spoke briefly with his guards and they selected three captives who seemed coherent enough to provide useful intelligence.

"Let's do this away from the injured," Varro said.

"Isn't it better that they see what awaits if they do not help us?"

Varro shook his head. "This is better done in isolation, so their companions don't strengthen their resolve against us. It also eases their shame for talking and speeds our work."

Albus stroked his chin. "You Romans know these things better than my simple folk. We would just cut off heads until someone spoke."

"And you might end up with a pile of heads that can no longer tell you anything."

They prodded away three captives from the others at spear point. Then, as they could not stand without aid, guards carried them to where Albus indicated—a blacksmith's forge. He gave a wicked smile to Varro.

"Just because we would normally kill our captives does not mean I've no idea how to make them speak."

Varro swallowed, dreading what was to come. The promises he made to his great-grandfather now echoed in his head, and he felt cold and empty. He hoped the captives would not resist and spare themselves suffering.

Inside the forge, embers shed heat and threw a faint red light over the terrified enemy dragged inside. The first one had a broken leg with bone poking out beside his knee. He hung between two men, and his gap-tooth mouth flopped open in wordless terror when he spotted the embers, tongs, hammers, and other tools arrayed around the forge.

"What do you want to know?" Albus asked. "Speak quickly, for I think our friend is going to die of fright before he answers."

"How many men does Diorix currently command, and how many might he call upon? What is the condition of camp? Do they have enough supply? How is the morale? Where are their lines weakest?"

"Stop!" Albus held up his hand, exposing the eagle talons tattooed on their backs. "We will go one question at a time."

Albus repeated questions, and the horrified prisoner shook his head. Albus then shook his own head and placed an iron bar in the embers. He repeated a question, this time emphasizing it with a punch to the man's gut.

Varro sat in the corner, observing Albus at work. The prince had been true to his word. He knew how to make men suffer. When the first prisoner had answered all the questions, his face was swollen and bleeding. Both eyes were shut and blood drooled from his mouth. Albus rubbed his raw knuckles and said he would spare himself on the others.

The first man was dragged out and Albus picked up a wood mallet while he awaited the next victim. Questions and answers were exchanged between hammer blows to the victim's joints and wounds until he was also reduced to a whimpering and bloody mess. The final prisoner corroborated all the gathered intelligence. Albus hardly had to work on him, since he had heard the screams and saw the conditions of the others who had been dragged from the forge. After a short time, he let that man go with minimal damage to his already substantial wounds.

Varro had watched it all, hating what he viewed as a lesser evil for a greater good. He told himself that through the agonies of three condemned enemies, he might ease the suffering of a greater number of people on both sides. For now, he understood Diorix's actual situation, and it was not as strong as it seemed. If the siege ended swiftly, would that not be better for all? A small voice told him it was weak reasoning and there were less violent means to gain the same knowledge. But Varro was learning how to silence that voice, which was exactly the fear his papa had for him.

For all Varro's introspection, Albus now seemed in high spirits. His hair was still clotted with blood from the afternoon's battle, and it was now freshened with spatter from his victims. The guards returned and beamed alongside their prince.

"I think we can count what we learned as the truth. All three said as much the same and had no time to come up with a shared story, if that was ever a thought for them. They are just farmers following promises of easy spoils."

"And finding the spoils are not so easily had," Varro said. "Diorix is desperate for something to show for his efforts. Today's attack was probably his best ploy, and it failed."

They cleaned up the forge, for Albus feared the smith's anger at what he would find upon his return. Teeth and blood spread on the dirt floor, and Albus had his men clean while he and Varro returned to the fort. As they walked, Varro reviewed what he had learned either through direct statement or implied from the context.

Diorix had tapped the groundswell of anti-Roman sentiment spreading through the province of Near Iberia. But rather than throw in with the gathering of tribes, he struck out on a personal vendetta against the Ilegertes. When he learned they would remain loyal to Rome, it was easy for him to gather every man with a hunting bow or spear to his side and attack.

The initial success drew more men to him, as easy victory often does. But now they find the real riches, which are all in capturing the Ilegertes's lands, not so readily plucked out of Bilistages's aging hands. There was considerable dissent among Diorix's followers, and many who thought they would be better served joining the main rebellion.

With the feverish greed that propelled his army now cooling off, his followers were also beginning to wonder how these so-called spoils would be divided, and Diorix had been evasive on this point. With morale already wavering, the defeat today might well cost him all but his sworn followers, which while not small were nowhere near enough to take and hold the Ilegertes' lands. He was proving to be more of a wonder of the moment rather than some fearsome and cunning foe that Albus and Bilistages seemed to believe him to be.

In fact, Varro learned just as much about the Ilegertes from this interrogation as he did about Diorix. Varro did not understand the complexities of tribal relations, but it was clear enough that Bilistages had instigated the troubles. It seemed Diorix was once a friend of the Ilegertes, and that he was even to be wed to Bilistages's daughter. But the king felt a better alliance could be made marrying her to another tribe, changing his mind at the last moment and at a huge loss of face for Diorix. He swore revenge and had his shaman cast a curse upon Bilistages for his perfidy.

That curse seemed to have had some effect, for the king had lived in fear of Diorix ever since. Whether Bilistages could counter this curse, Varro was uncertain. But it seemed to him that everyone believed in this curse and its power to bring ruin to the king.

While they walked back to the fort in thoughtful silence, Varro wondered if Bilistages hesitated to commit to battle because of this fear. Varro himself feared curses, and especially curses from the spirts of the dark woods. So he understood the terror that drove men to avoidance. But now the king was confronted with his deepest dread, and he wanted Rome to handle it for him.

And so Rome would, Varro decided. The path forward seemed clear.

He and Albus separated to clean up. Varro checked on Curio's progress, finding him in the final stages of composing a request for aid to the consul. He bent at a table and Falco stood over him with arms folded and scowling.

"You look just like our tutors did," Varro said. Falco shook his head.

"Now I understand why they were always so cross. This is painful work." He sighed, then took the papyrus sheet from Curio. "The king doesn't have many other sheets to spare. So let's hope you didn't make a mess."

While he reviewed the letter, Varro looked around and found no signs of a draft.

"He won't be able to pass the consul's test if you dictate the letter, Falco."

"And he won't learn to write if he doesn't have something to model." Falco looked up with a frown. "Why didn't you help him with the fucking letter and let me beat on those captives? Did you forget who's better for which jobs?"

Varro sighed, then sat on a stool while he explained all he had learned from the interrogation. When he finished, Curio's letter had been set aside and forgotten. Falco rubbed his temples.

"You think the way forward is clear? I don't see it."

"Diorix is ready to collapse," Varro said. "I now think he was serious about trading food for us. If he believed we could be ransomed for a good sum, then he'd have something to give to his followers. Right now, he seems to have tapped all the men he can. The rest of the tribes have joined together for a bigger prize."

"So he can't really win here," Falco said. "Are you thinking we just wait him out?"

Varro nodded. "It seems prudent. I believe once Consul Cato crushes the main rebellion, that news will scatter Diorix's men. Even the dumbest among them will realize their fight is over. Therefore, Rome will deliver the Ilegertes, but just not in the manner they wished for."

Curio scratched his head. "The king seems eager for results. I don't know if he'll like waiting. He's sending this letter, after all."

They debated what the king might do for a while longer, but then they were summoned to meet him back in his hall. The same advisors were present again, and their former scowls were now reduced to mild frowns. It was progress, Varro thought. Albus again stood by his father, smiling as if anticipating a great feast.

Varro presented his findings and recommendation to outlast Diorix. But this also came with the need for rationing. The scowls returned to the king's bald-headed advisors, and Bilistages's milky eye clouded with fear.

"We cannot sit by and starve while our enemy takes all the action. How can we know the situation won't change and Diorix is reinforced? No, we must send for help, and we must have a plan for action."

The argument continued in circles for what seemed hours. Even affable Albus eventually sat at a table and hid his face behind his tattooed hands. Varro pulled out every ploy he could think of, and even Falco and Curio joined in support of waiting out Diorix.

In the end, Bilistages finally conceded. It seemed more due to lacking his own plan rather than agreeing with Varro's. He stood up from his chair, weary and aged from the start of their meeting. His face seemed to sag and eyes drooped. Night was coming and he wanted to celebrate victory with his people.

"We will feast the victory tonight," he said, then held up a hand to prevent Varro's protests. "Such is our traditions, Roman. A victory must be celebrated, and if all is as you say, then we have defeated Diorix today. In your own words, he just has not realized it yet."

Varro had said as much, and so he closed his mouth and inclined his head. Bilistages gave orders to servants and Albus in his own language, then once more addressed the Romans.

"We will pray for Consul Cato's speedy victory, which by your expectations will become ours as well."

This served as their dismissal and they waited for the king to depart before also heading back to their quarters. As they did, Albus met them in the hallway.

"You three are a persuasive group."

"Thank you for supporting us," Varro said. "I realize it puts you in a difficult position. But the main battle is over, and now we wait for Diorix to fall apart."

"I believe it is as easy as you say." Albus brushed his long pale hair from his face and looked back toward where his father had exited. "Those captives did not lie, but my father is still worried."

"Is it for that curse?"

Albus's easy smile vanished, and he stared between Varro and the others.

"Maybe. It is not something we speak about. Our holy men have protected the king, but he still doubts them. It is his way to doubt everything that is not completely in hand. As long as Diorix still has men under arms, he cannot rest easy."

Then Albus's face cleared and he clapped Varro's shoulder.

"But that will change soon, yes? And tonight we shall feast one last time before tightening our supply. It will be hard, but the Ilegertes are a hardy people. If this is all we must do to defeat our enemy, then we do it gladly."

So the night came and the promised celebratory feast was prepared. Even some of the wounded were carried to tables which had been set up in the main yard of the stronghold. Strange songs were sung to even stranger pipe music. But Varro was glad for the wine and the meat, even if he believed such a feast might strain their supply if Diorix hung on longer than he should.

Men and women congratulated their Roman guests on their bravery and victory. And while they might not understand the words, they did understand the sentiment.

They sat at the far end of Bilistages and Albus's table. His queen and young daughter set to his left, and his son on his right. His face seemed less haggard than in recent days, and Varro was gladdened that he seemed to accept victory was at hand.

"Feels good to be treated like a hero for change," Falco said, leaning into him.

Curio continually stole glances at Bilistages's daughter, trying to act as if her youthful beauty was a mere passing interest.

"We've now sat at the tables of two kings," Varro said. "Not bad for us farm boys. But we've got to keep Curio from falling in love with every girl he sees."

"What? I was only thinking how much she looks like Albus, only with no ugly tattoos."

And so the laughter and celebration began, and Varro understood nothing of what the king said to his people. The wine was sour, but it seemed to Falco's taste as he twice drained his cup then held it out for a servant to refill.

Varro at last relaxed. While they were still besieged, with proper rationing, they could endure it. Diorix was not the main power in the region, and that power was occupied with Consul Cato's legions. In the end, he had drawn the better duty. For once, he was away from the real danger. He picked up his clay cup and touched it to both Falco's and Curio's.

"Here's to victory."

And then flaming arrows rained down into the yard.

16

Yellow streaks arced over the north walls in brilliant clusters against the night sky, then plunged into buildings and tents. The first volley landed scores of fiery shafts into the wooden roofs of outbuildings in a neat line. But a second volley came fast upon it, and these arced higher to land amid the yard and the scores of tables filled with celebrating people.

Varro blinked, his clay mug suspended in mid-toast to victory. He did not immediately comprehend the attack. Neither did anyone else, it seemed, as some people had already drunk enough to be slouching at their benches. The king and Albus both watched as if the flaming arrows were part of planned entertainment.

The time it took to react could not have been more than a heartbeat. But to Varro it seemed to stretch out indefinitely. With each flaming arrow that landed, a small fire sprang to life. Some shafts broke, then petered out. But enough scored hits on flammable material to send up ribbons of fire into the dark.

Alarm horns at last shattered everyone from their stupor.

But they were too late.

The third volley and a fourth right behind it sent burning clouds over their heads. The flaming shafts climbed to the zenith of their arc, then tilted down and plummeted amid the revelers.

Varro and the others had already leaped away from their benches, but not out of the radius of attack. Arrows plunged into flesh and wood, while others broke uselessly in the dirt.

Bilistages let out a horrendous cry. Varro was certain he had been impaled, but instead saw his young daughter batting wordlessly at an arrow sunk deep into her neck. Of all the gruesome things Varro had ever seen, little matched the horror of witnessing this young princess stoically grasping her neck as she collapsed at her father's feet with blood spray turning to smoke in the dying flames of the arrow. She did not even cry out, perhaps from shock, but simply died.

None of them were armed or armored. Warriors who had survived the morning attack now died with their faces in their dinner bowls and gray-feathered arrows protruding from their backs.

Albus threw himself over his father as a shield against more arrows. The queen stood in abject horror, staring at the blood that now spattered her Roman-styled stola. Yet the volleys had ceased.

But the fires had just begun.

Chaos surged through the crowd as fast as the fires that grew out of building roofs and tent rows. People scrambled for safety and for their own property. Albus crouched by his father and mother who hovered over their slain child while his guards, the only armed men here, encircled all of them with shields held overhead.

"They're going to attack again?" Falco had spilled his wine on his stomach, turning his gray tunic dark red. It was a bad omen, Varro thought, but he had no time to waste on it.

"So it seems. We need to get men on the walls."

Unable to speak their language, he shouted and pointed at the source of the attack to the north. Yet in the panicked rush, all shouts vied to be heard above the others. Fortunately, Varro was a Roman Centurion.

He leaped onto the table and cupped his hands to his mouth.

"To the north wall! Gather your shields and weapons! Prepare for attack!"

Even if no one understood, few could resist the sonorous bellow that commanded them. Even Albus sat up from his father's side, as if waking from a nightmare. He understood and leaped onto the table to repeat Varro's command.

"I've no weapon," Varro said. "But we've got to ensure they don't come over the wall.

"I will kill them with my bare hands." Albus's eyes were wide with hate, and the talons tattooed on his hands seemed as real and sharp as any raptor's.

"Fire," Curio pointed across the yard. "At the granary."

The large granary house was made of stone, but the roof and supporting beams were wood and thatch, and the arrows had done their work. Bright flames licked into the night, creating an orange haze around the building.

"Our food!" Albus put his hands on his head.

"We will handle the fire," Varro said. "Command the men on the wall."

They rushed off to their separate tasks. The cistern was close enough and men were already drawing water from it. But they worked as individuals, running into and around each other as they scrambled to reach the fire. Varro and the others arrived amid the confusion.

"This is not going to work. Falco, Curio, we need to get these men into lines. They know what to do themselves, but are too panicked. Let's get them sorted."

The heat of the blaze lashed out as Varro pulled men into

lines. They understood what to do, for anyone living in such a fort would have experience of extinguishing fires. They needed a guide to marshal their fears, and Varro and the others provided it.

Now they worked with organization, and all who rushed to help fell into the line and strengthened it. Varro filled in wherever he saw a need, either in drawing water or stepping into a slow line to speed it up. Each bucket tossed created a steaming hiss, and the fire was soon struggling for air.

Yet a section of roof collapsed into the granary. Falco led his team inside to put out that fire, but they soon spilled back outside with a rolling cloud of smoke chasing them. Even with the fire mostly defeated, the grain was likely spoiled.

The exhausting work continued, and Varro could not determine how the attack was proceeding. He did not hear the battle, but again he was surrounded by shouts, cracking timbers, and rushing flames. His eyes stung from smoke and the heat of the fire made his flesh feel taut.

The exhausting work continued until at last darkness returned and gray smoke clouds rolled away from the granary. They found other fires, the worst being among the packed tents. Most were made of hide and did not easily burn. But others were cloth and treated with oils against rain. These burned and spread smoke and fire through the encampment.

By the end of the night, Varro united with Albus again. He was black but for his pale hair, which now shined brilliantly white in contrasts to his soot-stained body.

"They never attacked," he said. "I think Diorix spent every arrow he possessed."

Varro shook his head. "A waste of resources if he did not follow up with an attack."

Albus's gritted teeth shined in the dark. "A waste, you say? Look at this madness. Final victory goes to him today."

Smoke rolled away from the granary and a half-dozen other buildings. The tent cluster from the refugees had a wide hole burned out of its center. People paced around in postures of despair. New casualties lay scattered around the site of the former celebration.

"And my sister is dead," Albus said. His eyes gleamed with both rage and tears. "I would say Diorix has had his revenge for this morning."

Varro clamped back on what he really felt, which was that Diorix had delivered one last blow before his personal rebellion failed. He could not even mount an attack, which would have caught the Ilegertes unaware and unprepared. If he could not claim victory tonight, then he never would.

But Albus was in no mood to hear this, and Varro knew to remain silent.

They all did what they could to help with the injured. Despite the terror from the flaming arrows, far fewer had died than in the attack on the walls. Albus's sister had been one of the unfortunate casualties. A good portion of the slain were from accidents after the arrow attack, either from the fire or from some other misadventure born of the confusion. Totally, they counted twenty-six killed and half as many injured.

Sleep was impossible that night, and the next day the ravages of the granary fire created panicked whispered throughout the fort. Varro could not understand what they said, but he saw people everywhere looking at the ruins of the granary and putting their hands to their heads. Everywhere, people were in a posture of despair. Diorix had not retreated during the night, but remained encircling the Ilegertes' fort.

They did not see Albus or receive any summons from the king. So Varro and the others used the time to wash and maintain their gear. Curio rewrote his letter to the consul twice more, and Varro was satisfied at his progress. But when he assigned a random topic, Curio lost all color in his face and did not finish but more than three sentences.

Bilistages had his daughter burned on a pyre that night. Varro watched as king, queen, Albus, and hundreds of shocked and bereaved tribesmen sang woeful tunes that weighed on his heart. No one cried, but that seemed to make their grief more terrible. He turned to Falco and Curio, and deep shadows thrown from the pyre danced across them as they too observed in silence. They remained long enough to be respectful, but then left the Ilegertes to their traditions and their sorrows.

"You can see it in their eyes," Falco said after they returned to their rooms. "Albus and the king want revenge."

"Wouldn't you?" Curio asked. "If someone killed my sister like that, I'd want to see them dead."

"You've mentioned your sister once in the last six years," Falco said. "How much do you really care?"

"Do I have to talk about my family to care about them? You never mention your mother. So do you hate her?"

"Of course I do."

"The problem," Varro said, cutting between them, "is that we'll have no choice but to fight now. I don't think we have anything to fear from Diorix in his current state. He cannot have enough arrows to do this again."

Falco dropped onto his mattress and folded his arms.

"You're sure about that? Maybe he has sent messengers to the main rebellion asking for a fresh supply of greedy men. He hit the granary, Varro. Food is running out. We can't just sit here now."

He growled in frustration, but Falco laughed.

"I know. If only he had been kind enough to just be defeated like we expected. But the bastard knew where the granary was, and targeted it."

"I've been starving since that attack," Curio said. "I'm used to fighting on an empty stomach, but I don't think that's true of these people."

"If we sally out to attack Diorix, I wonder at our chances now."

"Well, the chances were never good," Falco said. "That's why they came looking for the consul's help. So our chances now are probably complete shit. But what else should we do? Diorix knows he can starve us out."

"Which one of my letters do you think we should send to Consul Cato?" Curio sorted out the papyrus from the other two letters he had drafted on leftover animal skin. "I like the second one best."

"The consul is not sending anything," Varro said. "We can't look to the legions for aid. This is for us to figure out."

"Well, good luck with that." Falco stretched out on his mattress. "I say we just get stuck in and let the gods figure out the rest. Both Diorix and Bilistages are about to fall apart. Just have them shove at each other and one is bound to collapse. If we're lucky, it'll be the other side."

"While I agree in spirit," Varro said, sitting beside Curio at his table. "That idea is what you usually call complete shit. We don't just run into battles and hope it all turns out all right."

"Really?" Curio shifted to face Varro. "Then how come that feels like all we've ever done? Just form up a line and march into the enemy until they run away."

Varro shoved Curio's shoulder in answer to his question. "We need to find an advantage. Until now, it was this walled fortress. That granary was the weak point, but it's not all the supply Bilistages has."

Falco waved his hands, as if dismissing them.

"I'm going to sleep while there's time for it. You two should put out the lamp and do the same. I'm sure the king is going to have a belly full of shit in the morning and want action from us."

It was good advice, and soon they were all abed and the next morning were commanded to meet with the king. True to Falco's predictions, he and Albus were full of righteous anger. The king's milky eye now seemed to glow with white rage. His middle-aged and balding advisors were equally incensed.

"Diorix has sent a messenger to demand our surrender. I sent him the messenger's head as an answer and threw the corpse over the wall. Let it rot there for all to see."

"He must die for what he did," Albus said. "There can be no surrender or reconciliation. My father wants your advice on how to best attack his camp. How would the Romans defeat him?"

Varro felt every eye turn to him, including Falco and Curio. The night had not yielded any more productive options for him.

"Your highness, you are not asking if this is the best strategy?"

The king recoiled, and Albus's face folded in disgust. He spoke for his father.

"It is the best strategy. We have let him contain us, chase us off our lands, and now deny us food. Certainly, we cannot go to our deaths hiding behind walls like frightened children."

"Have you prepared that letter to your consul?" Bilistages recovered from his revulsion, as did his advisors who mirrored their master's every expression. Sycophants such as these men were found everywhere, Varro thought.

"Optio Curio has one prepared as you requested. Have you any news about the rebellion? Did any other prisoners have information?"

"We killed the prisoners," Albus said, brows furrowed in confusion. "We're not feeding our enemies, Centurion."

The room fell to expectant silence. Varro did not know what else he could tell them. They were not open to reason, and it seemed they were of the same mind as Falco.

"Are you willing to wait for the consul's answer, your highness?" Varro looked between him and Albus. "You must endure a further week of inaction, and then I expect you will be rebuffed."

"Ha! As I always thought!" Bilistages stood from his chair and narrowed his eyes at the Romans, as did his advisors. "You represent your consul, and you say Rome cannot help its allies. My daughter is dead for my loyalty to you. My people will starve, and in the end, when there is no one left to guard these walls, my enemy will sit upon this very seat and mock our memories. He will defile this hall with his filth. But Rome does not care and will not help. Perhaps I would've done better to join the allied kings against Rome."

"If you join the rebellion, then the consul will certainly come," Varro said. "But not as you wish him to."

Albus hissed. "Do not threaten us. You are but three among thousands, and three who I thought above such ploys."

Varro sighed. "Prince Albus, I am sorry to have spoken roughly. But you know I am correct. If we must attack Diorix, then it must be to our advantage. You ask how Rome would attack. Well, only with strength and allies on our side. I have learned your sister is married to another tribe. Can you not call on aid from them?"

Both Bilistages and Albus turned their heads. The king again sat, but leaned away as if avoiding a bad odor.

"They have joined the rebellion. We are as nothing to them now."

Varro raised his hand to calm any protest. "But this is not about rebellion. A sister has lost a sister. She must know, and then she must speak to her husband. Surely, some men might wish to please their queen in avenging her sister's death. Even a handful of men can do much if they come upon the enemy from behind his lines and under a moonless sky."

The idea Varro painted seemed to take shape in their thoughts. Albus looked to his father, who rubbed his gray temples in consideration. At length, and after murmuring with his advisors, he looked to Varro.

"Who can go to them? I cannot send my son, nor can I send

you, their enemy. I cannot even be certain they will answer our need."

"Do not state your need truthfully, your highness." Varro looked to Falco and Curio, who both raised their brows. "Diorix once thought to wed your daughter. When he has destroyed the Ilegertes and stolen all your wealth, he will come to take his promised bride by force. They must act now or else face a stronger threat later. That is the tale to tell. Make sure they have an interest joined to yours."

Again Bilistages and the others all conferred in their own language. But once more, the king fell back into his chair as if he had just been running for miles.

"We suffer the same problem by waiting for Rome's answer. How soon would they come? Would we even find them in time? For their warriors have gone to join the other tribes against your consul. It was a fair plan, but we have no choice but to attack."

Varro bent his head. "Then attack by night with all the force you can bring. You must be decisive in victory, or else all is lost."

"The scars on your face and your rank tell me you are a fierce warrior." Bilistages looked to Albus. "You three shall set the standard for the attack, and Albus shall command the army. I have grown too old to fight, as dearly as I want to. Bring me Diorix alive or dead. It matters only that I have enough of him to hang above the north gate."

Varro and the others gave shallow bows in answer.

And the next night, they went to war against Diorix.

17

The enemy roared at Varro across the dark night. He stood shirtless with only his short sword and round shield against Varro's armored might. Twisting blue tattoos covered his muscular body, rendered obscure from both shadow and body hair. Blood gleamed on his arms, lit by the blazes set throughout Diorix's camp. To his side a throng of combatants whirled against the flaming backdrop.

"Come on," Varro shouted. "Are you a man or a growling dog?"

The foe leaped the short distance, shield forward and sword ready. But Varro tilted his scutum, then slammed it into the attacker. He braced it with his left leg against the inside curve and felt it shudder as the Iberian tried to wrestle it aside.

His gladius slipped along the shield's edge and stabbed into the Iberian's ribs. A short, hard thrust was all Varro needed to topple his enemy. The magnificence of his weapon was in its deadliness when wielded by trained hands. The Iberians used similar weapons, and to stunning effect. But they were not a drilled military force and it showed in their lack of cohesion and fighting technique.

The enemy slid off his shield and collapsed, gasping for breath. Varro had punctured his lungs, and as an act of mercy he knocked the kneeling enemy to his back then stabbed his neck to speed his death. The big Iberian stiffened as blood sprayed over Varro's feet, then fell limp.

"You're too far out!"

It was Falco, along with Curio, who recalled Varro to the main battle. There was no formation to this attack, just a simple swell of howling enemies on both sides. Most rallied to Albus as he pushed toward the center of Diorix's camp. As such, the enemy also flocked to the middle.

Varro had tried to lead men to flank this mess and trap the Iberians between Albus and himself. But his warriors were led away by what they saw as easier targets, and he found himself alone.

"It was a good idea, sir!" Curio shouted above the screaming and slamming of shield on shield. His face shined with sweat from the surrounding fires. Albus had been determined to "return Diorix's flames a hundredfold," as he had said. But it came at the cost of surprise, which had been the entire rationale for a night attack.

"This is a fucking mess," Falco said. He and Curio hung back from the main brawl while waiting for Varro to extract himself from the failed flanking attempt.

"We don't command here," Varro said. "I'm reluctant to dive into that pile and sell my life to the confusion."

"They're blood crazed, sir." Curio pointed to Albus at the center of the fight. "He just wants revenge, not victory."

"Three of us alone can't give him victory." Varro scanned the firelit darkness. Small teams fought the fires raging among their tents. But these sensible men were the minority, and most sought to claim Albus's head instead. "But we can preserve his life. Let's get him out before he is completely entrapped."

They did not need to plan their next action, but understood what to do from their years of practice. They formed an arc of shields, with Falco at the center for his great size and Varro and Curio to secure the wings, then plunged into the press.

The three plowed a furrow through their own side, who in their blind fury struck at them without thought. Hollow thuds and slams vibrated through their shields. The packed combatants smelled of sweat and blood, and the horrible note of spilled entrails carried with it as well. Varro's steps skidded on puddles of gore, and he had to step across the fallen as they neared the center. Yet their unyielding shields, heavy armor, and powerful bodies drove through to where Albus fought.

The pale hair flowing from beneath his Roman style helmet made him seem like a raving ghost among the dark masses. His short sword plunged into his enemies as if they were awaiting death. But his mail was cut under his sword arm and terrible wounds showed his heedlessness.

"Prince Albus!" Varro guided their small wedge to reach his side. "You must retreat. We're being swallowed up. We will all die here."

The prince's eyes showed white in the dark. He sneered at Varro as if he were another enemy to kill.

But Varro interposed his shield wall before him and his opponents, with Falco and Curio muscling and stabbing their way into position.

"What are you doing?" Albus shouted. "I have not met Diorix in battle yet!"

"We must retreat." Varro pushed him back. "Now, before it is all lost."

"I have not taken revenge!"

Albus wrestled away from Varro and again plunged into the mass of angry, snarling faces of the enemy. Yet Varro insisted on shielding him, and in this brief contest the prince struggled, then slipped on a corpse.

He went down and a dozen enemies screamed for blood as they surged forward.

Falco and Curio both slammed their shields into the wave. But they skidded back from the impact.

"Fuck! Get him up now!" Falco groaned as he held the enemy surge at bay. Curio bolstered his flank, but it too started to crumble.

Varro hauled the huge prince up with his sword hand and a dozen of his own men did the same. Galvanized by Falco and Curio's protective actions, they formed a screen around their prince as he struggled to his feet.

Albus's long hair dragged through the bloody mud. He now cradled his wounded side and red spit hung from his lips.

Varro saw the horn and strap slipping from his arm, and he released Albus to grab it. Then he blew a long note into the roiling chaos of battle.

The prince whirled on him, still kneeling in the dirt. His teeth were clenched and stained red with his own blood. But the momentary fury eased, then he lowered his head and accepted Varro had signaled the retreat.

He handed the prince to his men to carry, then joined Falco and Curio to strengthen the rear guard. Extracting themselves proved a bitter struggle. Diorix had nearly encircled them. Given that Varro had assumed both sides evenly matched, this surprised him. Diorix had either found reinforcements or the interrogations had yielded poor information.

Yet they shoved back the closing trap, and Prince Albus stumbled along with his men toward their gates. Diorix never showed himself, at least as far as Varro knew. But his commands were felt, and the enemy did not pursue them. Instead, they turned to their own burning camp.

Once within the walls, Albus was met by king and queen along with the hundreds of noncombatants come to see if their loved ones had returned.

It was a confused scene and the Romans were set apart from it. Albus's mother fussed over his wounds while he pushed her away. The incongruous shouts of joy at safe reunions grated against the anguished cries of loss and the desperate calls of those still searching for their kin.

Varro thought to report King Bilistages. But without a victory to celebrate, he was surly and curt. He dismissed them without another thought and turned to his own people. In the end, they returned to their rooms to clean up and dress any scratches and bruises.

They stripped off their armor and set it on racks. Each tried to daub out as much blood and skin from the links as they could. Varro's helmet had lost another black feather, leaving him with a single one that he just plucked out.

Falco laughed at this, and Varro, twirling the feather in his fingers, joined him. He set his aside.

"We'll keep it to replace yours."

"This is weird," Curio said while trying to examine a bruise on his shoulder. "I've never just gone from a battle to my bed."

"The king doesn't want to see Varro," Falco said. "It'll remind him he was wrong to ignore his advice."

Varro had stripped to his tunic, which was unsullied but for sweat under the arms, then sat on his bed. His eardrums still throbbed with the noise of battle. He rubbed his temples in thought.

"Diorix was reinforced. Somehow, without us knowing. We don't even have scouts, it would seem, or else the king is so absorbed with his thoughts that no one is doing these basic tasks."

Falco gave a wry smile, then sat on his bed. "It's because he only calls us in when he wants someone to agree with his plans. If he would let us run things, we'd have men probing their lines all the time."

Varro shrugged. "We'd try to learn more about our enemy before attacking, that is certain. And Albus's inspired decisions don't help."

He hinted at the last-minute decision to burn the camp rather than sneak up on it. The ploy had worked as a distraction when Varro tried to lead them through the lines. But as an attack, all it did was reveal their presence in the bright light of the fire.

"I think he's jealous of you," Falco said. "He was impressed with the fire distraction you used."

"I don't see why he should be." Varro let his hands drop into his lap. "No matter now. Once we count the dead from tonight, I think it will become clear we have to rely on the strength of our walls from now on. Just as I had thought Diorix had spent his last chance at victory, I think we just did the same."

"Great," Falco said. "You mean you can't even come up with one of your mad schemes? We've just got to wait until Cato gets around to remembering us?"

Varro nodded, then began rubbing his temples again. When he closed his eyes, he only saw ghosts of the blazing fires and fighting shadows from tonight's battle.

"He never sent either of these letters," Curio said.

"What?" Varro raised his head and saw Curio holding both versions of his letter to Consul Cato. "I suppose you're right. He did read the letters. I remember that."

"He just handed them back to me," Curio replaced them on the desk. "He was to choose one to send."

"Wait," Falco said. "I thought he decided he wouldn't send anything?"

"He didn't make it clear," Varro said. "But I thought he would at least send another request. He'll need to now if he wants to attack again."

"But you'll keep him from making the same mistake again, right?" Falco now shifted to lying on his bed, setting both hands under his head.

Varro nodded, but now his mind started turning on these letters. He sat a long while, staring at the table where Curio had set them while he picked mud from between the hobnails of his sandals.

"There's that look again," Falco said from outside Varro's narrow vision. "You're thinking of a plan."

"We can't return to the consul. He'll not send aid unless he is finished with the rebels."

"Not to mention he'll flog us to death for breaking orders," Falco said. "That's an important detail."

Varro held up a hand so Falco would not interrupt his thinking. "King Bilistages already sent his only son to beg for help. Sending a note from us in the hands of a lesser messenger won't help. That message has to come from someone he respects and trusts. Someone who could persuade him to send aid."

His mind turned on this thought as he kept his hand up. Curio set his sandals down, then rested his chin in both palms to await Varro's conclusion.

Falco cleared his throat.

"Well, how are we going to get the ghost of Cato's father to deliver a message on our behalf?"

"Don't be foolish. I know who we could help us, someone who has the trust and respect of the consul. Centurion Longinus."

"The First Spear?" Curio asked.

"Exactly," Varro said, snapping his fingers. "I will go to him and explain our situation."

"I remember," Falco said, sitting up from his bed. "Seemed you made a sort of friend out of him? But do you think he'll stick his neck out for us? Besides, won't Cato wonder how Longinus knows we need help?"

Varro sighed, then slouched down. "I'm not sure if Longinus will help. But he is the only one I can think of who might have a chance. Cato clearly admires a good fighting man, and only the best soldier becomes First Spear. He has as much sway as a tribune."

"Which isn't much," Curio said. "Consuls do whatever they want."

"Cato is a bastard," Varro said. "But I believe he will listen to those he respects."

"Which was never us," Falco said. "He made that clear from the first day. Even so, Longinus might make a plea for us, but Cato will know we broke our orders to remain in place."

Shaking his head, Varro picked up one of Curio's letters. "I'll have to contact Centurion Longinus in secret. I have to be sure of his aid and the consul's response before I return. But the First Spear need only say he received this letter from a desperate agent of King Bilistages's."

"A small bit of lying," Falco said. "I guess it'll pass. As long as this Longinus fellow isn't as tight as our old First Spear, Fidelis."

"I don't know him well enough. But I have a good feeling about him. He can help, if anyone can."

"And if he can't?" Curio returned to cleaning his sandals.

"At the same time I return to camp, Bilistages must send word to his daughter's tribe. At least for mediation, if not outright aid." Varro clasped his hands behind his neck. "Otherwise, without relief from the outside, we can only hope to outlast Diorix."

Falco patted his stomach with a hollow sound. "Supply is already tight. There are many people here. We will not last for long."

"I fear the king's impatience," Varro said. "I hope this will stay his hand a while longer."

Curio looked up from cleaning his sandals. "At least until Diorix sends more fire arrows over the wall."

Varro hissed at the possibility. "It depends on his goals. If he wants to take and hold the land, and claim the people, he will not achieve it by burning everyone to death. But if he seeks nothing but destruction, it could become our doom."

Falco flipped his hand at the thought. "Diorix has been mostly posturing. He wants the people to rise against Bilistages. Totally humiliate him and take his lands. That's what he wants, not a pile of ashes."

The thought silenced all of them. For Varro, he could see that rebellion as a distinct possibility once starvation took root. Instead of shooting flaming arrows over the walls, all Diorix would need to do is offer food and forgiveness to the starving people. None could resist that sort of temptation, and the alliance with the Ilegertes would collapse.

It was such gloomy thoughts that occupied the remainder of the night. Even through stone walls the cries of anguished families reached him. His sleep was troubled, and when he awakened the next morning to a summons from the king, he felt more tired than he had before going to bed.

Albus stood beside his father, his side wrapped in a stained bandage. Scores of minor cuts crossed his face and hands. He did not smile at their arrival, as was his custom, but stood rigid behind his father's throne. The balding sycophants were ever-present, and they glared at the Romans' entrance.

After presenting themselves, they endured more glaring until Bilistages spoke in a thin voice.

"You were to deliver victory, yet brought us nothing but more loss."

Varro blinked, then looked to Albus who set his pale eyes at the far end of the hall. He then tuned to Falco and Curio, who seemed equally dumbfounded.

"Don't look elsewhere for blame," Bilistages said. "Where was your profound tactical advice last night? You had us attack in darkness, like thieves robbing a farm. Then you called the retreat while we were surging to victory."

"We were becoming enveloped, your highness."

Varro's hands shook and his breath felt like fire, but he knew better than to argue with a king.

"Albus was pushing through to the heart of Diorix's camp. Between the fires and his death at my son's hands, we would have broken the siege. But your rash actions cost us victory."

"No," Falco's voice boomed out. "We saved your son's life, which he seemed bent on throwing away."

"I was not in danger," Albus said, his pale eyes brightening at the challenge. "I would not have fallen had you not interfered. You tripped me, then stole my horn to sound the retreat."

"Cowards!" Bilistages's voice boomed across the hall, and now he rose from his chair. "And liars! When Rome makes a promise, it is as good as a promise whispered to the wind. What a fool I have been and what a price I have paid to hear these windblown lies from you Romans."

The sycophants behind the king joined in with their own curses, the words meaningless to Varro but their curled lips and narrowed eyes spoke clearly of their disgust.

"Your highness." Varro straightened his back and met the king's glare. "There was much confusion last night. But I assure you, I acted with the best intentions for your people."

"You acted to save yourselves!" Bilistages slapped the back of his chair with his aged hand. His milky eye seemed to glow with ire. "I will not hear your excuses. Too many of my warriors are dead with nothing to show for it. I have suffered my last insult from Rome."

Bilistages looked to his followers, his son, and the few men hiding from his wrath in the shadows of his hall. He spoke in his native tongue, hard and final words that drew deep nods from his listeners. Then he turned to Varro.

"The Ilegertes have no more need for you. As of this moment, all hospitality is withdrawn. Gather your possessions by the south gate. I hereby banish you from my lands. The Ilegertes stand alone."

18

Varro stood behind the south gates where not long ago he had entered as a welcomed savior. Men watched from the walls, their faces expressionless. Their hair flew in the wind of this overcast, blustery day. Neither Albus nor the king escorted them out. Upon the pronouncement of their banishment, they were under the constant guard of five spearmen.

None of them spoke, either to each other or to their guards. They collected their possession in stoic silence and followed their handlers to the gates. They now faced ejection into the enemy lines, with all the peril that entailed. Diorix's men still watched both gates.

So they drew up their shields, tightened their helmets, and checked their swords. Their guards regarded them with a mixture of pity and resentment. But none hesitated when Varro nodded toward the exit. The guards slid aside the bar and opened the gates wide enough for one man at a time to step outside.

Varro exited first, sliding through the narrow gap to come to the ravaged remains of Diorix's ram. The Ilegertes had wisely left it in place as an impediment to another attempt. Someone had dragged away bodies from both sides, but the ruins of battle remained in place.

He hid from sight behind the blackened ram as both Falco and Curio slipped out. Then the gates creaked and thudded shut. He heard the bolt drawn back into place.

"Fuck." Falco crouched beside Varro, as did Curio. "No friends anywhere."

All three peered out from where they hid behind the ram. Varro chanced a look back up at the walls, and none of the Ilegertes looked down on them. For now, Diorix's men had not spotted them.

"The moment we step out of here, we're caught. There's no cover in sight."

"Too bad we can't join Diorix," Curio said. "It'd be a pleasure to burn Bilistages out of his home."

Varro surveyed their options. The long slopes leading down to Diorix's lines lacked any concealment. The moment they stepped from behind the ram they would be seen. Their enemies did not appear especially vigilant, but their bulky outlines would identify them, and they would soon after become Diorix's prisoners.

"Under the ram," he said. "We'll hide here until dark. Then we'll have a better chance of cutting across those lines. They're not too deep."

They stuffed beneath the ruins with care. Varro looked again to the Ilegertes on the wall, fearful that their curiosity or misplaced rage might cause them to reveal their hiding place. One man watched, resting his cheek in his palm, but no other cared what happened once they were beyond the walls.

Inside the ruined ram shelter smelled of ash and death. The ram cover had collapsed, but still provided a screen that kept them hidden from Diorix's lines. They pressed together amid the tangled ropes, burned wood, and other debris. Falco nearly had his cheek against Varro's and Curio had wedged himself inside, keeping his shield between them and himself.

"We're going to sit like this until nightfall?" Falco whispered. "I either become crippled after this, or the stench of your breath is going to kill me first."

"Better die from my breath than become Diorix's prisoner." Varro shifted to relieve something pressing into his back. "Try to sleep now. We will have plenty to do after dark."

Pressed into the wreckage, Varro found no comfort. But boredom and weariness helped him doze. Both Falco and Curio snored at times, and he sat listening to birds and the distant sounds of camp life from the bottom of the slope.

At one point, Curio shifted and struggled behind his shield, prompting Varro to whisper what he was about.

"Practicing my letters," he whispered in reply. "I'm writing on the back of my scutum. You weren't joking about it, were you?"

Varro gave a stifled laugh. "That is determination, Optio. I like it."

Yet after a short amount of scratching Curio cursed under this breath and jerked back.

"I spilled the ink. Well, there's not much left now."

Falco awakened from his snoozing. "What's that? Something wet on my toes?"

Varro could not recall a more uncomfortable and boring day. Yet the time passed and the soothing darkness of night arrived at last. They peeled out from beneath the ram. They remained crouched to the ground and Varro looked between the walls and the line of enemies now defined by points of orange campfire light. No one seemed aware of their presence.

"What is the plan?" Falco asked. "I don't think we can do the fire trick again."

Varro strained into the darkness. The lines were heaviest by the gates, where any attempt to sally out had to be met in force.

But he suspected the western and eastern walls would be lightly guarded.

They hugged the walls where darkness clung as they followed it east. They clutched their bronze helmets under their tunics to prevent stray reflections. Their shields, however, were each of a different color and freshly painted and might reveal them. So they rushed in hopes the enemy was more concerned with his cooking fire than activity from the fort.

Once they settled in the shadows of the eastern wall, they found no campfires at the bottom of the slope.

"But that doesn't mean there aren't lookouts," Falco said. "We can't expect to just walk out of here."

Varro set his shield down and shifted his helmet to one side. He stroked his hands across the long grass, then smiled.

"We won't walk. We'll ride."

"Nice," Falco said. "You've got horses under your tunic?"

"We'll ride our shields to the bottom. Remember doing that as a kid? I used an old barrel my father had discarded. We would ride it down a grassy hill near the farm."

"Well, we had different childhoods," Falco said.

"The grass is thicker here," Curio said. "We should be able to do it."

"And the ground is more even," Varro added. "Not like the churned-up mud by the gates."

Varro set his scutum flat in the grass, then flattened out atop it. He shoved off, but did not travel far. Falco sniggered behind him. But Varro shoved again, and this time his shield launched halfway down the slope before it slowed to a halt. Curio followed him down.

After one last shove, he glided to the bottom where the grass leveled out to a short field leading to dark trees. Here is where Varro's cheerful mood ended, for he looked into the darkness of an inhospitable woods.

Both Curio and Falco rode down the slope to join him. He was about to speak when Curio rushed to place a hand over his mouth. All remained still, and Curio pointed toward the tree line.

Two vague shapes moved there, faces gray in the moonlight that fought against the heavy clouds above. Varro's skin tingled. His first imagining was forest spirits emerging from the dark to spread their evil. But more practically, they were Diorix's men on watch.

"I wish I had a pilum," Falco whispered. "They'd have no chance. But if we stand up, they'll see us and sound the alarm."

"It's a brief run," Varro said. "We've no other choice. It's still wide-open field here."

They crept forward, counting on the enemy's inattention. It seemed they argued over something held between them. It was an excellent distraction, allowing them to close the distance unseen.

Then Varro leaped up, Curio and Falco beside him, and the three rushed at their enemies.

The men screamed in surprise, a sharp noise that echoed through the woods. But Varro and Falco both plowed them to the ground, and Curio followed behind to run them through. They cried out in agony, but they did not sound an alarm. The violence had ended as abruptly as it had started.

"That was well done," Falco said. "What were they fighting about?"

"A wine skin," Curio said as he bent to lift it from between the dead men.

The horn blared jagged and bright in the darkness. It broke clear from Varro's left, jolting him ahead before he even recognized the threat. The others tucked their heads down, Curio dropping the skin. It wasn't until Varro heard the rasp of metal against a scabbard that he collected himself.

"Into the trees!"

Whatever he felt about the woods, he feared it less than being overrun by hidden enemies. He had heard more than half a dozen swords drawn, but as yet saw no one. As fast as they could, they bolted forward. Thanks to their youth, they were not completely out of marching condition. They were already at the tree line before the enemy shouts started chasing them.

"Eight of them," Curio called from behind.

"Head east to the shore. We meet there, then follow the coast to camp." Varro knew their flight would end in separation. So he set a rally point while they were still together.

Then he burst into the trees. He kept his scutum forward, blasting away dead bushes and bending saplings down. It would create a clear trail, but he knew of no other way. He was no woodsman.

The other two vanished into the dark clutches of the woods. The trees now seemed to come to life and fold around him. Angry shouts echoed among the black trunks. These came from behind and before him. He had miscalculated the enemy's vigilance and now paid for it.

He sped through the night-shrouded woods. His greaves protected his legs against the lashing branches he smashed through. His helmet, now back on his head, protected against the branches that clapped against it. Some he could see coming, and others he could not. Once more Fortuna guided his steps, as he had not yet collapsed over a hidden stone or broken his ankle in a ditch.

It seemed all of Diorix's men were on his trail now. He heard their lusty calls and the thunder of their pursuit. It seemed some even laughed.

Sweat blinded him, but moonlight now failed to breach the canopy. He was running blind. Trees grew denser, as if they were closing ranks on his passage. The enemies in pursuit were now atop him. He would have to make a stand. But this was not the place for it. He was blind here, and while his enemies would be as well, they would also only need to jab at him to overcome him.

So he pushed ahead.

Then the forest spirts attacked.

They seized him by the collar of his mail shirt, dragging him backward. He screamed in terror, and his enemies shouted in glee at this. Such was his fear that he might have blacked out for an instant. The spirits had such power that they flung him back as if he were only a child.

He did not land on hard earth, but plunged into a gully, rolling and crashing among the stones and bushes lining the slope, until he splashed into a stream.

Facedown in the cold water, he felt it rushing from his toes to his face. He had a terror of the water, as he had twice nearly drowned in his armor. The same horror engulfed him now, but he realized this was a shallow creek and even lifting his head he pulled out of it.

Instinctively, he rolled into the shadow of the gully wall. He was now swathed in mud and his shield lost. His helmet rested on the bridge of his nose. Shoving it back up, it still availed him no sight. Only the tiniest gleams of a tiny moon shined on the flowing water. Otherwise, he hovered in darkness.

From above, he heard his pursuers. They too had to be blind. So he held his breath and huddled in the mud, pulling his knees to his chest and wishing he could vanish. His heart thudded so hard he could feel his tunic jumping in time to it.

A stone rolled down the slope, splashing into the gully. Someone above commented on this, and a murmur of voices lingered while Varro hid. But soon they moved off, either following a misleading trail or having surrendered to the dark.

No matter what, if they returned with torches they would follow his trail to this spot. He could not remain. So after what felt like hours, but might have been far less, he extracted himself from the mud. His joints ached from all the strange positions he had held throughout the day. For all the terror of it, the run through the woods had relieved his stiffness. But now, having crouched in cold mud for so long, he again felt as limber as an old man.

The woods now seemed quiet compared to the earlier chaos. The gurgling of the creek was the loudest sound. Every hushed crack and crunch from the surrounding trees set his teeth on edge. What made those noises, he wondered? No matter, he had to get away so that he left no trail for Diorix's men to follow.

He reasoned the creek must lead him to the sea. So he followed the flow of it, walking through the water so he would leave no prints. His scutum was lost, though he still carried weapons, armor, and helmet. But he possessed nothing else. Already hungry from rationing food, he would be doubly pressed to care for himself in the woods. He would last until reaching the Roman camp, but then he could not draw rations as he normally would.

One problem at a time, he thought. He at last felt he had gone far enough in the water that he could follow the creek from its narrow bank. At points the canopy opened up to reveal the moon. When this happened, he found he had naturally emerged from the gully. But he did not know where he was. It seemed to him the edge of the woods must be near. It was not a deep wood, but a long and thin barrier between Bilistages's fort and the grassy plains that yielded to the coast. Thus far, everything seemed much as it had been, all twisting and dark trees joined by their armlike branches.

To continue ahead would only invite greater separation from Falco and Curio. All along the creek, he had been listening for human sounds but heard none. Instead, he heard the inexplicable cracks and rustling all around and he feared forest spirits stalked him. Though they might have saved him from capture by flinging him into a hiding place, he wondered if ultimately they did it so he would remain their prisoner and not Diorix's.

So he made a small, pathetic camp in the driest place he could find. He warded himself against evil as best he could, spitting and making signs all around himself. But these were temporary measures, and any spirit could catch him off guard.

This made sleep impossible. Exhausting as his flight through the woods had been, every time he closed his eyes he heard the wailing of the dead who wandered between the forests of the world, never finding their way out. His head would snap up and eyes stare into impenetrable darkness. But he was always alone. Only once the sun stained the eastern horizon did he find rest.

He awakened after only a few hours, and the sun was now fully risen. His stomach rumbled and his joints protested the contortions of the prior day, having been aggravated with chilly dampness all night. Varro felt a strange pressure in his nose and realized he might have fallen ill. No matter how he felt, he crawled to his feet and took stock of his situation.

Diorix would likely believe Bilistages had sent more messengers out during the night. He might think of capturing the messenger and searching the woods. In this case, Varro had been lucky to evade capture. But what if Falco and Curio hadn't? It seemed just as likely that one or both of them had escaped as was having been caught. In fact, the lack of any further pursuit during the night hinted one of them had been captured.

In the end, he could not know what happened. They had scattered to make it both harder to be captured and to ensure at least one of them could reach the Roman camp. But now Varro found himself more worried for his friends than for preserving the Ilegertes' alliance.

The only way to know their fate was to push east to the coast, and hope they reached the same spot. He had meant to indicate the cove where they had expected Tribune Galenus to land his men. Hopefully, they intuited the same place.

He pressed east into the sun and finally emerged to the fields of grass that rolled away like gentle waves to the horizon. As he proceeded, he smelled the salt air and saw the gulls against a bleak sky. Soon, he heard the waves and by noon had touched the Iberian shore.

He was alone. Worse still, he did not recognize this shore. Not that he precisely remembered the way he had come, but the huge black stones that grew out of the sea here created rough waters he would certainly recall. Therefore, he judged he had emerged south of the cove and so headed north once more.

But by late afternoon, he reached that sheltered landing spot and still found no one. Nor had he found any sign of human activity.

Seagulls squawked from tall boulders streaked with their waste. They turned their heads side to side at him as if judging this intruder to their homes.

Varro staggered to one boulder, causing several gulls to flee screaming into the sky. He slouched down against it, his mail shirt scraping the stone.

Were Falco and Curio captured, or had they just missed each other?

He rested his head in his hands and closed his eyes. He did not know what to do.

19

Varro scoured the beach and grass by the cove for any signs of activity. He was no tracker and anything but the most obvious signs would elude his detection. To his limited abilities it seemed Falco and Curio had not passed this way, though closer to the woods he found animal tracks and the trail they had followed to the Ilegertes' fort. They would not have taken care to cover their passage, and so he concluded they had not come this way.

If they were captured, he could do nothing for them. If they were lost, he likewise had no help for them. While it seemed impossible that they could have become separated, he chose to believe it rather than the alternative of their being captured. He also considered both outcomes were possible, with bigger and slower Falco captured and the more nimble Curio evading that fate.

He thought of the wailing voices from his dreams and shuddered. Maybe they were better off as Diorix's captives than as wanderers among the trees.

He had to push ahead, regardless.

Until now, his thoughts had been all for survival and linking up with Falco and Curio. Since that now seemed impossible, he settled once more in the grass by the cove to plan his next step.

Consul Cato had not given the order to return to camp and had not indicated what they should do if banished. The thought of that cold ejection and Albus's blank stare filled him with an anger that he wrestled aside only after a series of imagined curses at the two men. In the end, however, he realized Bilistages needed someone to blame who was not his son. From now on, their fate was their own.

Returning to his dilemma, Cato would not send help, as he had already showed from his blatant lie. He would also celebrate any ill fate that Falco and Curio met. So Varro could not count on him for aid there. That left him with his original plan to contact Centurion Longinus.

Whether he was part of Servus Capax, he seemed interested in friendship with Varro. If he would take serious risks to aid him was an entirely different matter. The First Spear had nearly as much authority as a tribune, and in Cato's legion probably even more so. He could detach men to help. Not the full three thousand which Albus demanded. Varro could achieve much with as little as a century or even fewer soldiers.

He would have to bring his highest charm and reasoning skills to persuade Centurion Longinus. Aiding Varro would be against all his rank stood for, but if he could be convinced doing so served a higher purpose for Rome, then he might be persuaded.

If this failed, Varro would be alone to help the Ilegertes and determine what had happened to his friends, not necessarily in that order.

Again his stomach rumbled and he looked toward the sea, wondering if the gods might send him fish to eat. It conjured up a vision of Neptune driving so many fish to shore that they leaped out into Varro's hands. The ridiculous thought made him shake his head in quiet laughter.

Then he caught sight of something unusual.

He had come higher up the cove and the slope in his search for signs of his friends. Toward the water, more tall gray stones served as resting spots for gulls. Some of these stones were far back from the surf, and Varro now noticed something flat and curved laying in the blue shade of one.

It looked like a scutum shield.

Leaping out of the grass, he rushed to the shore and found the shield obscured in the grass.

"Curio!" He shouted the name as if embracing the man himself. His shield lay facedown and wedged into the base of the stone. Along the top edge of the wood interior, Varro saw the childlike script where Curio had practiced his letters. Ink splatter showed where he had spilled his small pot.

But in the center, in bolder script, he had written a message. Varro read it aloud.

"No one here. Enemies in the woods. Returning to camp. Meet there."

Varro laughed, picking up Curio's shield and patting off sand and grass from the edges.

"Good man! Not the best composition, but it serves." He laughed again and set the scutum against the rock. He understood why Curio had abandoned it now. He would not only want to travel light but also needed to hide himself from both friend and enemy alike. The scutum was an amazing piece of war gear, but it was ill-suited to tasks requiring any measure of stealth.

Varro drew his pugio, then scratched a note under Curio's bolder one.

"Falco, follow us to camp." He read the simple message, then scratched his initials under it. The wood was hard and the carving shallow. But it was roughly done, and if Falco found this scutum, he wouldn't fail to see the splinters of the message.

Now Varro traveled with purpose and lengthened strides. Curio had a head start, but Varro doubted he would do anything more than hide in waiting for either Falco or himself to arrive. He did not possess the drive or initiative needed to be a centurion, even if he became literate. Perhaps after time as an optio in active command, he would develop those qualities. But for today, it meant he would delay meaningful decisions until he was certain no one else would make one for him.

After the burst of energy at his discovery faded, his pace flagged and his empty stomach reminded him he had not eaten in a day. He had gone longer without food, but he needed either wine or fresh water to sustain him. He regretted not filling his skin in the creek, but his thoughts had been addled. Now a burning thirst also plagued him. The vastness of the gray ocean seemed to mock him now.

Yet by nightfall he found freshwater enough to slake his thirst and refill his skin. He rested a short while, but pressed on during the night as the moon was full and bright. Expecting Curio over every rise, he never found him or any sign of his passing. He searched even when he thought he was simply focused on following the coast.

By the end of the third day, he saw the ordered lights from the Roman camp.

Despite what he felt about Cato, the sight of the camp nearly brought him to tears. It symbolized order and civilization. While the Ilegertes were noble and proud, and built a powerful fortress in stone, they were imitators of Rome and Carthage before them. Spread out before him was a camp laid out logically in the strategically best location for military operations. Thousands of soldiers lived disciplined, ordered lives in neat rows of hide tents. None of these Iberian tribes would stand against that, not for long, at least.

It took more than an hour to find Curio, despite a paucity of hiding places. In the end, he whispered to Varro from the shadows among a stand of trees. They rushed together, embracing as old friends while trying to keep silent.

"You got my note?" His youthful face, now full of scruffy beard, was bright with the moonlight.

"I did, and it was well written, Optio."

"Finally, some real reason to write." Curio held out the bronze ink pot. "It's empty now. But I'm keeping it as a memory of this crazy night.'"

"I left Falco a note, too."

Curio cocked his head. "Why did you do that?"

"For the same reason you left me one."

"Didn't I say he was with me?" Curio looked toward the camp. "He's down there trying to find a way to reach Centurion Longinus. Seems some of his former recruits drew guard duty and he's trying to work through them."

"Your note said 'no one is here.'" Varro shook his head. "That means you did not find me or Falco."

"I meant you weren't there. Falco and I met up after we lost our pursuers. You led them all on a good chase away from us."

Varro sighed. "Well, it didn't matter to what I needed to do. Really, Falco should've read that note and made it clearer. It would've saved me a few days of worry."

"He did read it."

"Then Jupiter save us if we survive long enough to take the consul's test."

They both stepped into Curio's hiding place among the trees and watched the distant camp. "How long has Falco been gone? And did you get any food?"

Curio grunted. "Nothing but a single rabbit I trapped. We had to go so far from camp to cook it we used up all the strength we took from it. Stringy little thing, too. Falco, he's been gone for over an hour. He didn't know when he'd return, but I've been watching. I figure if he was turned in, there'd be some commotion. But I've not seen anything."

Varro shifted from crouching to sitting. "We had coins in our packs once. They'd have been handy bribes for poor soldiers. I wonder if Diorix found them when he scattered everything all over the grass?"

"All this shit we're going through is because that one crazy Iberian didn't get the wife he wanted. I can't wait to kill him." Curio mocked strangling him. "And we've only seen him once. I wouldn't even know who he was if I found him."

"Then you'll have to strangle every Iberian surrounding Bilistages."

They shared a chuckle and settled into waiting for Falco. The camp seemed at peace, but he doubted Falco's arrest would create a noticeable stir. That would be like dropping a rock into the ocean given the size of the camp. They endured the silence, broken only by Varro's growling stomach, for what seemed another hour before Falco's distinctive shadow loomed up from the folds in the earth. He jogged at a crouch the final distance to the trees, making a noisy and clumsy entrance and bumping into Varro's shoulder.

"You found us," he said, his smile bright in the shadow. He sat beside them. "And in perfect time, too. I've got a message to First Spear Longinus. But now I owe a few denarii; nothing a rich man like me can't afford."

Curio leaned in and patted Falco's back. "I'm surprised they took your promise. I'd not do anything without the silver in hand."

"They're still young," Falco said with a cool smile. "And impressed by a centurion on an assignment so secret that not even their own officers or the tessarius can know about it."

"So when can I meet with Centurion Longinus?" Varro shifted closer to Falco to also pat his shoulder.

"He'll come here tonight," Falco said, looking back over his shoulder. "The boys at the west gate know what to expect."

Varro shook his head. "How much did you promise to pay them for that?"

"Three months' pay to each of them." Falco patted a nonexistent purse at his hip. "I'll give it to them out of my pay if I have to. But I figured we could split the cost three ways. It's only fair, and you all have the coin for it."

They traded whispered barbs about Falco spending their money, how much it would cost to replace their lost shields, and other costs that once would've crippled their finances but now no longer mattered. To Varro, this sort of good-natured teasing proved the strength of their bonds. It was their ability to joke together no matter what adversity they had to endure. He enjoyed the respite from fear and hunger that had dogged him to this moment.

Once they settled into quiet, they watched the camp for another hour. At last, a stout shadow separated from the natural dips in the land. This had to be Longinus. He looked across his shoulders, then toward the trees. When he drew close enough, Varro called his name as loudly as he dared. While the camp was too far for hearing, he remained wary.

Longinus spent long moments peering into the bushes before he joined them. Varro was struck that his memory of the centurion was not as crisp as he thought. The white scar on his face was unforgettable for knowing the cause of it. But he had forgotten the thick pad of black stubble that darkened his face and his stout size. Seeing him in person reminded Varro that the First Spear was essentially a stranger. Yet he had come, and at significant risk to himself.

Unless he planned to turn them in to Consul Cato.

"The three of you are like ghosts," he said. "I didn't see you until you gave yourselves away."

"Lots of practice, sir," Falco answered. "Looks like Centurion Varro was able to catch up. We're all here."

"Thank you for meeting with us, sir," Varro said, and Curio agreed. "I know you can't be away long. So I'll come to the point."

Longinus's smile faded to a concerned frown. "I know the task you were given, and if you are seeking me out in private, then it you must have desperate need."

"We do," Varro said. He shuffled forward in the crowded spaces behind bushes and thin trees. "The promised soldiers never made it to the Ilegertes. We have guided them as best we know how, but they have been defeated at every turn. Their supplies have been sabotaged, sir, and their people are considering surrender or worse."

Longinus lowered his head and rubbed the back of his neck.

"Those soldiers were disembarked a few hours after you left with the emissaries. It was all a ruse to send them away with false hope."

Varro widened his eyes as if surprised and hoped it seemed so. Of course, he had already guessed as much long ago.

Curio clapped his hands together with a light puff. "It's just like we—"

"We feared they had been intercepted." Varro drove his elbow into Curio's side and hoped the First Spear did not notice. "Or else they had been called to a greater need. I'm certain Consul Cato had good reasons."

Longinus lifted his head and gave a bemused smile. But he offered nothing more. Varro continued.

"We cannot let the Ilegertes fall. We will lose a firm ally, one we will need to help rebuild trust among the other tribes once the rebellion is defeated. Worse still, if the Ilegertes people depose their king and join the rebellion, we might have an even harder time taming these Iberians. This will only reinforce the belief that Rome is an unworthy ally. It would also force us to subdue an entire population. Tying up our legions when those resources would be better spent meeting the threats to the east."

"You are well aware of Rome's needs," Longinus said, his quizzical smile unchanged. "You speak like a consul."

"It's only because I served so long in Macedonia, sir." Varro tried to shift so that his pugio might be better exposed. But Longinus did not look down. "The Seleucids are certain to make trouble soon, as are some factions of the native Greeks. We cannot become distracted in Iberia or we'll cede an advantage to our eventual foes. Therefore, even if the Ilegertes seem unimportant today, their impact on the future may be far larger than their size suggests."

"Angry words spread like fire," Longinus said, stroking the thick stubble on his chin. "But words of praise never leave the atrium. My father told me this."

Falco now leaned in. "He was wise, sir. That fire is already spreading. When the king ban—"

"Sent us to beg aid once more," Varro cut in, speaking loudly enough that his voice echoed into the night. "Yes, when he sent us to make a final request, he was clear that his grip on the people was only so strong. They are not used to rationing, and their warrior culture means some men lay bigger claims to what food remains. It is a tentative situation, sir."

"I agree," Longinus said, looking between the three of them. "And you want me to intercede with the consul on your behalves."

Varro sat back, as did the others. While they had not rehearsed this moment, Varro at least felt they seemed at last united in their approach to the First Spear. They shared sheepish looks, as if unsure of what to do next. No one spoke, and Longinus tilted his head back at last.

"Ah, yes, you cannot return unless specifically recalled. I remember that from the consul's brief. He was clear about it, particularly to Tribune Galenus."

"Just so, sir." Varro again leaned forward, putting on a hopeful smile. "I could think of no one else I could trust except you. At least no one who would understand the complete situation we are facing and the consequences of failure."

Again, he twisted to bring his pugio forward. Even though it was dark, he hoped Longinus would notice the stylized owl's head inlaid in silver on the handle. But he just stared flatly at Varro.

"You overestimate me, then. I cannot order three thousand men. I have command of my maniple, but answer to my tribune. I'm not sure how I can aid you."

"I don't need three thousand men," Varro said. "I need only a century of veterans. The forces encircling the Ilegertes are about to collapse. A series of hard strikes will break them. We nearly did it ourselves but for the poor positioning of our own men."

Longinus sat back. "You are asking me to detach a full century of triarii to aid you? That is madness. We have found the rebels, and they've holed up in a fortress. We'll be attacking any day. Every man of both legions will be needed. In fact, I expect we will recall you in a few days."

"The messenger will not get through," Varro said. "We barely got out ourselves."

Shrugging, Longinus shook his head. "If we recall you, then whatever happens to the Ilegertes alliance is no longer in your hands."

Now Varro shook his head. "No sir. First, we both understand the three of us would be held accountable for that failure. But second, and more importantly, we have a duty to preserve their loyalty."

He now slapped his pugio, hoping that Longinus would recognize the symbol and understand that they both served a higher purpose. For Varro firmly believed the First Spear was also part of Servus Capax, despite carrying no symbols of membership. But the centurion only glanced down before shaking his head once more.

"I cannot do what you ask. Return to the king and tell him to be patient. We will finish the rebels soon and then may turn our attentions to his need. That is all your duty requires."

"Patience will not feed his people," Varro said. "But it will feed that fire of rebellion. All Diorix need do is offer food and shelter to anyone willing to join him, and the Ilegertes will be lost. There is no more time for patience."

They stared hard at each other across the darkness. Varro sensed the implacable will that made all First Spears the best soldiers in their legions. The muscles of his heavily shaded jaw worked as he thought and made his thin white scar dance.

"I cannot help you. Perhaps a man or two, but no more. I am sorry. I will honor your trust and give you whatever else I can give to help. But I cannot offer the men you need."

Both Falco and Curio settled back in dejection. But Varro had the past few days to think on what he would do if rejected.

"Then so must it be. I understand why you cannot give us men, and knew this request was a desperate measure. But are you truthful in your promise to help in any other way?"

Longinus sat back, his arms crossing over his broad chest.

"Tell me what you need, and then I will see if I can help.'

Varro gave a sly smile.

"First, the three of us are nearly starved. Provisions are our top need. But after that, what I will ask of you might seem both strange and impractical. Yet I will explain it all if you can grant what I ask."

Longinus's eyes lit up and he unfolded his arms. "Well, I'll be excited to know your plan. Please explain, Centurion Varro."

20

Miles from the Roman camp at the edge of the woods, Varro watched the wagon trundle across the grassy plains. It had resolved from a black spot into the complete shape of the wagon and driver. The mule drawing the cart held its head low, and the driver did little to encourage the beast to greater speed. Varro strained to see the cargo but found it hidden beneath a sun-faded black tarp.

"That's Longinus's man," Curio said. "He looks old enough to be one of the triarii."

"You've sharp eyes," Falco said, leaning against a trunk with his arms folded. "He still looks like a shadow to me."

"He's bringing what I asked for," Varro said, a warm glow spreading through his chest. "Longinus really did it."

Falco now leaned forward and drew his heavy brows together. "Still looks like fuzz to me. But there wouldn't be a wagon out this far if Longinus didn't dispatch it. I guess he was good on his word. You still think he's with Servus Capax?"

Varro shrugged and turned back from watching the wagon's

approach. "I don't know why he'd help us otherwise. But I nearly shoved my pugio up his nose and he did not remark on anything."

"But we're not supposed to give away our status," Curio said. "Maybe he's got the same orders?"

"Then if he has the same orders as us," Varro said. "He should be carrying some sign so we can recognize him. We're supposed to help out other members as we can."

"I don't know why this has to be a secret," Falco said. "It's not like the Ilegertes alliance is a surprise to anyone."

"Maybe not this time," Varro said. "But future assignments might require secrecy. We're acting in the long-term interest of Rome, not necessarily doing secret work."

"Whatever fills my purse," Falco said. "I'm a loyal Roman, no matter what we're calling ourselves."

By now the wagon had closed enough for Curio to step forward and wave both hands at the driver, who returned a crisp salute. They met him halfway to accept their delivery.

"Well, well, here are my three junk collectors." The old triarius had gray at both temples and was missing a front tooth. He had deep crow's feet, suggesting a man who laughed often. He slipped off the wagon and being dressed in his full battle gear landed with a dull thud on the grass.

"Thank you for coming at all haste," Varro said. The triarius laughed and patted the mule's flank.

"She was not up for a run this morning, but she was steady." The triarius's gap-toothed smile faded and he gestured to the wagon. "Let's have a look at the junk, then, and be sure it's to your taste."

They circled to the back of the small wagon and the triarius untied the faded tarp before casting it aside. Three large sacks sat on the bed along with bundles of straight branches. The old triarius pulled a stack of branches to the edge of the bed.

"These were harder to get than the other junk. They make fine stakes and poles. Someone is going to be angry tonight when he finds these gone."

"I hope you won't suffer for it," Varro said.

"I'm just following orders. I'm not asking why I had to collect all this and bring it to you three boys. I've been with Centurion Longinus on many campaigns. Doing what he tells me to do has kept me alive all these years. I'm sure he'll have all this covered for you."

The triarius stepped back to let them examine the rest of the cart while he unhitched the mule.

"She's not coming?" Falco asked.

"No one will miss a rickety old cart, but the pack master will have a fit if one of his mules is gone. Not even Consul Cato would be safe from him."

"But that means we're pulling the cart?" Falco looked helplessly to Varro, who smirked.

"It suits your personality. Besides, we can't carry all this into the woods."

Falco's posture of dejection brightened Varro's morning. He slapped his friend's back, then stepped into the wagon to examine the contents of the sacks. He pulled open the rope bindings and looked inside. The dull shine of bronze helmets reflected back to him.

"Is the rope and hook here?" he asked the triarius.

"In one of the bags. You've got sixty helmets, and not all of them are broken." The triarius dropped his voice now. "I wonder where the centurion got those? But it's all mostly junk. You've got some bent pila heads and all the tunics you asked for, at least what's left of them."

The triarius now led the mule around by its bridle and looked skeptically between all three of them.

"You've got everything needed for your straw man army. I am curious to see how you'll use all this junk."

Varro clapped his shoulder. "I'd be glad if you stayed."

"I've survived a lot of tight fights. But always with real soldiers, and not dummies on a stick. I'll be surprised to see you boys again if you're going to battle alongside straw men. If you do return, then be sure to share the story with me. It'll be the strangest tale I've heard in all my days with the legion."

They parted with the triarius and watched him lead the mule back toward the camp.

"You didn't say I'd have to be a mule." Falco kicked a wagon wheel. "And save your stupid jokes. This plan of yours has already ruined my mood. Having me do the work of a beast just makes me angrier."

"Maybe you want to write about it?" Curio asked with an impish smile. "You'll feel better after."

"We're all pulling the wagon," Varro said. He then shifted the sacks of broken and dented helmets that were slated to be repaired before Centurion Longinus appropriated them for Varro's plan. As he pulled the sacks higher into the wagon, he revealed a lockbox with a key inserted. "What's this?"

His question drew Curio up into the bed and Falco to look over the side. Varro turned the key and heard the rods shift and click in the lock. Opening the box, he gasped.

Curio slapped the wagon bed. "That must be over a thousand denarii!"

"Did you ask for that?" Falco said. He reached over and plucked a silver coin from the box.

"Even if I had, where would he come up with it?" Varro blinked at the mass of coins. Falco tossed his coin back on the pile with a bright chime.

"That's nice," he said. "But I'd rather have food than silver. What good will it do us in the woods?"

"This could change things for us," Varro said.

Falco's arms hung over the wagon side and he gave Varro a long-suffering look.

"Really? Who are we bribing with all that coin? Squirrels? Are we going to raise a legion of forest animals to fight against Diorix?"

"Squirrels don't need money," Curio said.

"By Jupiter's balls, Curio, I was joking."

While Curio and Falco traded barbs, Varro ran his palm across the cold, hard coins. He shut the lockbox and tuned the key, then secreted it under his mail shirt. His mind ran through a score of possibilities for using the silver.

A thousand denarii could pay a century of hastati for an entire campaign season. It would be a formidable bribe, but to whom? For King Bilistages, this was a paltry amount and unneeded during a siege. In fact, to offer it to him would be an insult at this time. So Longinus had not intended it to be used that way. Nor did it provide them with any survivability, as Falco so acidly pointed out.

But Iberians could be bought. Right now, the province was in rebellion and Rome could not be seen to buy their loyalty. It would only encourage similar extortion ploys in the future. But a small group of Iberians could be readily bought for a fortune in silver, and thereby create the century Varro had asked for.

Only he had no means to find these Iberian warriors or to communicate with them if he did. What Longinus intended for them to do with his gift eluded Varro.

"So, what are we doing with this silver?" Falco asked, ending his exchange with Curio. "We can have some exciting dice games for these stakes."

Curio mimicked throwing dice and collecting a pile of coins. Then he sat back on the wagon and scratched his head. "Why didn't Centurion Longinus say he'd give us this silver and what he thought it could do for us? Why does it always have to be a riddle?"

Varro shrugged. "Maybe he wasn't certain he could get it for us, or he had a late inspiration and just sent it along in hopes we'd understand its purpose."

"So," Curio dragged out his words and looked between the others. "Why didn't he write a letter to explain? After all, writing is so important that I'm going to be beaten to death if I can't do it."

Falco rolled his eyes. "He doesn't want anything connecting him to the silver."

"Then just don't sign the letter." Curio slapped his forehead. "Even I know that."

"This isn't a trivial amount of silver," Varro said. "So I think Falco is right. In any case, we need to get this wagon into the woods. We will think about the best use for the silver later."

They worked together to pull and push the wagon over the narrow, rugged trails. To ease Falco's shame, Varro had him push from the rear. Yet he groaned and complained just as much. Varro and Curio both pulled from the front. They made good progress for their first day, but would still need another to reach Diorix's line. That night, they ate dried and salted strips of goat meat, which Longinus provided. The meat was more than they would get on the march, but it was perfect for a stealthy meal while in hiding.

Curio stretched out under a tree and wrapped his cloak tighter. "It's too bad we've got all this stuff to start a fire, but can't enjoy one for our own camp. It's cold at night."

"A whole day pushing this wagon," Falco said. "And another one to come. This idea better work, Varro."

"It's a thin plan, I'll admit. But we've seen it work before."

Curio adjusted himself against the three, then yawned out his question. "Is anyone really going to believe they've been surrounded by a Roman century?"

"If they're panicked enough," Varro said. "We only need to

deceive a handful of men, and their reactions will fool the rest. But all our success is on you, Curio."

"I'll get back into Bilistages's hall," he said, rolling onto his shoulder and yawning again. "I won't mess up like you two and bring all of Diorix's men to chase us through the woods. I'm the real mountain ghost. Not you two giants."

"Is he insulting us?" Falco asked as he settled his own bedding for the night. "Because we can use that rope to hang him from this tree."

"No, he's stating the facts," Varro said with a chuckle. "But I've a new request of you, Curio."

"Sorry, sir, you'll have to run it by Centurion Falco first. He has so many opinions, you know."

Varro looked around at the darkening woods, and tried not to think about spending the night in it and instead focused on his plan.

"You must convince Albus to send us a guide and interpreter. That silver can buy us extra men. We need to find Bilistages's daughter and appeal to her tribe for aid and revenge. The silver will buy the men. With real warriors seeded among our dummy soldiers, Diorix will believe he has been outflanked and his destruction at hand."

Falco spread out his cloak and settled on it. "Well, he would be in that case."

"But not enough to truly break him. That is why Curio needs to deliver the message to Albus. You need to make sure he will attack when we are ready. If done right, it will shatter their flagging spirits. If we can kill Diorix during the attack, the threat will be ended for good."

"He's probably already attacked five more times since we left," Curio said. "That's all he wants to do."

"Good," Varro said. "Getting a guide out to us will be much harder. I'll give you silver to bribe someone if you must."

"We're banished," Curio said. "It's not like I can walk around town asking for help."

"We're banished until we bring hope," Varro said. "And that's what we are bringing."

They settled for the night, and Varro lay awake under his cloak, expecting yet another cold hand to grab his collar and fling him into despair. A fitful sleep overtook him deep into the night, and he awakened the next morning with his eyes heavy and crusted. Falco and Curio had already risen and had gone to refill their skins with water in a nearby stream.

By the middle of the day, they had cajoled the wagon as far into the woods as it could go and then surrendered. They made a camp on the highest ground they could find and near the stream. Curio slept while Varro and Falco worked to assemble armatures for the dummy soldiers. They chatted in low voices and constantly looked about for enemies either patrolling the woods or else foraging.

That night, they awakened Curio and huddled together in the purple gloom of twilight. Varro sat on the cart bed while the others leaned in to hear.

"Curio, here's a pouch of twenty denarii. It should buy the daring of one scout at least. He must be sent as soon as possible, tonight even. Be sure just to speak to Albus alone. King Bilistages is too consumed with grief and defeat to understand the possibility of victory."

"And Albus wants to be a hero," Falco added. "So now is his time."

Varro scratched at his beard, imagining a good shave once they handled this mess.

"Do not tell him about the dummy soldiers. He must believe we have brought him real men so it will embolden him to strike.

"Aren't you getting him real men from his sister's tribe?" Curio's youthful face still shone through his thickening beard.

"That's not guaranteed. We will weigh greed against patriotism and see what prevails. Greed is universal, and so I expect some will take enemy silver if they can justify it. Diorix has provided the justification."

"Have you thought it through?" Falco asked. "You're Roman and the enemy. Not to mention the Ilegertes are not anyone's friends these days. Maybe they'll get the idea to take your silver and try to ransom you as well. Don't let Longinus's gift interfere with your original plan."

"I understand the risk," Varro said. "But Albus has explained there is a vow of hospitality among all the tribes. Even if they are enemies of the Ilegertes, they will hear our request. They might take me prisoner, but I expect I'd be released soon. The consul is preparing his attack and will be victorious. Disorganized barbarians cannot stand in the field against Rome."

"Or you'll be killed, more likely." Falco shrugged. "It's not worth the risk just to bring back a score of warriors who won't hold if the fighting gets thick."

"They only need to enhance the appearance of a larger force. Then we can move into the camp and kill Diorix while he and his forces are distracted. Albus will shatter his front line. The siege will be broken and the Ilegertes will remain allies. Without real men to strengthen the illusion, we are relying on luck alone. I think the risk is worth it."

So they confirmed the details of their plans, even if Falco was opposed to every step. Curio was more relaxed, though he had the most dangerous assignment.

He gathered the rope and hook for scaling the fort walls, then he daubed himself with mud and dulled his mail shirt and helmet. After a round of blessings and well wishes, he set off into the dark to cross through Diorix's camp once more.

Falco and Varro both scouted the length of the enemy lines, finding no horses or animals at all. It was as thin as he expected, and he imagined Diorix and Bilistages as two old men slapping at each other. One would collapse from simple exhaustion and the other would claim victory, yet neither would land a real blow.

After they found what they believed to be Diorix's tent because of its size and the heavy guards around it, they retreated to their own camp.

They passed the night in rigid silence. Every stray noise or distant shout from the enemy camp drew both of them upright. Yet Curio seemed to have passed through the camp without notice and by now must be creeping upon Albus in his bed. Varro tried to imagine the scene.

Curio would dart from shadow to shadow, hide from passing men, then run behind before they could turn around. He scaled into a window, or else lay in wait for an open door to become unattended, then darted inside. Once there, he would again fade into shadow, hiding with eyes wide and ears straining to hear the world around him. After a long and patient wait, he would slip into Albus's room, find him abed and set a cool hand over his mouth. After some confusion, the prince would calm and the two would speak. Varro imagined the brightness of Albus's hair and the glow of Curio's face in the darkness as they discussed plans for victory over Diorix.

However, for all the vivid imagining, Varro stared ahead into darkness until sleep finally defeated him.

He dreamed of riding a horse through the blue night of a cold desert, his hair blown back and his chin free of any beard.

Then he jolted awake to something that bumped his foot.

He looked up to a dark shape looming over him.

Still on his side, Falco snored beside him.

Out of instinct, he reached for his pugio and the black shape fell into a crouch, reaching to his hip.

21

The shape hovered over Varro, already pressing down on him before he could draw his pugio. Sleep, however tenuous it had been, still weighed down his reaction even if his heart now thudded in his chest. It was just enough for the dark shape to clasp a hot, rough hand over his mouth.

"Don't cry out, Roman! I'm from Prince Albus."

The voice was deep and thickly accented, but the words were clear. Varro had half drawn his pugio and would have plunged it into his attacker's guts. But now he sheathed it with a click. The hand pressed over his nose and mouth, smelling of sweat and earth. But when Varro relaxed, so did the hand. Once the shadow withdrew, clean air flooded his nostrils again.

"You could've done that better," Varro said.

"I was to come tonight, yes?" The shadowed man tilted his head. "I had no choice but to find you asleep. My prince woke me like this, too."

"Then I am grateful you came."

Now Falco moaned and rolled aside. Varro slapped his shoulder to wake him, and he snapped up with a curse. When he saw the shadow of their visitor, he reached for his sword, but Varro slapped him again.

"He comes from the fort. Don't worry."

"I come from Prince Albus. You do not recognize me?" The shadow had been in a crouch to meet Varro's eye level. He now hopped forward and extended his head as if to display his face.

"You're a total shadow," Falco said. "Those all look alike to me."

The man leaned back. "Not even my voice is familiar? We traveled three days together, but then I spoke little. I was one of the prince's escorts to your Consul Cato. I am called Samis. You both are well known to me."

Now that the threat evaporated, Varro sat up and rolled his neck against the knot that had formed from sleeping on cold ground. Falco stretched and cursed the brevity of their sleep.

Samis now looked side to side as if expecting something, but Varro did not know what. He followed his gaze, eyes still heavy, and found only darkness.

"So Curio has reached Prince Albus and informed him of the plan?"

Samis grunted, but continued to search about. His face was consumed with shadow, and the same for Falco. It imparted a dreamlike feeling to this meeting where he conversed with unseen and unknown men.

"Then you know the plan? We must go to find the tribe of Albus's sister and gain their aid."

"You were to have sixty men with you? A full century of Rome's most experienced soldiers." The black shadow of the man called Samis continued to scan the surroundings. "But I walked all around the camp. There is no one else here."

"Well, we have soldiers of another kind." Varro smiled, then realized no one could see it. "But it is all part of our plan, which I will explain. In short, we will use the illusion of soldiers to create panic timed to Albus's attack."

Falco now stood, then picked off an armature from the stacks they had constructed earlier. He then stuck a helmet atop it, and it slid lopsidedly.

Samis stared in silence, perhaps not understanding.

"We could not get the men from our consul, but we bring the impression of sixty men. In the darkness of the woods, they will appear as actual soldiers who have come upon Diorix's line from behind. When Prince Albus drives his enemies back, they will see that they have become surrounded and break. During that time, we will slay Diorix if someone has not killed him already. The Ilegertes will be victorious."

Samis's enigmatic shadow rose up, then prodded Falco's dummy soldier and knocked the helmet around the armature.

"We have tunics and other gear to fill them out and make them appear more realistic." Varro now got to his feet, feeling like a hustler at a Roman marketplace. "Falco will prepare them while we are away. The other tribe will be seeded among these dummies, cutting down those who learn the truth. It needs only work for a short time. I've done this before, and it works. Men often see what they expect to see, especially in the confusion and panic of battle."

Samis flicked the helmet off the armature and it clanked to the hard earth.

"More Roman lies," he said. "Prince Albus sent me to count each man you were to have brought him. 'Don't return without learning all sixty names,' he said to me. 'I no longer trust Roman promises.' Well, it seems my prince was wise. All you offer are sticks and dented helmets."

Falco snatched the helmet off the ground, and it seemed he might smash it over Samis's head. Varro drew the Ilegertes scout aside and stepped before Falco.

"It is a small deception to encourage Albus to act. You have seen Diorix's lines. You just passed through them. He is at his weakest moment, a rotted wall ready to be shoved over."

But Samis had already shaken his head from the first word.

"No, you have lied again. Perhaps you work for Diorix now? Maybe you struck a bargain with him, and encourage us to foolish action so that he might defeat us in short order."

"You shit!" Falco pushed against Varro's back as if to attack Samis. "Do you know how much we are risking for you? I'm sleeping on the cold ground right on the edge of an enemy camp, preparing a trap that will probably get me killed, and you accuse me of being a traitor."

Samis turned his shadowed head aside, then spread his hands to indicate the camp.

"You promised us sixty men, but where are they? Albus will not attack. We must defend our walls and let Diorix fall apart on his own."

"And if he draws reinforcements?" Varro stepped closer, extending his arm as if to draw Samis into his confidence. "You will all starve. Come now, Samis, I begged to remain behind the walls when you attacked. And now I beg you to attack and you wish to remain behind your walls. Listen to me this time. I know your enemy, and he is not great. Whatever curse your king believes is upon him, it is not so strong that it cannot be defeated."

Samis stiffened and pulled out of Varro's hand. "What do you know of that curse? We do not speak of it lightly."

"How can it be broken?" Varro sensed an alternative approach opening. But Samis's shoulders sagged and his voice was weary.

"It cannot be broken, not even with Diorix slain. He put a doom upon the king, and so it would seem to come true. His daughter was slain, and his son defeated and wounded. One cannot fight magic with swords, Roman."

Varro stepped closer and put a friendly hand on Samis's shoulder.

"I agree, but thus far Diorix has carried the curse out. Surely, the gods work through him."

"And I agree with you, as well. That is why he goes from victory to victory and we suffer."

"I would not call him victorious," Varro said. "Not long ago, I called him defeated. We can still make that happen, but Albus must bring his men to attack. Our army of stick men will be worthless unless Diorix suffers real casualties."

Samis once more pulled back.

"Your plan is foolish. Your messenger promised sixty men, and it was a lie. I will tell my prince the truth. You are in league with Diorix now, and try to mislead us with promises of victory and false hope to lift King Bilistages's curse."

Falco had listened quietly, but now shifted behind Samis. His voice was too cool and level for Varro's liking.

"And what about Curio? What has your prince done with him?"

The shadowy form of Samis remained silent and he turned out of Varro's grip to face Falco. But he continued to look between them, and Varro noted his hands slipping toward his hip.

"He remains with Prince Albus."

Falco set his fist into the helmet he carried, as if he planned to use it to strike or shield himself.

"As a guest or captive?"

Samis did not answer, but grabbed his sword. Falco raised the helmet like shield. But Varro was the fastest of the three and pulled back Samis's sword arm.

"No matter your answer, you are in no danger with us."

"Draw that blade," Falco said. "And you'll be in danger from me. That's a promise, friend."

Whether Samis's action was a feint or failure, he relented under Varro's grip and let his arm be pulled away.

"The king banished you. Why would you believe yourselves

guests? Of course he will remain a prisoner until the king decides his fate."

Falco raised the helmet to strike, now like a cestus rather than a shield. But Varro warned him to peace, and he lowered his hand with a curse.

"You came running when you thought we could help," he said. "Your laws are flexible when it suits you."

"I will return to Prince Albus now." Samis stepped out from between them. "And tell him what I have seen, which is piles of sticks and old helmets that could not fool a blind man."

Realizing his soft approach had reached its limits, Varro hardened his voice.

"When you speak to Prince Albus, remind him that Curio is part of my delegation to you Ilegertes. As such, any violence or mistreatment of him is an attack on Rome. Further, the king may wish to revise his thoughts on banishment, for in his haste and clouded thinking he banished Rome. You seem a smart man, Samis. You have learned your Latin well, and must understand the Roman heart. Therefore, you know that Rome does not suffer insults lightly. There is still time to avoid the consequences."

Though still in shadow, he could hear the sneer in Samis's voice.

"My prince thinks your consul dislikes you."

"Whatever Consul Cato thinks of us," Varro said, stepping closer, "he must decide if you Ilegertes are loyal or part of the rebellion that will soon become little more than a bloodied and broken dream for those who survive its destruction. Be certain you help him decide in your favor, or the legions will wipe their sandals on the corpses of Diorix's men before tearing down your walls. Now return to Prince Albus and tell him to prepare for battle."

Samis did not answer, but stepped back a few paces before turning to run into the darkness.

Falco blew out a long breath, flinging the helmet aside.

"Fucking wonderful. Now Curio is a prisoner and we've got no way to help him. Why don't we join up with Diorix? At this point, he seems a better choice than these shits. Their moods change with the fucking wind."

"Diorix is a rebel, and the Ilegertes, whether or not we like it, are our allies. We've got to help them and preserve that alliance. Those were our direct orders."

Mumbling curses, Falco fetched the helmet he flung aside then dropped against a tree, vanishing into shadow.

Varro stood with darkness spreading around him, looking toward the Ilegertes fort he could not see and wished he had never known. He worried for Curio. As Albus had showed when interrogating Diorix's men, he had a cruel streak. Both he and his father were quick to lay blame for failure on anyone but themselves. Curio might become a handy scapegoat and suffer for it.

He had expected better from Albus. For all his friendly banter, he was indeed a prince and shared the same disdain for the common man as all other royals in history. This was one reason Rome ousted her kings and countenanced no more discussion of inherited royalty.

"This is my fault," he said into the darkness.

"It sure is," Falco said from his invisible spot against the tree.

"I counted on Albus's friendship."

"We don't have friends. We're Romans."

Varro rubbed his temples. "I guess I grouped him with Baku and King Masinissa. They treated us not only as allies, but as trusted friends."

"Numidia is far from here, Varro. Better leave those mountain ghost days behind."

"Of course, you're right. I thought the Numidians were barbarians, but truly that better describes these Iberians."

"So sad for us," Falco said, mocking Varro's dejected tone. "What are we going to do? That's the important question."

Varro sat on the bed of the cart and rested his hands on his knees.

"Is it too much for you to say something helpful?"

"I am being helpful. You're no good to us while you're sorry for yourself. So I'm telling you to snap out of that and become Centurion Varro again."

He exhaled a long, tired breath as his torso slumped forward. But Falco was right, and he set aside his feelings to consider their next steps. Falco allowed him to think in peace, announcing that he would close his eyes for a bit.

"Wake me up when you've solved this mess with an even more complicated plan than the first one."

"Maybe I'll just brain you and spare myself the misery of your company."

"Don't wake me too early."

It seemed Falco snored instantly, and Varro shook his head at his friend's ability to sleep under any circumstance. He crawled up into the bed of the wagon, bumping against the helmets still in the sacks. In the corner sat the box of silver. He grimaced at the thought of it, for it seemed a pointless waste. Centurion Longinus had doubtlessly gained it at some risk, but for no discernible purpose.

The hopes of finding and bribing another tribe left with Samis. Worse still, it seemed Albus had taken his defeat badly and now claimed a wound kept him from battle. Varro knew he had been cut along his ribs, and the wound could have become infected. But when he last saw the prince he did not appear to suffer much for it. it seemed more likely a fearful pride kept him from testing his skills in battle again.

With no help from the outside and now no help from the

inside, Varro could not think what he and Falco could do alone to break the siege.

He sat long in the dark, listening to an owl in the distance. The stress he felt had banished his fears of the woods. But upon hearing the owl, it reminded him that the woods held enemies both mortal and supernatural. Did Diorix's men suffer the predations of forest spirits? he wondered. They encamped at its edge, close enough for danger.

As he considered the idea, it led his mind down a clearer path of thinking. He had been considering Diorix's men, but what of Diorix himself? He was the heart of this problem, and his death would weaken if not dissolve the army surrounding the Ilegertes' walls.

Killing Diorix and fading back into the woods was all they could do.

Satisfied with the plan, he settled into a light sleep. When he awakened again, a thin light penetrated the canopy of leaves and branches. Falco was already up, having just been crouching behind a tree.

"I figured you needed sleep," he explained. "But I'm glad you're awake. It's dawn and enemies have passed this way."

Varro shot up from the bed of the cart. "I thought this was far back enough from their lines. Are you sure?"

"I sat very still and watched a man pass the bottom of this slope. Good thing he didn't think to climb this hill. I believe he was out here to set a game snare."

Cursing, Varro slid out of the cart, scratched his itching beard, and straightened his mail shirt.

"We've got to kill Diorix. That's all that's left to us now. If he dies, then the main force behind this siege ends and Bilistages might fear his curse less."

"Someone else might take his place," Falco said. "And nothing will change."

"That might be so. But will he have the same force of personality as Diorix? He drew these men together with promises of easy wealth. That has not come true, and a new leader will have a difficult time convincing them he'll do better."

Falco made a chopping motion with the edge of his hand.

"We kill Diorix and get out of sight before we're caught. Daring but simple enough for my simple mind. How about Curio?"

"When the siege is lifted, we demand his release. At this point, I don't care if we get credit for helping the Ilegertes or not. We just need to be sure of their loyalty until we can make it Consul Cato's responsibility once more."

They spent the morning relocating their campsite farther back in the woods. They piled their dummy soldiers into the cart and hauled it onto another hill where they hid it with bushes and debris. Finally, they went over their trail and tried to repair obvious signs of passage. After a rest, they donned all their war gear and headed for Diorix's lines.

Samis's passing must have been noticed, for Varro noted high activity in the woods. He heard the men calling to each other as they combed the trees, and regretted he could not understand their speech. At times enemy parties passed within yards of their hiding places. But they eluded detection and focused on scouting the layout where they had placed Diorix's tent, looking for the best entrance and exit points.

They never glimpsed Diorix himself, but did see what seemed his entourage entering and exiting the large tent at the center of camp. The lines were exceedingly thin, and Varro noted that many of the tents did not seem to have anyone inhabiting them.

"A deception of their own," Falco noted.

"I told you their forces are depleting. They only need one good setback and they'll break. If only Albus would strike now."

But nothing came from the Ilegertes walls, not that he would expect any signal. Shapes moved between towers, showing they still watched the walls. But nothing more.

They then hid away from the lines, evading those searching the trees for Samis. By nightfall, the searchers had returned to camp. Varro and Falco were ready to begin their attack.

Crawling back to the lines, they found Diorix's tent lightly guarded from the front. Only three guards were visible. Low fires provided guttering light, and true to their earlier observations many fires were outside unoccupied tents.

They looked at each other. The campfires reflected in Falco's dark eyes. With their swords loosened, they bent low and entered the camp.

22

After an entire day of planning an entrance and escape plan, Varro knew he must scratch it before even reaching the first waypoint. He gritted his teeth as he led Falco to hiding behind a lone tree in the fields behind the lines and hugged the rough bark. Whatever had set Diorix to searching the woods during the day translated to heightened vigilance during the night. The lanes they had plotted between tents were blocked off with spearmen. They had set a bonfire at the center of the camp, casting a wide sphere of golden illumination. The camp was on alert.

As he crouched behind the wide trunk, Falco piled onto his shoulder and whispered into his ear.

"We're not getting to Diorix his way. But we could cut across from over there."

Following Falco's gaze, he saw a dark area with no one standing guard. It seemed they could follow the back of the tent lines with minimal risk of being caught to get within reach of Diorix's tent.

For an instant, Varro considered calling off their attempt and waiting for a better time. But he also sensed a mood from the camp that spoke of impending action. Perhaps Diorix would attack again, and the activity observed during the day had been for the arrival of expected reinforcements. Not to mention the longer Curio remained a hostage to the Ilegertes the more likely they would make a terrible mistake.

He and Falco peeled away from the tree and followed their steps back into the woods. From there, they repositioned to take Falco's planned route. They moved with light, quick steps even in their armor. Only once did Varro's hobnails grind on stone, and both paused in fear of being heard. But this part of the camp was dark and mostly empty.

He glanced toward the Ilegertes' walls where orange torches flickered at regular points. Between them and Diorix was a wide but shallow ditch with a dirt palisade reinforced with wooden stakes. It reminded Varro of a Roman marching camp. This was a recent development since Albus's failed attack and showed Diorix's commitment to maintaining the siege.

Threading the camp in darkness, they moved with speed. But now they came within range of the bonfire. Its brightness and heat spread in a wide ball outside Diorix's tent. They hunched lower and moved with deliberation.

"How are we doing this?" Falco whispered as they both crouched shoulder to shoulder behind a weather-beaten and collapsed wagon. "We're not going in the front like we discussed."

Varro shook his head. "Is your pugio sharp? We'll cut open the back wall of the tent, get inside, and finish him. We both flee as planned."

Falco drew his dagger and replied with a sharp nod. They had planned on a light guard in place, which they could have eliminated prior to entering the tent. Now, they counted at least five men in the space outside Diorix's tent and possibly others out of sight. So they would use surprise to complete their murderous work, then each flee in different directions to reunite at their new campsite.

They waited patiently for the guards to look aside. Varro watched the men in front of the tent while Falco scanned the area for any other threat. The moment the guards turned aside to murmur to each other, Varro stepped out of hiding.

In a half-dozen long strides, he and Falco reached the rear of the tent. The deep voices of the guard in the front vibrated through the hide walls. No light shined from within, and if Diorix had anyone else with him, then they would share his fate. Falco put his ear to the hide wall, eyes glinting in the dark as he strained to hear anything.

He nodded to confirm someone was inside, then crouched to set his pugio into the bottom of the tent wall. The blade made a soft pop as it pierced the hide. With both hands gripping the pugio, he shot up and ripped open the back wall high enough for both to duck through.

Varro punched beyond it, the hide slit tearing wider as his shoulders forced it open. He stepped into near total darkness. The hide was thick and allowed only the faintest glow of the bonfire to penetrate the front wall like a glowing disc. He slid forward, gladius ranging ahead and searching the wide space for Diorix.

The tent was filled with all manner of things: crates and casks, stools, chests and animal pelts, pennants and other less distinct things hung from the support poles. It made for complete confusion, and were it not for the sound of snoring to his left, Varro might have missed his target.

The man's shape was barely visible against the piles of furs that comprised his bed. An armor rack shocked Varro, believing it was a guard lying in wait.

Falco shoved in behind him, and he found Diorix by following Varro's gaze. Thus far, they had not made significant noise and their enemy continued his rhythmic snoring.

Both now hovered over him, gladius and pugio points aimed at his prone and shadowed body. Varro's heart thundered in his chest and his head throbbed. This was murder, he told himself, even if Diorix was an enemy who had caused the deaths of hundreds. Killing a man in his sleep was a terrible thing, and Varro did not know how he would feel after it was done.

Falco had no such cares.

He stabbed down at the body, galvanizing Varro to follow.

Blades plunged up and down, impaling the man who awakened and flailed at the savage attacks. They stabbed as madmen, and Diorix barely raised a hand in his own defense before it fell to the side. In the darkness, Varro felt hot wetness pooling at his feet and splashing against his thighs. The body under their blades lay much as it had when he found it, only now the odor of death and blood reached his nostrils.

Despite the brutality of the attacks, they had still made hardly a sound. Diorix had gasped and yelped a moment, something that the guards outside could mistake for a bad dream. Varro's legs and arms were splattered with warm blood, and he held his breath, waiting for Diorix to move. He looked at Falco, a tall shadow in the darkness, and both silently agreed on their success.

They turned to exit through the rear of the tent.

Varro stepped on something soft and his foot slid.

A woman screamed in pain and that softness underfoot sprang to life and shoved against his legs.

Falco rushed out of the flap, but whoever Varro awakened now leaped up before him. Being off balance, his strike at the shadow before him went wide but still cut flesh. The woman let out a pained howl.

The tent flap slapped open and light spilled inside.

Varro now beheld the horror of his work. Diorix's body lay naked and bloodied, swathed in blankets that were sopping black. His face was unrecognizable from the wounds and blood.

A naked woman stood wide-eyed, brown and frizzy hair stained red on one side, and clutching her gashed arm. The light from the tent flap framed Varro against the corpse. The woman screamed again and the guard shouted at him, pulling his spear up as if to charge.

He rushed for the back flap, recovering his senses. But the woman, now recovered as well, snarled in rage and threw herself on his back.

Both staggered around as the guard pushed into the tent. She clawed at Varro's head, trying to wrest off his helmet but only digging the chin strap into his throat. The guard began prodding strikes at the two of them flailing around.

"Get off me!" he shouted, then flung the woman back. She made to scream, but her expression of rage turned to a wide-eyed look of terror.

The guard's spearhead burst out of her naked belly. Varro did not pause to see more. He left them both entangled and fled into the darkness.

But the camp had sprung to life. Alarm horns blared everywhere and men spilled out of their tents. No matter that Diorix's army had suffered heavy casualties, he was one man against hundreds and feared being cut off from escape.

He fled directly toward the trees, only to find warriors rushing forward to answer the alarms. Cursing his luck, he cut to the left. How had so many answered the alarm so swiftly? It seemed as if the alarm had sounded before Diorix had died.

Glancing over his shoulder, he saw no one in pursuit. Nor did the men rushing out of the woods have any interest in him.

The Ilegertes had come from their fort. Varro paused for a longer look behind and found the gates opened and warriors flowing down the slope to storm Diorix's camp.

If he was not so full of breathless panic, he could have cried. Even if not timed to any signal of Varro's, Albus had heeded his call to action. The Ilegertes would find their enemies leaderless and their ranks thinned.

Rather than flee, he turned to join the attack. He called out for Falco, but his shouting drew the attention of a cluster of warriors racing to defend their meager palisade. He dodged away from them, and they did not follow.

Varro raced alongside the enemy, who in their haste did not notice a Roman among them. Without a scutum or the distinctive feathers in his helmet, he could pass for an Iberian. As such, he had to be sure the Ilegertes did not cut him down.

Albus was easy to locate, standing a head taller than his men and his long, pale hair flowing out from beneath a Roman-style bronze helmet. He thrust his troops in a concentrated attack at the weakest point of the palisade.

Once at the front of the battle, Varro's real identity became apparent to his foes and he was soon desperate to escape a closing pocket.

Yet even without a shield, he held himself in combat against those who stood before him. One Iberian leaped at him with a spear, but he slapped it down and closed the distance to run him through. When he collapsed, Varro had barely enough time to steal the round shield for himself before another blow landed. However, it was a slash rather than a stab, and his mail dispersed the force of it.

So he dueled with his foes, ever retreating toward Albus's line.

He heard cheering and realized it was the Ilegertes. They were swarming the barricades, and some were in sight of Varro's heroic stand. Four bodies marked the path of his retreat and it seemed to encourage the Ilegertes to push harder.

Albus now appeared above his men. If he suffered from any wounds, he did not show it. Indeed, he seemed a god when he stood upon the palisade and pointed his short sword at the heart of the enemy camp. His men poured around him, and it seemed

Diorix's forces collapsed back. With no one to order them, they fought as individuals for their own survival and no leaders held the men in line.

Across the top of this madness, where men screamed and bronze slammed against bronze, Albus turned to Varro. When their eyes met across the line of interlocked swords, he raised his own in salute.

Varro did the same.

Then Albus's triumphant expression turned to a warning and a blow to Varro's shoulder knocked him flat.

Heavy clubs then beat him from all directions and while his enemies shouted in a foreign language, he was certain he heard the word "Roman" repeated with every blow.

Someone stamped on his sword hand, painfully crushing it open so that another snatched away his weapon. His face pressed into the dirt and he dared not turn over or else they would pound his face to mush. As it was, his mail could only help so much against blunt force weapons. His helmet protected his head, but his fight was lost. All he could see was a wall of sandaled feet surrounding him.

Then a net draped over his prone body and the blows stopped. Like a fool, he sprung upright and only further entangled himself. Peering through the loops of heavy rope, he discovered himself surrounded. Then someone swung at him with a long club. It connected with the side of his head and his helmet rang out and his ear felt as if it had been crushed flat.

He collapsed to the ground on his side, all his senses muted. Rough hands grabbed his legs, and he was aware of being dragged away like a prized boar. His vision swam and his ears were full of a painful wailing noise. He could not control his limbs and soon his captors lifted him from the ground. Through the keening wail that pierced his ears, he thought he heard Albus shouting.

His captors jogged with him away from the lines. Fighting

through his blurry sight he was aware of others running beside him. It seemed Diorix's army had begun a retreat to the safety of the woods.

They flung him into a cart, where a leather hood was thrust onto his head. The more he struggled against the net, the more it entangled him. In the end, he flopped down in exhaustion. The men in the bed of this cart laughed at his surrender. He grew aware of the rocking and bumping of the cart. His helmet pressed against the bridge of his nose, drawn down because of the tight sack over his head.

The captors spoke to him and among themselves. As he recovered his senses, his whole body now throbbing, he realized these men did not sound defeated. They sounded happy. One even patted Varro's leg as he bragged, reinforcing his own image of being a prized boar at long last brought down.

They traveled at great speed, and at points the cart lurched hard enough for Varro to bite his tongue and his captors to curse their driver. This torment seemed to last for hours, but he no longer had a sense of time. During this journey, he tested his limbs, and while they hurt, he found nothing broken. He thought of his ribs from his experiences at Sparta, and nothing felt as bad as that had. It seemed for all the Iberians' fury, their blows had struck the ground, and besides the hit to his head had never fully connected. His helmet had saved him there, but he felt blood leaking into his left ear.

At last, the cart rolled to a halt. The sack filled his nose with the odors of leather and dirt, but he could smell the sweet scents of cooking fires working through this. He also heard distant voices, including women and children. These voices grew louder and more excited as Varro waited. The captors in the wagon bed with him leaped off. He felt the shaking wood flex under him as they did. They sounded like braggarts even if he could not understand a word other than "Roman."

He lay still, entangled in the netting. His left arm had gone numb and cold from the constriction, and his fingers tingled. But shortly men jumped back into the bed and hauled him upright, bringing painful relief to his arm. They yanked off the sack, revealing dark, dirty faces of gap-toothed men leering at him. Behind them the dawn stained the sky pink.

One wild-eyed man kept a pugio to his neck as the others worked him out of the netting. It was clumsy work, and they shoved Varro around, cursed their own confusion, and restarted their work at least three times that he bothered to count. Throughout, Iberian villagers had come to see him, but the lengthy process of disentangling him caused many to wander away in boredom. The spectacle had passed, and Varro was now just a captive.

Once freed, he could stand again and flexed his legs and arms. The pugio was still at his neck, and he realized this was a native Iberian dagger and not a Roman weapon. All of his half-dozen captors were so armed. One removed his helmet and placed it on his own head. His gladius had been lost, but another man cut off his harness and claimed his pugio.

"I'll be having that back."

His words drew derisive laughter from his captors, who shoved him off the bed. He landed on his feet, but his sore knees gave and he collapsed flat.

Now he could see he was in a walled fort, nowhere near as large or sturdy as King Bilistages's was. The walls were stockade wood and the building of similar construction. The main fort was on a low hill, squat and imposing over a sprawl of haphazard wood and thatch homes. White smoked plumed up from each of these, turning everything to a milky haze.

After stripping him of his armor, they led him through narrow dirt lanes where chickens ran free and children followed the procession. Some teased him and others stared in awe. The higher up the hill they traveled, the fewer people they met until they passed the final distance alone.

His captors led him to a walled area beside the main fort, driving him at dagger-point across the bare ground. Trash filled the area, and one thin, sickly black dog wagged its tail as the men entered. It shoved its snout into Varro, but the men chased it off. There seemed to be nothing else here until he noticed a line of pits with heavy wooden grates set over them. Rickety ladders leaned against the low wall behind them.

The men opened a grate as the dog danced around them, barking at the open hole. One dropped a ladder into the pit, and it was clear Varro had to climb down. He glared at the man wearing his helmet, who laughed then spit at Varro's feet. But for all his anger, he was powerless do to more than descend the ladder.

"Welcome home."

Falco sat against an earthen wall, stripped of his armor. He held his hand to his head and gave a lopsided smile.

"Since I was here first, I claim this side of the pit. You can have the side with all the shit."

As soon as he stepped onto the soft earth, the ladder shot back up and the heavy wood gate thumped into place, cutting the sky to narrow squares of dawn light.

"Falco, this wasn't part of the plan."

"Well, unless one of us can fly, I'd say you don't need to come up with another plan. This is a fucking deep hole."

Varro nodded, staring dejectedly at his filthy corner of the small pit.

"A very deep hole indeed."

23

Late morning sun skimmed across the top of the pit, creating a checkered pattern against the grate. A choking odor of waste filled Varro's nose. His head still hummed with the ringing he had endured the night before. However, he still heard the barking dog and another captive dropped into a different pit. His pit was large enough for a third prisoner, though Falco's long body made it hard to stretch out when seated. Both of them stood then looked up at the squares of light above and waited for something to happen. The dog's barking trailed off and the light-hearted voices of Diorix's men receded with no one coming to their grate. The dog appeared a moment before vanishing again.

"Well, someone gets luxury accommodations," Falco said. He then turned to a corner of the earthen pit, hiked up his tunic, and let a heavy stream blast into the dirt.

"It already stinks enough," Varro said.

"Sorry, I couldn't wait to find a latrine."

"Why did it have to be a pit?" Varro pressed against a cold wall to avoid runoff from Falco's side. "We can't even see what's going on."

"That's the point." Falco finished up and looked around helplessly before wiping his palms on his tunic. "I can't wait for it to fucking rain."

"We've been in worse spots."

Falco chuckled. "Sparta will forever win all contests for the worst spots we've been in. But I don't see any way out of this. We can't climb these walls. They'll just collapse on us. Maybe if you stood on my shoulders, you could brush your fingers against those bars. But we're not getting out on our own. That's why they dumped us in a pit."

Punching the wall lightly, dirt clods crumbled to Varro's feet. He shook them out of his sandals, oddly wondering about the condition of his hobnails.

They passed the night trading stories of how they had been caught. Falco chided him for breaking the plan.

"You should've followed your own plan. Then maybe you could've escaped to do something for Curio and me."

Falco had fled toward the woods as planned, but did not realize the Ilegertes had sallied out for an attack. His capture had been less dramatic. He tripped on something in the dark, then sprawled out in front of men emerging from the woods. They knew him for a Roman immediately and one bashed his head with a shield, knocking him out.

"It was a perfect shot," Falco said, mimicking a shield slamming down. "Right to my temple. I woke up later and vomited all over the wagon. They trussed me up and we headed here. So at least those barbarians had to sit in a stinking puddle the whole trip."

"I told you to remove those helmet feathers," Varro said. "Maybe they wouldn't have recognized you so easily."

"Well, it didn't do you any good, did it?"

Now that morning had come, they spent it watching the sky color deepen and hoping for food and water, which never came. Both he and Falco dozed, their exhaustion finally conquering their fears. By midday, Diorix's men came to retrieve the other prisoner. Varro awakened to the barking dog during this time, but again dozed. However, soon after, shadows spread over the grate and voices reached them. They opened the pit and lowered a ladder. One shouted a command, which was unintelligible but a clear order to climb.

Varro went first, emerging to a different set of spearmen who kept their weapons leveled at him. The sickly gray dog growled and barked, but the spearmen kept the animal back. Once Falco clambered out, he inhaled a deep breath, as if enjoying the experience of fresh air and could not care less about his situation. Yet his antics drew a spear butt to his gut, doubling him over to be butted again on his head. He might have fallen back into the pit had another guard not caught him.

"Just behave," Varro said. "We're going to be ransomed soon."

Such was his hope as the guards corralled him and Falco toward the main fort. Whether to pay ransom was the consul's decision. While Varro did not doubt Cato would gladly see them dead, he was sure he would pay a ransom. Otherwise, Senators Flamininus and Galba, and whoever else was involved with Servus Capax, would know he had essentially killed their agents. Of course, this required any of those senators to actually care. He was uncertain of this part. So he went to the fort with a hard lump in his throat.

The interior was much the same as the Ilegertes' fort. They were driven into a wide hall filled with men with glowering dark eyes, brightly colored cloaks, and tattooed arms folded over their wide chests. Interspersed among them were women in modest robes of gray or green, children in dirty tunics, and old men who seemed shrunken versions of their younger counterparts.

The hall smelled of sour wine and sweat, plus that strange barbarian tang that Varro noted was common to all Iberians. Faint white smoke from a hearth fire at the far wall curled lazily along the rafters. He and Falco kept their heads up and shoulders back, even with spearheads pricking their flesh. They were driven across the wooden floor of the hall, then forced to kneel.

Only then did Varro realize he was kneeling before the man he believed he had killed.

Diorix sat on a plain chair, surrounded by his guards and advisors. His dark hair flowed wildly down his shoulder and a gold circlet pressed it flat around his head. His eyes sparkled with impish delight as he stroked a dark beard. He was younger than Varro expected for a tribal chief. For all the trouble he had wrought, he seemed an average and nondescript man. Perhaps that was his greatest distinguishing feature; his face was entirely forgettable.

But more shocking was the distinctive man kneeling beside him in chains. Prince Albus had been stripped of his armor and given a plain gray tunic. His striking pale hair was stained red and matted with clotted blood. His face was swollen and his hands bound. The talon tattoos lashed together now seemed more like chicken feet than the bold weapons of an eagle. Albus hung his head and did not look up at their arrival.

Diorix at last spoke, and his voice was unsettlingly deep for so plain a man. It was a voice of command, full and rich. When he last heard Diorix from the Ilegertes' wall, the distance had robbed him of this power. But now in his hall, it was apparent why men followed one otherwise so unimpressive. The power of that voice compelled Varro to listen even without understanding the words spoken.

Now Diorix turned to him, his smirk deepening, and spoke in heavily accented Latin.

"Fate has been kind to me, Romans. Today I have everything I wanted kneeling at my feet."

Falco sneered. "You don't have the Ilegertes' land."

The spearman behind Falco slammed the spear butt into his head, bending him over his knees. The guard shifted the point of the spear to the back of his neck, so that if Falco sat up again he would impale himself. Diorix chuckled.

"That will come, of course. You see who I have captured as well. The only living son of King Bilistages. But the Ilegertes are no longer your concern, Romans. Worry only for the value of your own lives, for that will determine what I do with you."

Diorix shifted on his chair and his smile vanished. He now looked to the silent crowd of his tribesmen and addressed them in his stentorian voice. Whatever he said, his words drew growls and angry shouts. Varro felt the eyes all around him, but focused ahead while Diorix's speech fed the anger of his people. He could not see past the crowd of guards piled behind their king, and so looked through them as they glared back.

At last he gestured to his left, indicating a woman in a black robe with long, graying hair who dabbed at tears on her sharp cheeks. Two boys clung to her, looking fearfully between the woman and Varro on his knees. Diorix spoke softly to them, and the boys nodded as they stepped back from her.

"You thought to kill me," Diorix said, leaning forward on his chair. "But instead you murdered my brother in his sleep. Cowards! See his poor wife and his sons. See the sadness you have brought them. No matter how much your lives are valued in silver, how can I leave my brother's death unavenged? His widow and sons demand it and your crimes of murder must be punished."

Varro knew better than to speak. Falco was still doubled over with a spearhead ready to pierce the base of his skull if he so much as sneezed. Instead, he tried to act as defiantly as he could though his hands were icy with the thought of torture and execution. Diorix was a king with responsibilities to his people, and Iberians were a vengeful sort irrespective of their tribe. Varro understood little about Diorix other than he was a greedy and prideful man. Pride would demand he punish his enemies, but greed would drive him to sell his captives to Consul Cato. Thus far, Varro had seen more greed in him than pride and counted on that for survival.

Diorix looked once more to Albus.

"I shall have the wealth and lands of the Ilegertes. They have no more strength to fight me behind my own walls." He paused to chuckle. "Had they not left their own walls, it might be different today. But now Bilistages must trade with me for the life of his son. I will demand a mighty price for it."

"You forget Rome supports the Ilegertes."

Varro braced for the impact to his head, but Diorix held up a hand. He heard from behind sandals scratch to a halt across the wood floor.

"I have not forgotten Rome. In fact, I have been asking myself a question since I first learned three Romans entered the fort of my enemy. Why did Rome just send three? Why not three thousand?"

Varro leaned back at this. Did Diorix know what Albus had requested, or was it just a poetic expression?

"Of course, now there are only two Romans left." Diorix held out two fingers on a tattooed hand to emphasize his words. "For your companion is dead."

Now Falco tried to raise his head and cried out in pain when the spear jabbed him. Varro shook his head, his throat constricting. Their reaction brought joy to Diorix, who joked in his own language with his people and drew their laughter.

Varro dared to ask, "Is it true, Albus?"

But before the prince could answer, Diorix slapped his chair and his voice boomed out.

"Do not speak to my prisoner again or your tongues will be cut out where you stand. If your companion lived then he would be kneeling alongside you. Do not pretend you did not know this. He was lost in the forest, and killed by wolves. We found his shield not far from what remained of his body."

Diorix nodded to a wall, where men parted to reveal a black scutum shield propped against it. Varro tried to mask his relief, for that was Falco's scutum which he had lost in the woods. Whatever body had been found near it was not Curio's. So Diorix continued to gloat and Varro feigned tears, which were easily summoned just thinking of their predicament. This display set Diorix aglow with malicious glee.

"Your sorrows are nothing compared to the suffering of my people. To my own suffering at King Bilistages's hands!" Diorix thrust his finger at some indistinct point, as if the king were lurking at the back of the hall. "Had he not humiliated me, treating me like a lame mule to be cast aside, then none of this would have come to pass. Do you think to avenge your friend, Romans? Look to your own ally instead. There you will find the real blame."

Falco, still bent over with the threat of a spear through his head, gave Varro a look as if begging him to do something. But surrounded by enemies, he had no chance to fight back. Words were his only weapon now, but he could not find any that would affect Diorix. He had truly plucked victory out of defeat.

Composed again, Diorix relaxed into his chair. He spoke sharp, bass commands to his men. They snatched Albus off the ground and led him away with his arms tied. While he did not look up, as he passed Varro he could see beneath the long hair hiding his face. His teeth were gritted and eyes wild with rage. If he were released from his bonds, he would extract a terrible vengeance. But as it was, he shuffled away with four spearmen herding him out of the hall. Diorix now shifted back to them.

"I know the value of Albus, and will keep him for later. I

summoned him here to show how badly you have failed. Perhaps the best punishment for your crimes would be to send you to your own consul."

"Albus is a Roman ally," Varro said. "And a prince. You'd do well to see no harm comes to him."

Diorix's laughter boomed, shared by his men who likely did not understand what had been said.

"Defiance is admirable, but useless. Do not educate me on how to run my affairs, Roman. I know the value of my goods, both you and him. So let us speak of your value, eh?" He stroked his dark beard and again muttered to his guards. Several left with his brother's widow and sons, and Diorix waved off Falco's guard to at last allow him to kneel upright once more.

"As I said, I wondered at why Rome would send only three men when there are so many under your consul. But then I realized, Rome has none to spare. It seems your consul is pressed for resources. Thus have I told my fellow kings and they have rejoiced. For very soon, perhaps even today, they will crush your consul and burn his ships. Rome will be banished and our lands will become ours once more."

Varro considered correcting his naive assumptions, for Rome would send even more men in the wake of Cato's unlikely destruction. Iberia would never win until all of Rome was completely depopulated. So instead he blinked away the last of his false tears and held his tongue.

"Now, if your consul sent only three of you, then you must all be great men. You must be the best of his warriors. Indeed, after you arrived King Bilistages seemed to grow in strength. I don't doubt it was you three who guided him to be a better enemy than he truly is. And once you were gone, look at what happened? He gave me his only son and lost the best men Rome could provide. He stumbled around like the old man he is. Therefore, you are truly great men and must be worth much to your consul."

"You flatter us," Varro said. "But we are hardly better men than the rest of the legions."

Diorix fixed a doubtful eye on him.

"I do not understand what modesty will gain you, Roman. I need only set a price for your lives. If your consul does not pay, then I will sell you as slaves. Death is too easy for you, and maiming you reduces your value in trade. So for now I think you shall live. But still, I must consider my brother's death."

Here was the greed Varro counted upon. Even if Diorix pretended to debate his options, simply by escorting the widow and her sons from the hall indicated he had already settled on coin over the intangible rewards for revenge. Varro dared to steer Diorix with his lust for coin.

"You may call us murderers for the death of your brother. But this is war. He was asleep on the front lines of it and so suffered for his lack of vigilance. This must be understood by all."

Diorix's nostrils flared and he leaned forward. But he did not speak and it seemed the thought took hold. It was a solid argument against revenge to consider the death a result of the siege rather than the work of his Roman hostages. For it was clear to Varro he did not care about his brother's life, his widow and sons, or anything other than what he could claim for himself. He just needed an explanation to his people for his choice, which Varro had now provided to him. So his posture softened and he nodded.

"It may be as you say, but still he was my brother. I owe it to him that he be avenged."

"There is a price set for important soldiers," Varro said. Falco now looked to him, but caught on to the lie and turned back to face Diorix. "Rome says it will not pay ransoms, but we all know that is not true. I've seen tribunes captured and ransomed back in Greece. It is done quietly, so that the common soldier does not think to surrender rather than fight to the last. But agents such as us two are in the same league as tribunes and we do have a price."

Diorix set his hands on his knees and leered at them.

"I imagined so," he said. "Then what is that price?"

"Five pounds of silver for each. Less if we are injured and nothing at all if we can no longer serve due to our wounds."

Since Varro fabricated the entire scenario, he conveniently selected the approximate weight of the coins Centurion Longinus had sent along—perhaps for this very purpose.

"Five pounds each?" Diorix seemed ready to leap out of his chair. "Then what would be paid for a tribune or a consul?"

"Perhaps ten times more," Varro said. He suppressed a smile at the terrible fires of greed shining from Diorix's eyes. He nearly drooled on himself.

"Perhaps I should go hunting for tribunes," he said. Then he snapped his fingers at his men before giving crisp orders in his bass voice. They lifted Varro and Falco to their feet. Diorix stared hard at them.

"You think you have convinced me to treat you as honored guests? Then you are mistaken. You will go to your consul unharmed, but you shall live in the pit as the snakes you are. You will eat whatever I choose to feed you, and you shall be covered in your own filth. None of this reduces your value either as a hostage or slave. Either way, I shall have a good price for you both."

With those words, Diorix's guards drove them at spearpoint back to their pits. When the heavy wood grate slammed shut and the guard dog ceased barking, they both sat down. Falco rubbed the back of his neck, then checked his fingers for blood.

"That was close," Falco said. "He was ready to spill my brains. Well, you set a good price for us. Do you think Consul Cato will pay or just die laughing?"

"I think Curio is alive, and he can produce our ransom even if the consul won't. But we must help Albus."

Falco rolled his head and stretched, then gave a long groan.

"There's nothing we can do for him. Let his father trade land for his son. It's out of our hands now."

"The mission doesn't end with our freedom," Varro said. "You wanted Centurion Varro to return. So here I am. We need to save Albus or the Ilegertes will be lost as allies, if there is even such a tribe left after Diorix sets his demands for Albus's return."

"Would Bilistages trade his whole kingdom for his son? I don't believe his people would support that. He's cursed, after all. Seems like time for a new king."

Varro wiped his face with both hands. "A new king not loyal to Rome. If we save Bilistages from ever having to make this choice, then he will remain loyal. So that is what we must do, Falco. We will succeed in our mission and keep the Ilegertes allied."

Falco stared at him from the shadow of their shared pit. Soon, he turned his head away and muttered something about impossible missions.

For his part, Varro set his head against the cold earth wall of their pit and looked to the squares of gray sky above. He had no idea how to bring Albus along, but he must devise a plan or else Consul Cato and even Senator Flamininus could rightly punish them for failing in their mission.

And he knew who would have the first opportunity to enact punishment and how terrible it would be. He could not leave Diorix's fort without saving Albus. He just could not see how.

24

Long days of monotony followed their meeting with Diorix. Varro and Falco remained packed together in the pit, each drawing into their own thoughts. Despite their long friendship and bonds forged in shared trials, the cramped, stinking pit wore away at their mutual patience. If one touched the other, he would recoil as if struck. Every movement became an encroachment on personal territory They could not escape their own filth, which by now had soiled their clothes and flesh. Only once did their keepers lower a bucket along with their meal, and they scooped out what they could before sending it back up to a waiting slave.

Diorix did feed them surprisingly fresh bread. It pained Varro to eat with dirt-encrusted fingers but he was thankful to have anything to eat. A small skin of wine accompanied the loaves lowered into the pit, and this caused more fights between him and Falco over who took more of his share. Flies settled over everything, and by now Varro squirmed at the light touch of their dances atop his exposed legs.

Counting from the frequency of their meals, a week had

passed without any change. Were it not for the guard dog barking and the daily appearance of slaves to serve them bread and wine, it seemed as if Diorix had abandoned his fort. With nothing else to do or say, both speculated on what this lack of activity could mean. In the end, they concluded that they were not so important that the world turned on their crisis. A demand from Diorix would need time to be sent to Consul Cato, considered, and a reply returned. If Cato was occupied with a larger problem, then that reply might take days before he composed it. From there any settlements would still require more time to complete.

They took turns exercising within the limitations of both space and their own meager diet. One would press into a corner while the other did deep squats, pushed against the walls, shadow boxed, or anything else to stress their joints and muscles. This minor point of cooperation always improved their moods and whatever aggravations afflicted them before such sessions dissipated by the end. Both wanted to be flexible and strong enough to exploit any opportunities, rather than stiff and bent from a long confinement.

Over these torturous days Varro lost the thread of his own plan. Falco had to remind him that he hoped to devise a way to save Albus. But he was uncertain if Albus remained a prisoner, as they had not heard any activity from the other pits even after calling for him. He might not be held in the same area, or else Bilistages had already ransomed him back.

This worried Varro the most. Knowing the king's mourning for his recently slain daughter, Varro imagined he would do anything to secure his son. If he surrendered lands or wealth, then he would surely be bitter enough to end his alliance with Rome—if he even remained king. So Varro prayed it took as much time to arrange Albus's ransom as it did theirs.

By the evening of the eighth day, Diorix's men rather than his slaves arrived at sunset. They lowered ladders into the pit then waited for them to climb out. As Varro set his foot on the springy wood rungs, he realized he did not hear the barking dog.

"This is our time," he said to Falco. "They've taken the dog away. We're not coming back here."

Falco followed at his feet. "If we're not ransomed back to Consul Cato, then we go down fighting. I'll not be a slave or live another day in a pit."

"We die as soldiers."

Varro reached the top and impatient hands grabbed him out of the pit. Fresh air struck him with the intensity of a slap. He had grown accustomed to the stench of the pit and now nothing smelled or tasted fresher than the air outside. His guards flinched away after seeing his condition, then laughed among each other. He guessed from their gestures they joked about using their spears to guard him and keep distance from his stink.

Once they also collected Falco, they left the pit enclosure and guided them outside to where a large wood tub shimmered with water. While the guards forced them at spearpoint, neither of them required any prodding to enter the tub. Their guards mocked their desperation. Varro did not care, but dunked into the cold water and scraped what filth he could from his hands, face, beard, and body. He was still wearing his sandals, and even cleaned mud from between the remaining hobnails. They stepped out for slaves to drain the dirty water, then rinsed once more before slaves presented them clean gray tunics.

"We've been ransomed," Falco said, his heavy brows finally lifting after a week of constant frowning.

"I've not thought of a way to free Albus," Varro said.

"That's because he's already gone. Just focus on saving ourselves."

The guards broke up their conversation with shouts and butts from spear shafts. Finally recovered from the shock of cleanliness, Varro looked around the yard. It was early evening with stars already hanging in the violet sky. He smelled pleasant cooking fires and heard voices in the distance. Diorix's fort was alive with activity, but buildings and other obstructions kept him from seeing why. He hoped to catch sight of a Roman delegation, but saw only Iberians rushing about in the distance.

The spearmen escorted them back to the hall where Diorix had judged them days ago.

Albus stood beside him, now seeming more like a guest than a prisoner. That thought plucked Varro's spine with icy fear. Could they have joined forces? But then he remembered Albus's look of hatred and decided it could not be. He was a prince, after all, and had just received better treatment. His pale hair was clean and brushed, and even his black fur cloak had been restored to him. But for lacking weapons and armor, he seemed as strong and hale a warrior as always. He folded his hands at his lap and gave them a faint nod. The tattooed talons once more were freed.

Diorix remained seated in his chair and unchanged since their last encounter, even down to the plain tunic he wore. Were it not for his golden circlet he would seem more like an everyday servant than the king of a minor tribe. Seven broad-shouldered men in mail and armed with spears flanked him and Albus.

"Looks like the prince has made a new friend," Falco whispered, but was still rapped in the head from one of their guards. He glared with an unspoken promise of revenge for that knock, but fell silent.

Once more they were compelled to kneel, and Diorix stared down at them with hooded eyes. He spoke in his deep, commanding voice.

"You look well rested," he said, then extended his hand for a slave to place a silver cup in it. He sipped while studying them. "Perhaps I have been too good to you. Such mercy does not suit a king."

"Then you suffer no shame." Varro winced at the anticipated

blow, but Diorix tilted his head and did not understand the jab. Albus, however, surrendered a faint smile at the missed insult.

"I should have you beaten for speaking out of turn." Diorix flashed a wicked smile. "But it is the night of your freedom and so I will be generous."

Varro felt Falco looking to him for a reaction, but having expected this he simply inclined his head.

"Then Consul Cato has paid our ransom?"

"Indeed," Diorix said, his voice touched with mild surprise. "He answered my demands within days and did not debate your price. I should have asked for more."

Now Varro looked to Falco. While he could not be certain what he thought, it seemed both felt Curio's hand in this matter. Fortunately, Diorix only seemed to consider how much coin he was about to gain from their release.

"But it is a good price still," he said, straightening in his chair. "And your consul has sent a delegation to pay for your release. I have guaranteed their safety in my lands and hall. Indeed, I have fed and rested them. After all, I must show my generosity as I am soon to become one of the great kings."

Diorix gave a sly look to Albus, who only narrowed his eyes in answer.

"I have persuaded Bilistages to renounce his kingship in favor of his son. Now King Albus and I have negotiated a mutual peace. It has taken many days to conclude, but we have an agreement, don't we, King Albus?"

Varro blinked in astonishment. Albus gave no reply except a nod.

"The Ilegertes have renounced their allegiance to Rome?" Varro looked pleadingly to Albus. "Prince Albus, have you agreed to this?"

But Diorix raised his hand to prevent Albus speaking. "This is not your concern. Your ransom will be satisfied shortly, and you will be free to join Cato's shattered legions."

Now Varro and Falco both snapped their heads to Diorix, who laughed at their surprise.

"Oh yes, word has come from my own scouts that the Romans have been forced back to the sea. This is why I am surprised your consul still paid your ransom. You two must be incredibly valuable to him. Maybe he believes you will help him recover from his failures. But I am only sending you to your eventual deaths when your armies are totally destroyed."

Fear is easy to engage and bad news always accepted as fact over any better tidings. Varro knew this and still quailed at the thought of Cato's defeat. He was facing a force of superior size, but it was outmatched in training and discipline. Capricious fate could have dealt him a defeat. But Varro believed Rome would carry the day, particularly when the Iberians did not even have unified leadership. Perhaps Cato might have experienced a setback that Diorix now exaggerated.

Diorix issued commands and Varro's guards picked him and Falco off their knees and shoved them beside Albus. All told, the hall was filled with twelve fighting men, as many servants, and both kings. Varro could still not reconcile what Albus had done. He held such bitter hatred for Diorix, especially after the death of his youngest sister. However, a different set of rules governed nobility. Perhaps this alliance was his best choice, even if it meant aligning with an enemy. Varro avoided glancing at the giant prince standing beside him. Instead, he focused on the open door at the end of the hall.

Diorix adjusted himself on his throne, straightening the gold circlet on his head and setting both hands on his knees in a powerful pose. He tilted his head back so that his wild hair curled against his shoulders. Varro resisted rolling his eyes at this attempt to puff up his authority. No matter what Diorix thought of himself,

Rome would never regard him as better than a barbarian chief. He was not of the same stock as Philip the Fifth of Macedonia or King Masinissa of Numidia.

One of Diorix's men introduced the Roman delegation, and he waved them inside.

Varro and Falco did not flinch at the appearance of the Roman delegation. But Albus shifted and looked away. Fortunately, Diorix only had eyes for the Romans entering his hall in what he considered an inferior position. To him, it was as if he had defeated all of Rome. But in fact, his situation was far different.

Curio led the delegation, dressed in a polished mail shirt, bronze greaves, and a three-feathered bronze helmet that shined with the hearth fire burning against the side wall. With him came Samis, dressed in his own mail shirt and staring straight ahead. Neither man was armed, but they wore long gray cloaks that Varro recognized as belonging to the Ilegertes warriors.

But what caught his attention were the twelve Roman soldiers who followed him in. They all wore the battered helmets Varro had intended to use in his ruse. They had been cleaned and set with new black feathers. The men wearing them were clearly not Roman soldiers by their footwear alone. Yet this costume would readily dupe less familiar onlookers, which certainly included Diorix and his men. Curio must have had a hard time selecting Ilegertes warriors who did not have obvious tattoos that could not be hidden.

They carried a heavy crate, two men to each side holding it by thick rope handles. Curio himself carried scales in one hand and a rolled papyrus in the other. A clean shave had restored his youthful appearance. He sported nicks and cuts, as did the other false legionaries who must have cursed shaving off their proud beards in order to appear Roman.

Varro turned to Falco, who gave the vaguest smile in acknowledgment.

Whatever the plan was, Curio would have to somehow inform them of it.

"Welcome!" Diorix said in his booming voice. "Have you rested? Are you well fed?"

Curio's imitation of a haughty centurion nearly set Varro to laughing. He raised an eyebrow and sniffed before answering.

"Sufficient, King Diorix. Now, I assume the two men under guard are Centurions Varro and Falco. I have brought you the required silver and I have scales to measure the weight. Here is a letter from Consul Cato addressed to you. Please read it and we will proceed to certifying the ransom payment. I will require your seal upon that bill when we are done. There can be no misunderstandings when terms are agreed upon."

With each precise and overacted statement from Curio, Diorix's posture slumped fractionally lower. From his angle, Varro saw a redness tinging the king's cheeks even under his dark beard.

Curio stepped forward to present the papyrus to Diorix. This set his guards on edge, each one rattling their spears. But Diorix waved his hand and Curio continued to approach.

Knowing trickery was in play, Varro scrutinized Curio for any hint of what he planned. But he acted his role so coolly that nothing indicated he intended anything more than delivering a message and ransom.

Diorix accepted the papyrus in trembling hands, then Curio stepped back. In that moment, his eyes flashed toward the letter. Knowing Curio as well as he did, Varro recognized his uneasiness as a slight flush in his cheeks and a gentle tightening of his brow. That letter or something tied to it was significant to his plan.

The hall held its breath as Diorix unrolled the papyrus and scanned it from top to bottom. Varro strained to see what it contained as did Falco, but the oblique angle prevented him from seeing more than indistinct lettering. Diorix rolled it up faster than he could have read it.

"I'm sure you would not be foolish enough to cheat me in my own hall. And you have scales to weigh the silver."

"Your seal." Curio indicated the papyrus now nearly crushed in Diorix's trembling hand. "You must ratify the agreement so that later there can be no question on our arrangements."

For such a deep voice, Diorix laughed with a light and trembling tone. "Ah, well, that is not the way of our people. We have no use for letters and writing. That is a Roman pursuit."

Curio frowned. "I don't understand. You speak our language with such command. Certainly you understand the importance of written agreements. My orders are to obtain your seal and exchange this silver in return for the centurions and that agreement."

Diorix growled and pinched his brow, clearly pushed past his patience.

"I speak but do not read your language. It is good for a king to speak Latin, when lately you Romans have governed here. But that will soon change, then writing and documents will have no meaning for us. Take your papyrus and those words back to your consul."

His face reddening, Curio searched around the hall.

"King Diorix, I must have that document signed. There is no one among your people who can read? Who taught you our language? Perhaps he can help?"

Diorix slapped his hand on the armrest, his deep voice booming through the hall. "Enough with this! In my hall and in my lands, you obey my orders. Set your silver down and let us weigh it out. Then I will keep my promise to you. Forget your letters and seals!"

Curio's flush deepened, and he ordered his men to set their crate on the floor. As he did, Albus leaned beside Diorix's ear and whispered. He nodded impatiently at Albus's words then thrust the papyrus at him as if glad to be rid of the burden.

Curio smiled now and he ordered the crate opened as Diorix leaned forward to behold his prize.

Albus unrolled the letter, stepping back and allowing both Varro and Falco to read alongside him.

Diorix gasped when the lid thumped to the side. Silver denarii shined in the hearth firelight, piled to the top of the crate. "That looks like more than I thought it would."

Both he and Curio continued to speak, but Varro did not listen. Instead, he, Falco, and Albus all stifled their surprise at the letter's contents.

It was one of Curio's draft letters written to Consul Cato on behalf of King Bilistages that begged him to send men to relieve the siege. Varro scanned down the page to where Albus pointed with his thick finger. He highlighted a fresh passage added to the bottom.

Weapons are in the silver. Arm yourself when the attack begins. Fortuna bless us all.

25

"You may safely put your mark to this," Albus said as he proffered the letter to Diorix. "It simply outlines what you have already agreed upon."

Diorix took the rolled papyrus and tossed it to the floor beside him. He leaned forward to see his prize in silver, as did his spearmen. The reflected glow from the coins cast strange shadows on their faces.

"I will place whatever mark that satisfies the Romans. But first we will weigh my prize."

He then spoke to his men in their own language and they laughed greedily at whatever was said.

Varro stood back and his mind raced to what would happen next. Curio would signal the beginning of an attack, probably by just launching into a fight. They would have been checked for weapons upon entering Diorix's fortress. Therefore, at least a dozen weapons were hidden under the silver. It seemed impossible that all of them could retrieve weapons without first being run down by Diorix's men. Therefore, a distraction or total surprise was needed.

He looked to Curio, whose flush had ebbed and now seemed more at ease. They met each other's eyes, but Varro could not read his intent. He simply looked down to the chest as if to emphasize what his note had already indicated.

"You will have your own scales?" Curio raised his scale and a heavy bag of associated weights. "And a level surface? This will take some time to complete."

Diorix leaned back and frowned thoughtfully. "I do have scales and a table. I should have thought to prepare them."

Curio gave a smile that reminded Varro of the real man under this facade. "Take your time, King Diorix. We should conduct the exchange properly."

"Yes, you Romans have your procedures." Diorix chuckled then snapped commands to his slaves waiting at the dark edges of the hall. Two ran from the room on their master's errand.

As they waited for the slaves to return with the table and scale, Diorix rose from his chair and approached the Romans. His guards remained in place, surrounding Varro, Falco, and Albus in a semicircle behind them. Yet they rested their spears at their shoulders while they murmured to each other, likely planning for a share of the silver.

Falco tried to whisper without moving his lips. "The plan?"

"Follow Curio."

A low groan escaped Falco and he rolled his eyes. But Varro did not know what Curio planned. He had clearly spent time devising a careful one. Varro feared disrupting those plans with one of his own, and so waited for an opportunity.

"Now these are the riches I have sought," Diorix said. He spoke again to his men, and his grand gestures seemed to describe a monumental achievement. His guards agreed to this with claps or lusty bellows. But Albus simply remained standing, though Varro saw the eagle-taloned hands were now balled and the usually jovial cast of his face tightening with anger.

"And the lands I now possess, or will soon," Diorix glanced to Albus with a cunning smirk, "will gain me the prestige I deserve. Your father should have kept his promise to wed your sister to me. What is her husband now in comparison?"

He laughed, then crouched down to run his hands through the silver.

"Stop!"

Curio's shout was panicked and in his own voice, not the feigned voice of a bored centurion.

Diorix froze and his spearmen snapped their weapons into their hands. He hovered over the silver and looked to Curio standing over him with his hand holding the scale extended as if to beg him to pause.

"Are you afraid I will steal these coins? They are mine, Roman."

Curio stammered until he shook his head and recovered his false voice. "Not at all, but no one should touch the silver until it is weighed. I must be sure you do not try to lessen the weight."

Diorix scoffed at this. "And by what magic would I achieve that? My shaman is dead thanks to this long battle. Only he could have made silver lighter with a mere touch."

"Even removing a few coins could make the difference," Curio said. But now it was Diorix's face that reddened.

"You are brave to accuse me of being a cheat in my own hall. Be glad that my men cannot understand you, or I would be forced to punish you for that insult." He turned back to grin at the pile of silver. "But I'll not ruin this moment. At last, I have all I deserve."

He plunged his hands into the silver as if both were aflame and the coins were water.

Then he thudded against something hollow and cried out in shock.

"What is this?"

"The bottom of the crate," Curio said.

"That is too shallow." Diorix's powerful voice was full of desperation. It reminded Varro of a child who had his favorite toy taken away. He began to scope out the coins, streams of them tinkling to the wood floor. Varro couldn't see what he had revealed.

"What trickery is this?" Diorix sat back on his heels, folding over in dejection. "Do you wish to die, Roman?"

"I suppose I must one day." Curio looked up to Varro and Falco, his face bright with anticipation. "But today, I think you will."

Curio slammed the heavy bag of weights into Diorix's skull. The blow struck with a dull thud, snapping his head to the side and knocking the gold circlet askew. He gave a shriek and collapsed to his side. For an instant, the entire room hung in a state of disbelief.

Varro and Falco whirled on their stunned guards. Both immediately seized the spears in the hands of their enemies.

The hall erupted into screams and battle cries. With his back turned, Varro could not see how it started. Instead, he wrestled nose to nose with his armored guard. Despite being surrounded by them, none were prepared for an all-out attack. Varro shoved his enemy out of the line toward the rear wall.

The Iberian recovered, however, and drove his heels against Varro out of instinct. His yellow teeth flashed as he growled and wrested the spear from Varro's grip.

But he was not without a weapon of his own.

The venerable caligae, his hobnailed sandals, were as good a weapon as he could ask for. He stamped down with all his might on the foot of his enemy, and the hard nails drove into the bone and broke the arch of the Iberian's foot. His eyes flashed with the burst of pain from crushed bone and torn skin. Caligae were often the tools to finish fallen enemies on the battlefield. Varro and his fellow hastati would stamp prone bodies, killing the injured underfoot as their line advanced. Now, the bare feet of his enemies were vulnerable and just as crushable as a fallen enemy's throat.

Varro shoved into him, sending him crashing to the floor, but not before he snatched the spear out of his grip. With a deft thrust, he slipped the blade into the exposed armpit of the prone Iberian and yanked it free to disgorge bright blood onto the wood floor.

He whirled to face the others. But rather than any concerted attack on him, he found mayhem in the hall.

Diorix had staggered to his feet and seemed to have sustained several blows from Curio before escaping into his men. A line of the Ilegertes who had posed as Romans swarmed upon Diorix's spearmen, attacking with their bare hands and using their heavy cloaks to entangle the enemy spears. Behind them, their other brothers along with Curio retrieved their weapons.

Albus grabbed for Diorix and pulled him from the protection of his men. But both fell to the floor, slipping in the silver that Diorix had spilled. They vanished behind the melee.

Falco had wrestled his man back to the wall, and while he tried to stamp on the exposed legs and feet of his foe, the Iberian dodged out of this.

Varro ran the enemy through from the side, and his spear caught deep in the torso. Falco released the gasping man, and when he fell the spear followed.

"Get our weapons," Falco said. "We've got to escape fast."

The fight between Curio and Diorix's men blocked them from reaching the other side to aid Curio and Albus. Side doors led from the hall, and Varro glimpsed the fleeting shadows of escaping slaves.

"The hall will be overrun shortly," he said. "Whatever Curio's plan was, it's broken now."

"The plan is to get out of here," Falco shouted. "And we need real weapons, not these fucking sticks."

He kicked at the spear his enemy dropped, picked it up, and

charged into the line of fighting men. It was as good a plan as Varro could conceive. They could have followed the slaves outside, but that would be the way of a selfish coward. So he followed Falco into the press.

Falco's furious charge landed him against one of the Iberian guards. The spear plunged through his back and sent him onto the sword of the man before him. Varro threw his weight alongside Falco and the two of them staggered through to the other side of the battle line that bisected the hall.

Curio kicked a gladius to Varro's feet. "Relief is coming! Get to the front gates."

Falco protected Varro as he bent to retrieve the sheathed sword. He then pulled him back and faced the battle.

The surprise Curio had achieved had granted them a sure victory. However, Diorix's men seemed to disagree. They were better armored and fought to save their king's life. But no matter, for Curio's false Romans now curved their line around the remaining defenders, stepping across the bodies of the dead bleeding on the floor. Samis, the Ilegertes' envoy who had once accused them of working for Diorix, led the attack with Curio urging them from behind like a good optio would.

"A sword!"

The call drew both Varro and Falco to face the hearth where the cry came from.

Albus and Diorix wrestled on the floor, flailing and punching at each other. Despite Albus's massive size advantage, slippery Diorix had kept out of his grasping hands. However, his head bled from Curio's pounding.

Once more, Albus called for a sword and extended his hand.

Varro rushed to place the handle of his weapon into Albus's waiting palm. He pinned Diorix by his knee against the hearth and barred an arm across his neck. But Diorix had one free hand that clawed at Albus's eye.

Once he gripped the sword, he flipped it about and rammed it into Diorix's side as he shouted a curse.

Diorix bucked and screamed, returning Albus's curses as he tried to escape. But Albus drew the short sword back and stabbed a second time. Now Diorix slumped against the hearth and his screaming stopped.

In the same breath, Samis and his warriors proclaimed their own victory shouts when the last of Diorix's men fell under their blades.

However, Curio did not seem pleased. He turned from the pile of bloody corpses that looked as if a giant hand had swept them to the wall. His eyes were wide and he looked over the men on the ground. Three moaned and rolled, but only one was from Curio's men. He rushed to the man and Varro followed while Falco tended to Albus.

"What is wrong?" Varro asked as he joined Curio over the Ilegertes warrior. He had been stabbed twice in his chest, and while he bled terribly, he had not died. Instead, he gurgled and coughed as if drowning in his own blood.

"This went too fast. The attack hasn't happened yet."

"What attack?" Varro helped Curio pull aside the wounded man's tunic. Dark blood pooled at the pit of his neck.

"The covering attack." Curio tried to staunch the wounds with his bare hands, clearly unable to save the man. Varro pulled his hands away.

"He cannot be helped. Tell me the plan so I can help you."

But before Curio could elaborate, more men rushed into one side of the hall, their swords drawn and their faces grim. They paused in confusion at the carnage, searching for but not finding their king.

The Ilegertes, however, were prepared and lunged at the new arrivals, penning them to the doors they tried to enter.

"That won't hold." Varro pointed to the other entrances and Curio understood.

"Help me carry him," he said, putting his arms under the dying man.

Rather than argue, Varro helped lift their man off the floor. The clangor of crossing swords and shouting of fighting men ringed throughout the hall. Yet Albus stood with Falco over Diorix's corpse, both strangely serene for the carnage enacted mere feet from them.

"We've got to reach the front gates." Varro grabbed Albus by his shoulders. "Curio says a covering attack will come. I don't know the way to the gates."

Albus looked up, his face speckled with blood.

"I will lead us."

He then called to Samis and his men. They peeled back while holding their enemies in place.

Albus snatched Diorix's crown from his bloodied head. Varro glimpsed his plain face a last time, his eyes wide in horror and disbelief at his own death.

"The coins!" Curio shouted. "We can't leave it all here."

Varro hefted the wounded man on his shoulder. "The coins or your man. We can't carry both."

They exited from the front, and Varro transferred the wounded man to the others leaving before him. He remained behind until Samis and his twice victorious men followed. Then he looked to Falco.

"The hearth," he said. "Burn the hall and that will distract them."

The once grand hall was now a room of bloodied corpses heaped in random piles. But both he and Falco scattered burning embers from the hearth in hopes to start a fire.

Falco uses his short sword to flip burning logs onto the floor.

"Funny how a spark will burn a house down when you don't want it to, but we can't get a fire going like this."

"It's enough," Varro said. "Fire or no, we've got to rush to the gates before the alarm traps us here."

They left coins, blood, and bodies in their wake, and Varro hoped fire as well. Diorix's proud hall had devolved into a ghastly scene that would give even veteran soldiers nightmares. Outside the hall, Albus and Samis embraced while Curio looked over his men who had formed a wedge before them. Eleven of the original twelve were red-faced and bloodied. They had lost their cloaks and some had lost their helmets. The looked far less Roman now, except for their clean-shaven faces.

"Albus, lead the way." Varro pulled at him, and he laughed. He now wore Diorix's crown but it did not fit his head.

Horns sounded in the distance, and Varro knew this was not from the chaos in the hall. It came from the walls.

"They're here," Curio shouted. "Thank all the gods a thousand times!"

Varro did not know who had come, more Ilegertes he supposed. Diorix's folk rushed into their homes while his warriors climbed onto the stockade walls. Since they rushed toward the walls as well, Diorix's men did not seem to recognize them as an enemy.

But they would soon.

Albus led them down the twisting paths toward the walls. The men still possessing helmets realized to cast them aside so their profiles would not draw attention from a distance. When they did meet enemies, they were run down before realizing the threat.

"There are the gates," Albus said, towering over his men. "What do we do, Curio?"

"Open them!" he shouted while slapping his helmet in disbelief. "Let our allies inside."

Arriving at the gates, they found Diorix's men already engaged with enemies scaling their walls. All around swords rang out and shrieks followed. Scores of men were surging over the wall, overrunning Diorix's thinned out force and knocking them off the parapet. Also, without firm leadership to direct the defense, they had failed to set any receiving force in case the gate was breached. The gates were unguarded.

"The way is opened," Albus shouted, smiling and laughing. "And the hall burns. Look!"

Varro looked back up the slope they had just rushed down. Black smoke billowed into the night air, lit from beneath by orange flames.

So Curio and his men piled onto the door and hauled the bars aside. From the outside came blood-thirsty calls that Curio's men returned.

Battle along the walls continued in a fierce clash, where bleeding bodies slumped on the parapets or else plummeted to the ground. But Varro saw desperate glances from the defenders to the gates and heard the panicked shouts that followed.

"We have won," he said to Falco.

The second bolt slid aside and the gate opened. The horde outside burst through, red-faced men with shields and swords braced for combat.

Albus shouted in joyful surprise at the men rushing into the fort.

"Who are they?" He looked to Curio, who stood with Samis by the fallen gate bars.

"Your sister's tribe." He gave a sly smile. "And some of your own."

So Diorix's fort would fall. His people would be dragged out of hiding and the surviving warriors all killed. All others would become slaves and the entire fort would be razed. Varro had witnessed these atrocities scores of times and never enjoyed this dark side of victory. No one ever stopped at simply defeating the enemy army, but tormented everyone who supported them as well.

With their work done, Varro and the others stepped aside to let the victorious tide surge into the fort.

He let the tension flow out of him and blew a long breath.

"That should settle things with the Ilegertes."

Falco smiled at Albus greeting the arrivals pressing though the gate.

"If he's really king now, then he owes us to keep the alliance alive at least until we're not responsible for it."

They both looked to Curio, who stood with his arm around Samis's shoulder. Like Albus, they cheered the men flowing in from the gates and now those declaring victory from the walls.

"He did well," Falco said. "I wouldn't have expected this from him."

"If you want to be critical, you could say he took too long," Varro said. "And if we're going to be recalled soon like Longinus said, then he better be able to write more than scribbled messages."

"Ah." Falco nodded and rubbed his chin. "There's that part yet. Fuck Consul Cato. Isn't this victory enough for three men to achieve?"

Varro looked up the hill to where flames now reached over the tops of houses between him and the hall. While they had victory tonight, Consul Cato had been defeated and Rome's position in Iberia was endangered. He scratched the back of his head.

"It's never enough."

26

Varro still found sounds of the Roman war camp a comfort to hear even days after returning. He sat at the narrow desk in his tent, a yellow light shining through the roof from the sun in the noonday sky. Somewhere a centurion had spent his reserve of patience and was bawling out his men. Elsewhere, soldiers chatted as if on a market stroll. Varro smiled and folded his hands.

Falco sat on the ground, leaning against the tent pole. He rubbed his shoulder idly. Both dressed in plain clean tunics, had gotten their shaves and baths, and swore to never grow beards again. He narrowed his eyes at Varro.

"You're awfully confident in him."

"Why shouldn't I be?" Varro spread his hands wide. "He has shown himself to be more resourceful than we could've imagined."

"People doubt him because he's short." Falco shifted against the tent pole. "And he can look like a boy when he wants to."

"That won't always be."

With a derisive snort, Falco shook his head. "Especially if he doesn't pass the consul's writing test. He'll die young. We all will."

They had all been confined to their tent since answering Cato's summons. The consul had only briefly visited them and wanted a full report before they were allowed to mix with the regular army. So they produced a written report of everything that had occurred, summarized diplomatically and omitting all of their trickery. It was as much a work of fiction as a report when completed. But it seemed to satisfy Cato, as he had sent no comments back to them.

Varro was not certain if Bilistages remained king or not, but he had been overjoyed at the safe return of his son. Both pledged friendship to Rome, and Albus promised to speak to Consul Cato on their behalf. It had been a hard assignment, but ultimately the alliance held despite Cato's crude deceits.

Varro's plan to defeat Diorix had somehow worked, even if not according to his initial design. Albus had led the attack on Diorix at Curio's prompting. He was still eager for revenge and to prove he was no failure. In private, they had discussed the attack plan and feelings that Bilistages had given up hope. The raid did break the siege, as the death of Diorix's brother ended any organized leadership of the besiegers. But Albus fell when he overextended his line in pursuit of enemies.

"After that, I expected to be killed," Curio said. "Bilistages blamed me for everything. But Samis, who was ready to have me strangled when I first showed up, actually defended me. I can't figure out these Iberians."

According to Curio's recounting of that week after the raid, Bilistages had negotiated with messengers from Diorix and all the while had cursed Rome for bringing him problems. But Curio had dared to correct him, and then offered him a plan.

Varro recalled how Curio's face lit up as he described his actions. Typical of him, he had acted it all out like he was putting on a one-man play.

"I convinced him to go to his daughter for help," he said. "We had to pay that silver to her husband for their aid. So it didn't help that you burned the hall over it."

"I'm sure they can dig it out," Varro had said. "And it was hardly the full amount anyway."

"No matter," Curio said. "They were eager enough to join. The silver was just to bind them to their promises."

As it turned out, the news of Cato's defeat was also Curio's doing. They had captured a messenger bringing the opposite news to Diorix. Consul Cato had decisively crushed the disorganized rebel army. But in order to keep Diorix in place and hopeful for rewards, Curio promised the captive protection if he would trade sides to join the Ilegertes. As he was a practical man who realized Diorix's rule was ending no matter what and the Ilegertes were on the victor's side, he delivered the false news.

Curio mimed a legionary's punch and stab maneuver as he spoke. "If Diorix knew Rome was just a few days away from plowing him under the earth, then he might have killed all of you and fled. I needed him to hold on until we could organize the breakout plan. So we fed him lies about the real situation. Good thing Consul Cato didn't actually show up before we did."

Bilistages's son-in-law was eager to be on the right side of Rome's victory. In exchange for their support against Diorix, Bilistages promised he and his people could shelter in his lands and he would guarantee freedom from Roman reprisals.

"I won't tell the consul if you two won't." Falco had spoken in jest, but it was a deadly serious one. Perhaps of all Bilistages's risks, this deception was his most dangerous.

So once Curio knew he had superior numbers, he just needed a way inside that would keep all the hostages alive.

Curio shook his head as he recalled the danger. "The whole time he kept telling Bilistages that he would just as soon kill all of you if he could not have exactly what he wanted, which was three-fourths of Ilegertes' territory and an oath of loyalty from Bilistages and his son. I couldn't take a chance with an assault."

He hatched a plan to smuggle in weapons hidden under the ransom, and took Albus's personal guard inside as disguised Romans.

"That was actually Samis's idea," Curio said. "He thought of getting the helmets and tunics we got from Centurion Longinus, but it was all gone when we returned to your camp. We'd have been faster if we didn't have to go searching the woods for them."

Varro laughed and explained why they moved.

"If you're talking about risks, then writing down your deceit and handing it to the enemy has to be the worst I've ever heard."

But Curio waved it off with a smirk.

"Diorix can't read or write. I confirmed that with King Bilistages himself. None of these Iberians can, even if they speak Latin. They see no value in written records. Albus and the king are exceptions. So I knew Diorix would need Albus to read the letter for him. Even if he didn't, I planned to demand that you read it aloud. There was never any risk."

Falco sniffed at this. "Well, the moment I saw you, I knew you had to be hiding weapons somewhere. If wasn't under those cloaks, then it had to be under the silver."

Curio seemed offended that Falco claimed to have figured out the plan and folded his arms.

"Well, it's a good thing I've learned to write even if you were so clever to guess the plan right away. I thought you might have believed we were paying your ransom, which would've been easier than a fight. But King Bilistages warned that Diorix would take the ransom then have us all captured again to be sold as slaves. After all, he believed Rome was broken and unable to strike at him. Besides, the Ilegertes wanted Diorix dead. Aren't we supposed to be making our allies happy? That was the best chance to kill him, and it worked."

"You did well," Varro said. "And both Falco and I are grateful for what you did. Now, you have to pass Consul Cato's test so we can all enjoy the results of your careful planning."

So that day had come now. Messengers summoned Curio alone to the consul's tent. They searched him before taking him away, presumably looking for anything that might help him cheat. Both Varro and Falco waited impatiently for hours, filling time with idle conversation.

Varro had felt strangely calm about the test, and Falco had paced the tent and slumped to the dirt floor repeatedly. It was a reversal of their usual roles. But Falco claimed Curio had not been earnest in his studies and that he was bound to fail. Varro disagreed.

At last, the same messenger retuned to them later that morning. Grim faced and speaking no more than his orders required, he led Varro and Falco the short distance from their tents to Consul Cato's command tent. The three of them walked in a stiff line, straight-backed and silent. Whoever they passed stepped aside to stare at them. But no one turned their heads.

Varro's confidence was about to be tested.

Entering the tent, he was immediately assailed with the odors of an old soldier—leather and bronze, polishing grit, oils, and the less common odor of cabbage. Curio sat at a small desk, his fingertips of his right hand stained black. Being washed and shaven, he had been restored to his youthful looks. He gave a faint smile as they passed inside.

Varro and Falco both presented a salute to Consul Cato. He sat at his desk in his austere command tent, piles of wax slates prepared for him on his left and stacks of completed slates on his right. His deeply lined face and bald head gleamed with the lamplight, even though a mellow diffused light seeped through the cloth of his tent. Once more, Varro had the distinct image of a cabbage sitting atop human shoulders. The consul dressed informally in his white tunic with purple hems to denote his senatorial rank.

When the messenger left, the four were alone in the tent. Cato stared between them, then pinched a yellow papyrus between his fingers and lifted it off his desk with a scowl.

"If Optio Curio could write so well today, I cannot believe so recently you two had to deceive me as you did. No one improves that fast."

Unable to hide his relief, Varro smiled at Curio. This drew a click from Cato's tongue, as he was still to remain at attention until otherwise instructed. Cato let the papyrus fall back to his desk, then waved them down.

Both he and Falco let their shoulders slump in relief. Cato gave a humorless smile.

"You three did an admirable job. I have to admit that you might have an actual use to me. The Ilegertes seem well pleased, and have reaffirmed their alliance with Rome. Nor am I bothered with their troubles any longer. Their enemy has been defeated and his forces scattered. Something I am told you had a major role in."

Varro tilted his head. "Have you had word from the Ilegertes, sir?"

"Well, I've read your report," Cato said, searching his desk as if it were right before him. "I can't find it now. But you were clear about killing this minor king. Diorix, was it?"

Varro nodded. "To be clear, sir, it was Prince Albus who killed him."

"Yes, well, he did come to declare his loyalty. He asked to see you three again, and I promised he would soon. But for now, you were to be sequestered. He looks forward to that day, and he was very clear that you three were responsible for saving his people. I cannot recall the exact words, but he claimed that you never gave up even when all of the Ilegertes had. So, again, excellent work."

A warmth spread in Varro's chest. He had seen the best and worst of Albus's personality. He was proud of what they had achieved, and glad for Albus's words. But he also wondered if the prince would have been as lavish in blaming them for failure had things been otherwise. He chose to ignore that thought for now, and enjoy the rare praise from Consul Cato.

"So I have had your report, and Optio Curio has written a good summary of the same today. I will forgive your trickery since you have done Rome and me good service with the Ilegertes. We'll need more of that, as this rebellion is not yet fully extinguished. When the season is right, we will move out and ensure the rest of Nearer Iberia is pacified and be certain Far Iberia remains in hand. Throughout, we'll need strong alliances. I will be counting on you three for help in that regard."

"Thank you, sir." Varro and Falco both spoke together, but cut short as Cato's brief smile turned to his customary scowl.

"But if any of you lie to me again or think to deceive me as you did, I don't care what your achievements are. You will be flogged and, if you survive, will be stripped of your ranks. Do you understand?"

Again, all three stood to attention and saluted as they confirmed their understanding. Cato glared at them, then softened as he looked to Curio.

"It won't do for your rank to be at odds with these two. Your risks are shared, and perhaps you've been undervalued. You meet the qualifications, so I am promoting you to centurion."

Curio blinked, looking to Falco and Varro as if seeking their permission to accept. "Thank you, sir. I won't disappoint you."

A blithe smile crossed the consul's jagged face. "Well, none of you have a command yet. But we shall sort it out. For now, you remain assigned to my staff. The rank will help you get things sorted when I give you commands. For now, you are dismissed."

Before saluting, Varro asked, "So we are free to move about the camp, sir?"

Cato had already picked up a wax slate, then paused to consider.

"Yes, you've answered my questions. Take the next days to reacclimate and recondition. Repair your gear and be inspection-ready. I will have new assignments for you soon. Oh, and peaking of gear, take these." Cato reached beneath his desk, then clapped a leather-wrapped bundle atop it. He pulled the tie and three pugiones spilled out, two smeared with soot and dirt. "Prince Albus recovered most of your belongings from Diorix's fort, which you can pick up at the armory. I pulled these aside to ensure you got them. You're not supposed to be without these."

Varro collected the bundle with a grateful nod, then handed Falco and Curio their daggers. Cato watched with a sour frown as they set them on their belts, and when finished he waved them off.

"I've work to do. Dismissed."

Outside the consul's tent both Varro and Falco slapped Curio's back and laughed together.

Curio straightened to his full height, which was not much between Falco and Varro. "Centurion Curio. I like that title."

"You're going to be doing a lot of reading," Falco said. "Fuck me, but we take all the risks and get all the administration. Seems a bit unfair."

"Where did you learn to write so well?" Varro asked. "I knew you had improved, but I didn't see you practicing."

Curio touched his temples with both fingers. "I was always thinking about it. My father said to imagine a thing before you do it and it will go easier. So I imagined writing reports all the time. Then, I tried to make it real when I practiced. And I did practice! You think I didn't?"

Falco slapped his back again. "Well, however it worked, you did it. Once more, you saved us all, Centurion Curio."

"We should celebrate," Varro said. "And the wine is all on the new centurion. That's the rule, Curio. Get us something good to drink, and invite all your friends as well."

"We don't have any friends." Curio shared a laugh with Falco, but Varro's mood darkened. He remained smiling as they chatted up Curio while returning to their tent. But he felt a stab of loneliness. When in Macedonia, he had many friends in the legions. Now that he was in Servus Capax, he had only Curio and Falco. Their work set them apart from the others, and they did not share the same dangers even if they faced the same enemies. He regretted that trade-off.

"I have something I want to do," he announced when they arrived at their tent. "I will be back later. Curio, don't forget it has to be the best wine and plenty of it."

"Well, we can't get drunk on duty," he said.

Falco burst out laughing. "Now that's a centurion's answer for you!"

Varro left them to search deeper into the camp. He passed rows of ordered tents and into the first legion camp. After asking about, he found Centurion Longinus drilling with his men. He stood to the side to admire him at work, but soon the stout man with the heavy shadow of beard noticed and called for a break.

"Centurion Varro," he shouted across the distance, striding forward with a bright smile. "I had been hoping to see you soon."

They clasped arms as old friends, and Varro felt a keen pride at being so warmly greeted by who was essentially the hero of the legion. They exchanged pleasantries until Longinus at last dropped his voice and guided him away from his men who now rested in the trampled grass.

"I am eager to know the details. You made good use of what I sent you?"

"Maybe not in the way I had planned, but it all served."

"You fooled the enemy with those helmets? I had to hush a couple of smiths who were overloud in searching for them."

"I appreciate what you did for us. Say, Curio was promoted to centurion today. We're celebrating with some good wine. Why not join us and you can hear all the details?"

"At least the details you can tell me." Longinus rapped Varro's shoulder with the back of his hand. "But maybe the wine will loosen up your story, eh? I'll gladly join you."

They shared a laugh, but Varro grew serious.

"I did not know what to do with the silver you sent to us. At first it seemed a waste, but it proved to be just what we needed. I don't know how you go it, but I thank you for it."

Longinus's smile vanished and he titled his head. "Silver? I didn't send you anything like that."

They stared hard at each other, and Varro felt his throat constrict and his hands grow cold. For an instant, he even thought Longinus might draw his sword. It was a strange feeling, and neither moved for their weapons. But it felt like in some way both had.

"Ah, I'm confusing that with a different part of the plan," Varro faked a smile and slapped his forehead. "A detail that I shouldn't have said, and I'm not even full of wine yet."

Longinus's broad smile returned. "Then I can't wait for what you'll reveal tonight."

Both laughed off the awkward moment. They then spoke of the battle against the rebels, and Varro learned the details of what had been a nearer fight than he expected.

"Our right flank crumbled," Longinus said. "Consul Cato had to physically drag men back into the fight. It was not a proud moment. But these are still young recruits for the most part. After that, he sent in the second legion to mop up. That would've been your fight were you not busy elsewhere."

"I still would've traded positions to be in that fight. I'll tell you why tonight."

Their talk having run its course, Longinus looked back to his men.

"If I'm gone any longer they might actually start to think nice things about me. Can't have that."

Varro smiled, and before Longinus left he grabbed his arm.

"Before you go, I've wanted to show you something." He twisted his hip and indicated his Servus Capax pugio. "What do you think of this?"

Longinus stared with no expression. Then he shrugged. "Standard-issue pugio. It needs a good cleaning. Am I missing something?"

Varro let him go. "Nothing. It's just a new issue, as I lost my other one. This has a different handle design. That's all."

With a doubtful look, Longinus returned to his men.

Varro let him go, then walked back toward his own tent. It seemed Longinus had no connection to Servus Capax. But he had seemed somehow threatening at the mention of the denarii. Varro cursed himself for being so careless.

Whoever had provided the silver had slipped it into Longinus's shipment without anyone knowing. That person or group would have also had to know their plans. He did not know who that could be and why they did not come forward with a direct offer of help.

But that was a worry for another day. He had satisfied his duty to Rome and earned what might be the start of a grudging acceptance from Consul Cato. Not every reward had to be in coin. Tonight he would celebrate his friendships and give thanks he lived another day.

And that would be reward enough.

HISTORICAL NOTES

In the summer of 195 BC, Rome sent Consul Marcus Porcius Cato to Nearer Iberia to crush a rebellion of the Celtiberian tribes that had been raging for nearly two years prior. Consul Cato, also known as Cato the Elder or the Wise, was a hardline conservative who came from a Plebian family noted for its military honors. He was more than ready for the task of quelling the rebellion, which he accomplished with blood-chilling effectiveness.

Cato was about forty years old at this time, and had just won some fame in his opposition of the Oppian Laws, which were under protest by the women of Rome. Being a staunch conservative, he opposed lifting these draconian restrictions on women's rights such as being allowed to wear colorful clothing or to drive a horse carriage within one mile of the city, among other such ludicrous restrictions. However, the laws were repealed despite his efforts to keep the old ways. His opposition, however, did not seem to be a stain on his reputation. Though it is interesting that Livy takes great care to describe Cato's failed opposition. Surely someone was displeased with his stance!

Cato was an interesting figure from Roman history. He was renowned for his devotion to simple living, and spent much time on his farms when not serving his city. As a consul he was famous for sharing the daily hardships of his men, and would directly supervise the execution of his orders whenever possible. He was also famous as a staunch opponent of Hellenization, a trending fashion among some Romans such as Flamininus. As a curious side note, he had a love for cabbage and believed cabbage could cure any malady or condition.

Cato's campaign against the rebelling Celtiberians was swift and decisive. Upon landing in Iberia, he ruthlessly gathered intelligence through the capture and torture of locals and pinpointed his enemy, then formulated a plan to destroy them. His 20,000 men were outnumbered more than two to one, but in the end he crushed the rebellion near the city of Emporiae which is in modern day Catalonia, Spain. Cato inflicted about 40,000 casualties on the rebels, ending their uprising and bringing Nearer Iberia back under Roman rule.

However, before this battle he was visited by Rome's only allies among the tribes, the Ilegertes. King Bilistages sent three envoys, including his own son, to beg Rome for three thousand men to chase off the enemies besieging him. At first, Cato cited his own meager forces and declined the envoys. But he wanted to keep the Ilegertes in the fight, so he made a show of granting them the requested men. He had soldiers board ships as if ready to sail to battle. The Ilegertes envoys went away encouraged, but later when Cato was sure they had left, he disembarked the men and returned them to the ranks.

Historians have excused this as Cato's ploy to keep up the Ilegertes' spirits. Of course, I have depicted a far different situation. It is entirely possible they waited for help that did not come and felt the sting of betrayal.

While King Bilistages and his predicament are historical facts,

Albus and Diorix as well as all that happened between them are fictional. Additionally, the Roman taking of the fort at Rhoda is more of an interpretation of historical events. Cato did fight a battle there, but a different one than what this novel described. In any case, it was a minor point in his campaign that merely announced his intentions to retake the province.

The battle of Emporiae may have ended immediate resistance in Nearer Iberia; however, Cato's campaign at this juncture was far from complete. The final pacification of Iberia would take many more years and continue long after Cato's tenure. But those are stories for another time.

NEWSLETTER

If you would like to know when my next book is released, please sign up for my new release newsletter. You can do this at my website:

http://jerryautieri.wordpress.com/

If you have enjoyed this book and would like to show your support for my writing, consider leaving a review where you purchased this book or on Goodreads, LibraryThing, and other reader sites. I need help from readers like you to get the word out about my books. If you have a moment, please share your thoughts with other readers. I appreciate it!

ALSO BY JERRY AUTIERI

Ulfrik Ormsson's Saga

Historical adventure stories set in 9th Century Europe and brimming with heroic combat. Witness the birth of a unified Norway, travel to the remote Faeroe Islands, then follow the Vikings on a siege of Paris and beyond. Walk in the footsteps of the Vikings and witness history through the eyes of Ulfrik Ormsson.

Fate's Needle

Islands in the Fog

Banners of the Northmen

Shield of Lies

The Storm God's Gift

Return of the Ravens

Sword Brothers

Descendants Saga

The grandchildren of Ulfrik Ormsson continue tales of Norse battle and glory. They may have come from greatness, but they must make their own way in the brutal world of the 10th Century.

Descendants of the Wolf

Odin's Ravens

Revenge of the Wolves

Blood Price

Viking Bones

Valor of the Norsemen

Norse Vengeance

Bear and Raven

Red Oath

Fate's End

Grimwold and Lethos Trilogy

A sword and sorcery fantasy trilogy with a decidedly Norse flavor.

Deadman's Tide

Children of Urdis

Age of Blood